The
Sunday
Hangman

James McClure

The Sunday Hangman

PANTHEON BOOKS · NEW YORK

For Allen Cook

Manufactured in the United States of America
First Pantheon Paperback Edition

Built of attractive brown brick, it looks more like a modern office block. Heavily barred windows are set into the walls. White marble steps, flanked by lush, colourful flowerbeds and rolling lawns, lead up to the huge door of highly polished wood. The door is heavily studded. On the outside is a shining, polished brass door-knocker, and an eye-slit, inlaid in brass. The only indications of the function of the block are the watchtowers at the corners. Inside the block, the prisoners awaiting execution are under observation 24 hours a day.

—*Pretoria News*

1

TOLLIE ERASMUS LOOKED AT the room in which he was about to
die, and saw there the story of his life. Nothing had ever turned
out quite the way he'd imagined it.

For once, however, he was very relieved to find this was so. In
nightmare after nightmare, he had seen himself in a harshly lit
execution chamber that had whitewashed walls and high
fanlights, a scrubbed wooden floor and a crude beam, a long
lever and a thick, bloodstained rope. Whereas, in fact, the
chamber was far more like a hospital corner, screened off by
green curtaining and lit by a warm orange glow; there was a
clinical sparkle to the brass pulley, and the rope was so clean it
must have been specially sterilized, assuring him of a swift,
certain, scientifically humane end to his days.

Tollie was thinking very fast; absorbing all this in a twinkling
while, on another level, wondering what had happened to all the
in-between bits. He couldn't remember his arrest, the trial, or the
passing of sentence. It was like coming round in a dentist's chair:
you knew where you were and why, but you didn't want to probe
too much for fear of the onrush of pain.

His other senses were recovering now. He smelled the prison

1

stink of disinfectant and tasted brandy. In his left hand was something squarish. His hand wasn't visible. None of him was visible. He had been rolled up in a sheet so expertly he couldn't move. A sheet wrapped round and round and round, and pinned neatly down the side with safety pins. He was sitting in a chair, bound to it by a wide, soft bandage that went round and round and round.

This couldn't be right. Think, Tollie, think fast.

The shape of the room was wrong. Every weekday morning at Pretoria Central he'd waited in the soccer yard to be marched off to the workshops with the others. Facing him, as he stood there, had been two and a half stories of solid wall with only a fanlight near the top. If you didn't guess right away that this was the gallows building, you soon enough learned, because on Tuesdays and Thursdays there was often a delay while they finished nailing down the coffin lids. Inevitably, you came to know its dimensions pretty well, and this room just didn't go with them at all. Think faster.

The pulley for only one rope was another thing—and so was the amount of floor space. He knew for a fact that sometimes they strung up six kaffirs at once, and no way could six stand side by side on that area of trap door. Naturally, the warders liked to exaggerate the figures they dealt with, but he had seen the evidence of a multiple hanging with his own eyes. After leaving the soccer yard, you went up some steps at the side of the gallows building and along a passage between the door to the laying-out room and the door they brought them out of, over sawdust sprinkled to keep the drips of blood from sticking to your feet. And one Thursday morning, after an unusually long delay, he had actually seen six pairs of soggy khaki shorts being dropped outside the door for collection by the laundry. He recalled the warder winking at him, and wiping a hand on the wall.

He had ears as well. He couldn't hear the sound that never ceased within the walls of Central—except, very abruptly, when the traps went down: the sound of the kaffir condemneds singing hymns and chanting in the great cell in B2. They always sang even louder before a hanging, making "Abide with Me" last all night, driving A and B sections crazy, which served the privileged bastards right. Although even in C, which was that much farther away, they got to you when the lights came on at five-thirty and there was that final upsurge before the long, empty silence.

Fighting to impose his sanity on an insane situation, Tollie put a simple question to himself: If I'm not in Central, then where the sod am I?

It wasn't a dream, and logically he couldn't be anywhere else, despite all the—

Tollie knew exactly where he was, and just why things hadn't matched up to his experience. He had been away from Central a good while, and had forgotten the new building for the condemneds which had been going up on the rise just behind it. A really modern place, the papers had said, with all sorts of up-to-date ideas; the inmates had nicknamed it Beverly Hills.

In that same instant, everything slotted into place. The idea of having one gallows for all races had always surprised him; this was the gallows reserved for whites, which explained the curtains and the single rope. The constant hymn-singing from B2, back in the old block, had worked on everyone's nerves; now the kaffirs had been put in a new section that was sensibly soundproofed. As for the sheet around him, it was an improvement on the old straight jacket, which, as the warders had often complained, had never worked all that well on the really stroppy cases.

Having resolved the immediate conflicts set up by his awakening in a room like that, Tollie suddenly realized he'd never had a mental blackout before. In fact, he could remember quite distinctly—

"Don't be frightened, son, you won't feel any pain," said a deep voice behind him. "We're all here and it's half-past five on the dot."

2

IN HIS TIME, Lieutenant Tromp Kramer of the Trekkersburg Murder and Robbery Squad had been asked to believe many things. But when they told him that Tollie Erasmus had hanged himself, he simply shook his head.

"See for yourself," said the new man in Fingerprints, dealing him a photograph from the batch in his hand. "I took that myself this morning, as you can tell from how nice and clear it is."

Kramer used an apathetic finger to bring the picture round the right way up on the bar counter. Sure enough, that was the face of Tollie Erasmus, all right: a sleekly handsome, pointy face, with small, close-set eyes; the sort of face a bull terrier would have if it were human. A dead face, moreover, and there was a rope around the neck.

"Where?" he murmured, glancing up to see who else had come across to the hotel from police headquarters opposite.

He really should have guessed. Why, it was none other than Sergeant Klip Marais, the gladdest bearer of ill tidings in the Criminal Investigation Department, and an obsequious, sometimes quarrelsome, little runt to boot.

"Lieut' Gardiner said to inform you immediately," explained Marais, his tone repenting the levity shown by his companion. "We saw the note you had left in your office for Zondi, and so..."

"Where?" Kramer repeated.

"Ach, upcountry," said the new man. "They had him unidentified at Doringboom, and the Lieut sent me to get prints, et cetera. Then, when I got back just now, the other blokes all recognized him straight off, and I was sent to find you in CID."

He seemed amused by his present surroundings.

"So Doringboom is handling this?" Kramer said, pocketing the print. "When are they doing the P.M.?"

"This afternoon, I hear."

"Uhuh. The body was found when?"

"Today."

"Where?"

"In one of those picnic places for cars alongside the national road, about twenty kilometers this side of Doringboom. His car was there also, a green Ford, and he'd strung himself up on a thorn tree just by the fence. Some umfaans made a report to a family that had stopped for breakfast with their caravan. He hadn't been there all that long; only a few hours—or that's what the doc says."

"Doc who?"

"Don't ask me—the local district surgeon, whoever he is."

"Uhuh."

Kramer stared at this new man, and then decided that he was not going to be an asset to crime detection in the division. Shyness made some people cocky, and so did being the minimum required height of five foot six, but here was an object that was neither of those things: if anything, he was almost as tall as Kramer himself, a lot bulkier, and his swagger showed even in the way his greasy quiff was combed back.

It was curious how the unbelievable had this effect, tempting you into thinking about petty irrelevancies, while, deep inside, certain adjustments were made.

"Are you offering?" the new man asked, nodding at the drink in front of Kramer.

"Why not?"

"Um—I think I'd best be getting back," said Marais, edging away. "Um—see you, hey?"

They watched him go.

"By the way, I'm Klaas Havenga," the oaf announced, snapping his fingers for the Indian barman. "A brandy and orange, no ice, and the officer here is paying for it."

"The same," Kramer added, noting how automatic his responses had become.

He took out the picture for another look at it.

"So what's this all about?" Havenga asked, after using his first sip as a mouth rinse. "Marais was trying to tell me as we came across, but you know how that bugger talks, nineteen to the dozen like a bloody coolie."

The barman, a sensitive soul, moved to the far end of the counter, taking his newspaper with him. He'd been writing some interesting names into the crossword when the two jokers had arrived, armed with their bombshell.

"I was looking for him," said Kramer, feeling nothing as yet.

"Oh, ja? Is it true he tried to take a pot shot at you once, only your boy went and buggered things up?"

"Three months ago," Kramer replied, taking some ice from the plastic barrel. "We got a late tip-off there could be a raid up on that rise in Peacevale where there's a line of Bantu business premises—ach, you know, along that dirt road that runs parallel to the dual carriageway. They were trying out the idea of a small bank there at the time. Right on noon, our informant said, but when we rolled up, the bloody thing was already in progress."

"Yirra!"

"Not that it looked like it. The people outside didn't even know at that particular moment, he was so quick. They were used to seeing armed whites going in, carrying the bank's money—and the same went for the bank employees. The stupid bastards took him right up to the safe and opened it. Anyway, Erasmus comes running out with his gun up before we realized the position. Mine was still in under here, so Zondi spins the car around, to give me time to draw. As he comes on to Erasmus's side, he gets a thirty-eight in the leg, straight through the bloody door. That was it."

"How do you mean?" asked Havenga, frowning.

"The leg went stiff, onto the accelerator, and we went into the front of this fruit shop—glass, grapes, cabbages everywhere. The owner was killed outright."

Never, so it seemed, had the man heard anything funnier. Kramer smiled indulgently as he came up for air.

"Jesus Christ! C-c-cabbages everywhere!" Havenga gasped, rejoicing in such a vision. "Man, you'll have to excuse me a sec."

And he used the back of his inky hand to smear the tears from his eyes, before beckoning for the barman.

"Same again," he ordered. "Only this time I pay."

"Like hell," said Kramer, and the matter rested there.

While the barman saw to their refills, a bright splash of reflected light began to flutter across the bottles and glasses on the shelves behind the counter.

"Who's *doing* that?" muttered some old bugger irritably, following its progress back and forth.

Nobody could answer him, so he slid off his stool and went over to the mullioned windows behind them, which gave the bar its spurious look of a Tudor tavern. But the frosted panes defeated his attempts to peer through, and he went out onto the pavement to do some shouting.

"So go on," Havenga invited Kramer, clinking glasses. "While your boy was making a damn fool of you in all those grapes and bloody mangoes, Tollie got clean away?"

"Uhuh."

"This is the first time you've heard of him since?"

"The first. His home town was Durban, but he didn't go back there. We've had a running check going in all the big centers—Joey's, Cape Town, P.E.—without any joy so far. What plates did he have on his car?"

But Havenga was distracted at that moment by the return of the old misery from the pavement.

"Who was it?" asked a visiting farmer, who'd apparently ordered them both fresh lagers in the meantime. "Some kid left in—"

"No, some insolent little black bastard, waggling his tobacco tin or something about over the other side. Just grinned at me—you know the type. Dressed up like a dog's dinner in a bloody suit he must have swiped. I don't know. This for me? Very good of you, old chap."

"If you like, I'll go and kick his backside," the farmer offered, being a much younger man.

"No, no; I've sent him packing! Best of health!"

Havenga grinned cynically and turned back to Kramer.

"Sorry, what was that?"

"I asked you about his sodding plates."

"Ach, I never saw them. Don't these bloody English kill you?"

The splash of light crossed Havenga's face even as he spoke, slipping from it to move like a butterfly from the Oude Meester brandy over to the till.

"What's he playing at?" exploded the old man, banging down his tankard. "Just who the devil does he think he is?"

Suddenly Kramer came to, and realized he knew the probable answers to both those questions. Not only this, but that he'd now made his adjustments, and the time had come to act.

"Duty calls?" asked Havenga, puzzled to see him rise so purposefully for no obvious reason.

"Duty, Sergeant? I came off duty officially at six o'clock this morning."

"But I . . . you mean, Marais . . . ?"

And the new man in Fingerprints looked at the glass in his hand, before coming the old comrade with a slightly uneasy laugh: "You aren't going to report me, hey, sir?"

"Naturally," said Kramer, just for the hell of it.

Over on the other side of the street, just as he'd supposed, leaned the jaunty figure of Bantu Detective Sergeant Mickey Zondi, still overcoming his problem of access to the bar with the aid of a spare 9mm magazine, angled to catch the sun. An instant later, however, this had stopped, and the fly little sod was on his way across.

"How goes it, Mickey?"

"Not so good, boss—and not so bad. I was two hours with Mama Makitini, but she swears to God she never had one drop of that vodka in her shebeen. Then, by chance, I find Yankee Boy Msomi round the back of Pillay's place, and I get a tip for us to watch where the Mpendu brothers go tonight, because maybe there is a connection. I am sorry you had to wait so long."

"That's okay; just got a bloody gutsful of the office. I've been talking."

"Who with? The old guy with the fine command of the Zulu language?" Zondi joked, waving a shaky fist. "Only it would be a kindness to explain to him the difference between bhema and bhepa. He crudely told me to go and smoke myself."

"Hmmm."

"Boss?" asked Zondi, quick to match moods.

"Forget the bloody vodka and the Mpendus. I'm going to have a word with the Colonel, while you get the car filled up. Be in the yard at one."

"Where do we go?"

"Doringboom. A post-mortem in Doringboom."

"*Hau!* This is a murder inquiry?"

"Well, at the moment," Kramer said, "that seems to be a matter of opinion. Here, you tell me what you think."

"He handed over the photograph.

Zondi's fleeting scowl was involuntary. He returned the picture, gave no sign of what was going through his head, and took a step away.

"I get the car, boss."

"Fine."

Kramer set off in the opposite direction, heading for the CID building, then side-stepped into the shadow of an off-loading Coke truck. That limp wasn't getting any better; in fact, when Zondi thought you weren't looking, it tended to become a lot worse.

"I've heard," said Colonel Hans Muller, without glancing up from his blotter, where he was making daisies with the juice tapped from his pipe stem. "I've also been having a word with Dr. Myburgh, the young DS handling the case at Doringboom. Putting him in the picture and so on."

"Oh, ja? What does he have to say?" Kramer inquired, taking his usual seat on a corner of the big desk.

"Careful! No vibrations, please. This isn't as easy as it looks. Anyway, as I was saying, Myburgh sounded an intelligent fellow. He gets a lot of hangings, of course, being in a rural area and the Bantu not having sleeping pills and all that rubbish to play around with. Quite a lot of experience for his age."

"Uhuh."

"Interested in what we had to tell him about the deceased. Said it would account for Erasmus carrying no identity—which shows he isn't a fool."

"And?" prompted Kramer, wary of the build-up.

"Well, he told me he'd visited the scene in person. No signs of violence, no strangulation prior to suspension, and a nice little fork in the tree to jump off. Nothing to make—"

"But, Colonel—"

"Ach! Look what you made me do! I don't want bloody *sunflowers*, hey? If you'll just let me finish. . . . The one slightly unusual feature was Tollie's bust neck and his use of a drop—most suicides just sort of strangle."

"Slightly unusual? Christ, I'd like to hear what our own DS has to say about that," Kramer retorted, confident that his doubts would be shared by Dr. Christiaan Strydom, the gifted if eccentric garden gnome with whom he generally worked.

"Your wish, Trompie," murmured the Colonel, good-humoredly, "is my whatsit. I checked with the very same not five minutes ago, and Chris agreed that a fracture was rare—although far from impossible, given the circumstances I described. He also made a couple of very sound observations, one of which Doc Myburgh had himself already noted."

Instead of explaining what this was, the amateur artist gave his undivided attention to the spread of the next disgusting yellow stain.

"Do I have to just guess, Colonel?"

"Hmmm. You could try, if you like: what have—or had—Doc Strydom and Tollie Erasmus got in common?"

The answer he received was deservedly coarse.

"Then let me give you a clue: where have they both, in a manner of speaking, served a term?"

Kramer kept silent, regretting he'd ever bothered to pay the bastard the courtesy of a quick call. But his mind childishly insisted on solving the riddle: Strydom and Erasmus had both spent time in Central Prison, Pretoria, the site of the Republic's gallows and, for this reason, one of the few places blacks were able to share the same amenities, however briefly.

"Full marks," Colonel Muller continued, taking Kramer's correct assumption for granted. "... where it would surely be impossible for a man to remain in ignorance of what takes place there on Tuesdays and Thursdays. Every warder has to witness at least one little send-off, and I'm sure he then feels it his duty to pass on the deterrent effect to those maximum-security prisoners in for rehabilitation. Tollie must have heard their stories dozens of times during his last stretch—and maybe even the sound of the trap going down. And so, when he felt in need of an instantaneous death, guaranteed by the government itself, then—"

"Tollie? That's crap!" snapped Kramer.

"Then I hesitate to ask you to bear it in mind, Lieutenant. Nonetheless, such an approach would be entirely rational on Tollie's part, especially if he'd thrown away his gun and left himself just with a tow rope. Don't let the statistics fool you: very few members of the ordinary public know anything about a drop or more would use it."

"You'll be saying he did it out of conscience next!"

The Colonel looked up. "Now who's in the crap business?" He chuckled, leaning back. "That's one kind of trouble our friend never got himself into, having a bad conscience. But you've got to admit that, in this context, there's nothing inconsistent about the method used."

"I'd be surprised if he hanged himself any other way, sir—which doesn't mean that I think, for one minute, he did it."

"A feeling in your water?"

"Other inconsistencies, beginning with—"

"Hold it; point two coming up. Doc Strydom shares your respect for precedent, you see."

"Oh, ja?"

"Hanging, he reminds us, is a form of violent death that's different to all the rest, inasmuch as the forensic presumption is, for once, that death was self-inflicted. In his strange mind, even judicial hangings are self-inflicted, but we won't waste our time going into—"

"Ach, why not?" Kramer was niggled into saying.

"Watch it. You should be asking why this presumption is made. Simply because self-inflicted hanging has millions of precedents—going right back to Judas, if you like—whereas homicidal hanging is a crime that's virtually *unprecedented*. Follow? In fact, the only case Doc could cite offhand was one in Paris in 1881."

Kramer lit a Lucky Strike and rode out a few waves of doubt in that water of his. For a moment there, this talk of precedent had impressed him, then he'd realized that the Colonel's whole argument depended solely upon the number of homicidal hangings that had been actually detected.

"A handy presumption," he remarked dryly. "Hell, if my love life ever gets too complicated, I might give it a whirl myself."

"You do that, Tromp—providing you're picking on two-year-olds these days, or on junkies stoned from here to bloody Christmas. Because the DS will still be making his routine check, and is certain to note any signs of secondary violence, such as might be needed to control your victim. Erasmus was conscious at the time, and there was no evidence of recent bruising."

"Fully conscious? How could Myburgh tell?"

"Ah," said the Colonel, appearing shifty on purpose, "here is the unbelievable part of the story. It seems that Tollie had in his left hand a small, leather-bound copy of the Holy Bible. He must have been holding it hell of a tight, and then the fatal spasm kept it there."

Of course, Kramer could believe that: sudden and violent death was capable of many tricks. He had once spent ten minutes trying to free a hair drier from the grasp of a skinny typist electrocuted in her bath. He had found a brier pipe, not unlike the Colonel's, clenched in the teeth of a steeplejack impaled on a parking meter. And if anyone was to turn to Jesus in extremis, then it was invariably the scum of the earth—see the prayers scratched on any cell wall.

But he said with conviction: "Ach, somebody stuck it in afterwards."

The Colonel wagged a hairy finger.

"Sir?"

"The truth of the matter is, Trompie, that you wanted this

Tollie Erasmus for yourself. And now you can't get him, you want someone else to take the stick."

Kramer shrugged.

"Furthermore, it's no use you and me jumping to wild conclusions, and saying Tollie was too psycho to ever think of such an idea, because we aren't qualified to make that kind of judgment—I would go so far as to say that nobody is. Let us keep to the facts, and both our feet on the ground. I don't want you going to Doringboom and forcing a confession out of Dr. Myburgh, for instance; or some other bloody thing, equally typical of you in a frustrated state. The facts, the hard facts, and how they concern us as of now—understood?"

"There's the money, sir."

"Just what I had in—"

"I meant: would you kill yourself if you had twenty thousand rand still to spend?"

"God in heaven!" protested the Colonel. "Since when was that known to you as a fact?"

"Ach, sir; we'd have at least heard as much, if Tollie had been giving it a tonk. It's obvious that he was waiting for the pressure to come off first. Probably shacked up in a flat somewhere with a little goose to do the cooking and run errands for him."

"Ja? The same little goose who maybe ran away with his golden egg one night? After doctoring up his curry? That has happened before—and it can leave a man very depressed."

Much to the Colonel's evident satisfaction, the telephone rang at that moment, creating the right sort of pause.

Or so he thought.

"Hey, when are you going up to Doringboom?" the Colonel asked a few moments later, cupping a hand over the mouthpiece. "Your old pal's on the line, wondering if there's a lift for him available. I thought it wouldn't be long before he wanted to get his nose in there! You know how Doc is about these matters."

Kramer frowned; he also knew that Strydom had an official car of his own, which made the request seem rather odd, and that he didn't like the idea of being tied down to bringing the silly sod back again.

"Tell him I'm sorry, Colonel, but I'm not even waiting for lunch. We're leaving straight away at one o'clock."

"Hello, Chris? He's charging out of my office right now."

The Colonel listened for a second or two longer, chuckled, and then replaced the receiver with a flourish, thereby regaining Kramer's undying loyalty and respect.

"All fixed up, Tromp," he said blithely, flicking the rest of his tobacco juice at the wood paneling behind him. "You'll find Doc waiting on the corner of Parade and Ladysmith Street on your way round the block. And the next time you try to cut short a briefing with me by saying you're leaving town at one o'clock sharp, make sure that it isn't already after bloody ten past."

A total adjustment, it seemed, had been asking too much.

3

THE VELD ALL AROUND them was as parched as an old tennis ball and much the same color. Apart from some thorn scrub, there were no trees except those gathered together for a definite purpose: to shade a tin-roofed homestead, or to provide a trading store with its windbreak. The sort of God's own country where every farmer began his day with a very deep sigh.

Wearied simply by looking at it, Kramer turned his gaze back on the road ahead. Puddles of mirage water shimmered across the asphalt, putting a wobble into the broken white line, and, a long way off, an oncoming bus glinted like a pinhead in the bright sun, before looming huge. Then the buffet and shake of their passing was over, and a distant Volkswagen entered the lists. Soon it, too, was left cross-eyed behind them, and the one-horse town of Doringboom drew that much closer. Mickey Zondi was driving as he always drove: not as though the Chevrolet were a taut extension of mind and body, but like a man who has given his bolting horse its head, being content to merely rake it in the ribs now and then. Kramer personally found the technique stimulating, yet he could tell—from the awed silence on the back seat—that their passenger thought differently.

"Do you get up this way often, Doc?"

"Er—not what you would call a lot."

"Then it must be nice for you, hey? Especially when you can just sit back and enjoy the scenery."

"Very nice," said Strydom, whose narrowed eyes never left the road. "It was one of the main reasons I asked the favor."

Not that he'd put forward any other reasons so far, the devious old bastard. He had mumbled something about a radiator and water leaks and then let it trail. However, once you had a few minutes to reflect, it was simple enough to guess his strategy: by actually traveling with the investigating officer, he felt able to gate-crash Myburgh's morgue party, and no ethical questions asked. That young bloke had better watch himself, or he'd find a paper being poached from right under his nose.

A signpost flashed with DORINGBOOM 22 KM.

"Look, sir," murmured Zondi. "This is maybe the place."

The road had just twitched into a straight and level section that arrowed across a bleak plain, brushing a dark smudge at about the halfway mark, before disappearing into the drifting haze of distant grass fires. And the vulture-eyed bugger was right: in no time at all, the smudge had resolved itself into three concrete picnic tables, a large refuse bin, and half a dozen flat-topped thorn trees—plus a police Land-Rover, parked with its doors left open. Two Khaki-trousered Bantu constables were crouched with a tape measure, while a white constable, in his blue tunic and shorts, made notes on a clipboard. As a roadside attraction, it was too good to be missed.

They came to a sliding halt, waited for their dust to clear, and climbed out. The white constable approached, treating them to a full measure of rustic caution. He was a scrawny lad, knobbly at knee and elbow, and heavily reinforced by the revolver sagging at his side.

"Lieutenant Kramer?"

"That's right—and this is Dr. Strydom, senior DS."

"Van Heerden, sir," said the youngster, shaking hands with the civilian. "Hell, you were quick! When Sarge warned me to get down here and finish my plan, instead of finding those sheep, I didn't see what the panic was about."

He had an engaging innocence that wouldn't get him very far in the force.

"Let's have a look, then."

"Please, sir, it's only in rough. If you will wait a minute, I'll—"

"Ta," said Kramer, jerking the clipboard from him. "I see what you mean: lots of nice sums and pretty letters, but no bloody plan begun—let alone finished. You are an idler, aren't you?"

"Very idle, sir. Only there's this sheep business to worry me, and the tape's got no meters, so I'm having to convert. My boys brought the wrong one."

"So relax," Kramer grunted, handing the board back.

Then he went over to where the dirt met the tar, and looked to the right and to the left. You could see a considerable distance in either direction, and at night, any approaching vehicle would give at least sixty seconds' warning before its headlights became effective.

"How about the whatsit itself?" suggested Strydom, who was showing a decided stubbornness regarding precedent.

"Doc, you think of everything."

"Out of the officer's way!" barked Van Heerden, bustling through a wide gap between his black assistants. "This is the tree in question, right here. And to be strictly fair, sir, if you give my plan another look, you'll see that I have called it *A*."

The tree called *A* was the second tallest of the group. It had a very hard, grayish-yellow bark, and supported an umbrella of tiny, dusty leaves, protected from long-vanished giraffes by clusters of big thorns. The trunk, which was roughly the thickness of two telephone poles, rose fairly straight, dodging a few imaginary redcoat shells near the top. There it divided into a spread of twisted spokes, with the stoutest branch going off horizontally, away from the road. And then, because asymmetry was a quirk of all thorn trees, the neat look of the thing had been spoiled by a secondary trunk, sprouting out of the main one at head height, on the other, picnic-spot side.

"Shall I explain, Lieutenant?"

"Uhuh."

"The deceased was dangling over this exact area where you see the red ants going in and out of their nest. His toes were almost touching, because of the stretch in the neck—it was terrible. So, as you can see, the rope went up and over that biggest branch, and down to where it was tied on the main part."

"Just hold on," Strydom interrupted, his head tipped back. "How could he have got it over a branch as high as that? He couldn't have thrown it, with all the rest of the sticks in the way."

"That was also a bloody long tow rope," Kramer added.

"Not really, sir; usual double-length. Can I show you?"

"You're about the right size."

Grinning, Van Heerden went around to the far side of the tree and sprang onto a large boulder. He reached up, took a grip on the offshoot from the main trunk, and hauled himself into the air. Then he slipped his foot into the fork, swung round and stood triumphant, with his underpants showing.

"Very clever, Van. You worked that all out for yourself?"

"Didn't have to, Lieutenant. This is where the end of the rope was tied, after he'd dropped the noose part over the branch. In line here with my face, when I'm upright, you see. Actually, it was Sergeant Arnot who said how obvious it was, when we were undoing the knot this morning."

There he went again; no idea of tact at all.

But Doc Strydom seemed delighted, and took out his notebook to make a quick sketch.

"Don't you see, Tromp? That must have also been how he achieved his drop. There's nothing else he could have been standing on."

"What about the rock?"

"You couldn't swing off from there, man! Talk sense. The tree's in the way, for a start. Van Heerden, will you try something for me?"

"Anything, Doctor, sir."

"Stand on the fork with one foot only and see if you could jump out this side."

The experiment was nearly a traumatic success.

"Excellent! And the Bible was in his left hand—yes, that would be in perfect keeping; he'd grip with his right."

"Erasmus," muttered Kramer, "was left-handed. One reason we didn't spot his gun the moment—"

"Ach! Van Heerden, can you do the same the other way round the trunk?"

This was attempted and then aborted, when Van Heerden's

head engaged some minor branches.

"I'm sorry, Doctor, but a bloke can't manage it if he isn't standing up straight; you get too bulky, if you understand. You don't have to grip hard though—just a touch to keep your balance."

"See, Tromp?"

Kramer glanced around for Zondi, and picked him out in conversation with the two Doringboom Bantu constables. Then he beckoned to the young demonstrator.

"Okay, Tarzan, it's time for walkies, so down you come. I want that sketch plan, correct in every detail, on your sergeant's desk before I leave today. In inches as well, okay? Because all this metrication business gives me a pain in the arse."

"What would you estimate the drop at?" Strydom said, stepping back to improve the perspective. "I'd say it was approximately two—er—six feet. Pity we didn't ask the lad to take the tape measure up with him."

Van Heerden laughed as he overhead this, and tapped his clipboard. "There's no need for all that fuss, surely? You measure from where his foot was, on the fork, and then down to a couple of inches from the ground, where his foot ended up! Five foot ten, I've got here."

This time Strydom did appear somewhat put out, but Kramer, who enjoyed the triumph of common sense over rare idiocy, was forgiving. He even offered Van Heerden a Lucky Strike, while firing a sudden question.

"What car's tracks are these?"

"Them? They must come from the ambulance—from when it was backed in under here this morning."

"Didn't anyone check the ground?"

"In what way, Lieutenant? It was all trampled by the umfaans and who's going to—"

"I am, Constable Van Heerden. You have seen a cowboy film, I suppose? Where they make the bloke sit on his horse with the noose round his neck?"

"Now, now, my friend," Strydom intervened. "You are going too far! Even if you are suggesting he stood on the top of one! How could he be made to meekly do that? We must stick to the facts."

That could have triggered something unpleasant if Zondi hadn't chosen to sidle up then, his brows raised deferentially for permission to speak.

"Let's hear it, Hopalong," said Van Heerden.

"Thank you, sir. Lieutenant, I have been talking with one of the others who interrogated the children this morning. Would you wish to do likewise?"

"Which one is it, Sergeant?" Kramer asked.

"Agrippa Ngidi, sir."

"Hey, Fatso! Over here, man—at the double!" Van Heerden bawled. "Your boy had better interpret; this one's useless."

The larger of the two jogged up, stamped to attention, and Zondi had to sway out of the path of a sledge-hammer salute.

"Suh!" boomed Ngidi, who bore tribal scars on his plump cheeks.

"Carry on, Sergeant Zondi."

As melodic Zulu became Afrikaans, Strydom stirred restlessly, but Kramer was determined to hear the man out. Ngidi had arrived with Sergeant Arnot a little before eight, and had been detailed to deal with the farm laborers' children who'd found the body. These children came to the picnic spot early every morning, to see what food might have been thrown in the food bin, and to wait on in hope of begging scraps off motorists who paused there for breakfast. The body had frightened them badly, and only the smoke of the caravaners' fire had lured them back. At this stage, the body hadn't been noticed from where the tables were, being hidden by the tree, and the morning rather misty. After showing the whites what one of their kind had done to himself, the children had watched the family pack up and go. Uncertain if they were not entitled to the bacon left untouched on the stones around the fire, most of them had stayed on to see what would happen next.

"Did he ask these kids if they'd seen the dead man's car here before?" Kramer broke in. "Or anything about any other vehicle that was familiar to them?"

The question put a worried frown on Ngidi's face, and he whispered his reply apologetically.

"He says, Lieutenant, that his only orders were to make sure that the children had stolen nothing from the deceased's clothing, or from the motorcar, which had been left unlocked."

"And then?"

"He was instructed to chase these children away. His superior waited here for him to return, and that is all. They then returned to Doringboom."

Kramer fell into a ponder.

"You can bugger off now, Fats," Van Heerden told Ngidi. "Be sure you're ready with the tape when I come, because the boss has still a lot to do."

"No, first ask him where the kids live, Zondi."

"To hell and gone," declared Van Heerden, "and there's not a road anywhere near that I know of. Five kilometers, at least."

"Lieutenant," Zondi said quietly. "Ngidi can show me the path they have made."

"Fine. Then you see you have a proper word with them. Hitch a lift in the constable's van afterwards, or we'll pick you up on the way back. Okay?"

"Sir."

"Excuse me," Strydom butted in, "but are you sure that sending him such a—"

"The lazy bugger needs a walk," said Kramer, making for the car.

Zondi could have chosen which path to follow without any assistance from the Doringboom bumpkin: it was so obviously a children's path. The veld was never as flat and featureless as it looked from the road, and a path made by adults' feet, trudging through the same dry grassland day after day, would have taken the line of least resistance. A four-gallon tin of river water, balanced on the head, was far easier to bear up a slope if the incline was climbed crookedly, and an outcrop of rocks was tedious when your feet were heavy. And so, whereas a path worn away by grownups would have skirted and meandered and turned, the path he was following ran straight. Dead straight, and as uncompromising as the hunger that sent small bare feet, numbed fleet by the frost, scampering down it each morning.

He cursed the children for the straightness of their path. There was, of course, nothing to prevent him from finding a less strenuous route, except his pride. Over the past three months,

Zondi had learned many things about pride, and in particular, how much strength it took.

But he could be weak and shameless, too. This was when he permitted himself to imagine all sorts of nonsense, just as he was doing right then. The thief Erasmus, his brain said, had fired a rat, not a bullet, through that car door and into his leg. By mistake, this rat had been sewn inside him at the hospital, trapping it there in the flesh and the dark, and making it very afraid. If left undisturbed, then the rat endured quietly, and all he felt was the sting of the urine it passed. All he had to do, however, was to take a single step, and the jolt would startle the rat, forcing it to twist and bite and then gnaw on the bone, until he stopped. Oh, yes, it was a clever rat, this frantic, burrowing pain in his thigh.

Zondi limped on.

Then stopped suddenly, aware of how foolish he was being. Why, this was what pride could do to a man! It could lead him to act without thinking, and not for a moment had he given the Lieutenant's actual order any thought. He'd been far too busy proving to the doctor what a tough little kaffir he was.

If I were a child, he thought, then I would have been greatly excited by what I saw today. It was a dead white man, and now I know that a white man can die, the same as my father. I have seen this frighten other white men, and I want to see why the police come here to do so much writing. There is no food at home until tonight, when perhaps my father brings a little, and I don't have to go to school like the ones whose parents have the money—why should I go home? Let this big fool chase me, if he likes, for he will surely not come all the way. I will steal back, like I did the day I first saw the big snake, and perhaps I'll even share in that pig meat. I will steal back, with the cunning of my uncle's dog, lying low in the grass. It will be—but see, another man is coming this way. Come, let us follow! What strange things are happening. . . .

And sure enough, now Zondi had taken his eyes from the path, and had allowed them to pass casually over the long grass surrounding him, he was able to see three places where the seed tufts leaned against the press of the wind. His ears then snatched at a muffled giggle, and he knew himself for the bumbling idiot he must have looked. These had to be the children he sought—they could hardly be anyone else—and the rest was simple.

No, it wasn't; by slipping himself back into their skins again, he knew that, at the first sign of the hiding places being spotted, they'd be up and off and running like spring hares, leaving him far behind. His next move would, in fact, have to be judged most carefully.

With a strangled cry, Zondi pitched forward in his second-best suit and lay very still.

The speedometer needle gave no hint of the loss of momentum that Kramer was experiencing. Doringboom lay within sight, and the copper steeple on the Dutch Reformed church grew taller by the second. But his own interest in reaching the town seemed to be diminishing proportionately, for he was not an unreasonable man, and the evidence, presented to him at the picnic spot, had worked on his gut reaction like a dollop of milk of magnesia.

"Speaking objectively," he said, lighting another Lucky, "and forgetting about the drop for a moment, is there *anything* unusual about the case in your eyes?"

"Only that such a high point of suspension was employed—but that's part of the drop bit, anyway."

Then Strydom went on to explain that a surprisingly low point of suspension was very often the popular choice, as when a table leg or doorknob was used, involving less than a meter.

"Talking of which, Tromp," the DS added, going off on one of his tangents, "it bloody amazes me how stupid some coons can be! When I borrowed that tape just now, the one Van Heerden was complaining about being in inches, I found it had meters marked on the underneath side. You would have thought his boys would have looked!"

"Perhaps they had, Doc," Kramer answered with a slight smile; he'd suspected as much from the start.

"Hey? I don't get that. Anyway, where was I?"

"Getting the Nobel Prize for bullshit."

"Ach, no; that isn't a nice attitude when a bloke's doing his best. You can't have seen as many as I have, and it's quite true what I'm saying."

People who *played* at hanging—sex deviants and so forth, even kids copying from banned comics—were often caught out by how quick and easy hanging was. It took a pull of only 4.4 pounds to close off the jugular veins, for example. At 11 pounds the carotids closed, too, and at 33 pounds the windpipe was buggered. Now, when you knew that the same 33 pounds approximated the weight of the head and shoulders of a 140-pound man, then it didn't take a genius to work out what could be achieved simply by sitting on the floor and leaning back a bit. Unconsciousness would be almost instantaneous, and death, whether you liked it or not, could take its time.

Nor did it take a genius, Kramer conceded a little angrily to himself, to work out that only Tollie Erasmus would have had a compelling interest in going, as it were, according to the book. Anyone else could have achieved the same result with a minimum of fuss, effort, and imagination—and have been back in their car before the next lot of lights caught their reflectors.

WELKOM!—WELCOME! said the Doringboom boundary board.

"Get stuffed," said Kramer, hoping that Mickey wasn't going to a lot of trouble for nothing.

4

Constable Van Heerden must have radioed ahead some dire warning or other, because when Kramer and Doc Strydom drove round the back and into the Doringboom vehicle yard, at least half of the station's white complement just happened to be there. Five of them were crawling on, under, and through a green Ford, while the remaining three sixteenths, in the rhinocerine person of Sergeant Cecil Arnot, stood directing operations.

"Hello, gentlemen," he said, begrudging the obligatory smile that went with it. "As you will see, I have not been letting the *grass* grow under my feet."

"I don't think the car's where you'll find the money," Kramer replied, puzzled by that strange emphasis, "but it's certainly worthwhile having a look. Hell; Johannesburg number plates? Nobody bothered to bloody mention that to me. Have you—"

"I'm checking with Johannesburg, sir, and they'll be reporting back shortly. The plates themselves seem genuine."

"Uhuh."

"Is Dr. Myburgh here yet?" Strydom asked in English, as a courtesy.

27

"Ready and waiting, Doc! I passed on your telephone message at lunchtime, and he said there was no need to ring back; he'd be honored."

Funny, thought Kramer, watching the DS toddle off to where the mortuary, a Victorian relic, stood quietly on its own in the far corner. If Myburgh had known all along that he was having a visitor, then... But there wasn't time to take this any further.

"Sir," Arnot was saying, his heavy head lowered, "although I cannot explain how I sense this, I've reason to believe that someone has been *casting aspersions*."

He made it sound as horrible as anything an incontinent dog did, and then waited for his answer, little eyes aglint.

"Really? You must tell me about it later. Meanwhile I want to catch up with—"

"Sir, this is a serious matter. Perhaps all I need say is that a very careful inspection of the site was made by me this morning. It was, after all, my duty to ensure that the umfaans had not in any way interfered with the body. I saw no indications to this effect; the grass beneath the deceased bore no signs of trampling, and there were no other marks of a suspicious nature either. Furthermore, I am quite certain that no vehicle had proceeded beyond the prescribed parking area—it took seven of us to move the tables aside for the ambulance to back up. A precaution I personally organized, as it allowed us to work behind a screen without any inconvenience to the passing public. To summarize, the scene of death was given every scrutiny, in accordance with the—"

"Cecil," said Kramer, "I never doubted it."

"Hey?"

Arnot's ire missed the quick swerve, and came lumbering to a halt; you could almost hear the tail swishing behind the folds of his immense baggy trousers.

"You didn't, Lieutenant?"

"No. So now your question must be: who did?"

Kramer left him with that to think over, a process certain to waste several more minutes, and hurried on in the good doctor's wake. There was, of course, one thing you could always safely say about Sergeant Cecil P. Arnot, and that was, setting human nature aside, the man knew his job. If he claimed that the signs of disturbance had been minimal, quite unsuspicious, and in keeping with the situation as he saw it, then this just had to be so. Sod him.

For one wacky instant, as Kramer passed through the double doors of the old-fashioned post-mortem room, with its high ceiling and quaint skylight, he expected to hear lightning strike, and to see the prone form rise jerkily from the marble table. Then the tall, aristocratic figure on the left of the head, and the hunched, shaggy-haired dwarf on the right, dissolved back into two district surgeons, intent on examining a neck. The air still crackled, however, when Kramer stepped forward to introduce himself.

Myburgh looked up and nodded, tight-lipped; he was, as the Colonel had guessed, young and intelligent-seeming, with more than a resemblance to a celebrated Cape heart surgeon, which was bound—once he'd saved enough for a city practice—to stand him in good stead.

Mildly surprised by his reception, Kramer turned to Strydom and found him equally distant, as though withholding something you didn't say in front of natives.

"Doc? What gives?"

"Er—I'm afraid you somewhat misled me, and that has—um—resulted in an embarrassment of a professional nature."

"You called me a bloody fool," Myburgh reminded him.

"For which I have already apologized, even though when I said 'you fool,' I was really referring to myself, Dr. Myburgh. But, Tromp, isn't it true you said that scrawny bloody constable and the deceased were the same build?"

"No, I only said the same size, meaning height," Kramer replied, taking his first look at the corpse and hearing his voice trail. "Because Erasmus was average, around the 150-to-160-pound mark...."

"*Was,*" echoed Strydom, prodding the dead paunch. "*Was* being the operative word. What would you care to place his weight at now? Another fifteen? Another twenty, perhaps? Maybe more?"

"Around 180, 185. Christ, how did he get like that?"

"Not through being a nervous wreck," Strydom said cynically.

"But . . ."

"Ja, Tromp?"

"This means he must have been living very easy and drinking his bloody head off, night and day. Look at that tan, too, and the new haircut. . . . Hell, I don't understand."

"Nor do I," murmured Myburgh.

"You don't? This bastard was supposed to be on the run, Doc, with blokes in every—"

"I meant that I still don't understand what Van Heerden has to do with this. Will you explain, sir?"

But a reply from Strydom wasn't immediately forthcoming. He was engrossed in a calculation that he crossed out impatiently—and then returned to, repeating it twice over, with what appeared to be the same result. He slipped the notebook into his pocket, gave a cheery, meaningless smile, and suggested they begin the examination without further ado. His explanation could, if it was still required, be given later, he said.

Kramer, feeling acutely aware that the bluff held more than either he or Myburgh imagined, managed to contain his curiosity. He gave his attention instead to the equally placid, equally inscrutable features of the late Mr. Erasmus, and thought it a shame that he hadn't been strangled a nice deep purple. Hanging, with its kindly attitude to the complexion, wouldn't have been his choice at all. Two other things struck him, one snide and one ironical, which also helped to provide temporary distractions. The first was that Erasmus had an appendix scar exactly like the little white line on the Widow Fourie's sweet, peach-fluff belly, and finding it here smattered of very poor taste on the thief's part. And then there was the wince Kramer gave when the body, into which he'd dreamed of driving soft-nosed slugs, preferably at point-blank range, was slit open from chin to pubic arch.

Myburgh did all the heavy work, and, to judge by Strydom's grunts of approval, he did it well. His cutters soon had the ribs and breastbone freed from the flayed chest, and he took out a dangle of organs in one. After a time, the old man started carrying bits and pieces across to the sink for him, and their relationship settled down.

"Methodical," confided Strydom, noticing Kramer now at his elbow. "I could show you hundreds twice his age who would have gone straight for the neck."

He turned on the tap to sluice the viscera.

"Anything interesting?" Myburgh inquired, proffering his long knife. "That heart was good for another twenty years, I reckon."

"Liver was shot. No, man, you go ahead."

Myburgh opened the stomach: the smell was, if you'd encountered it often enough under those conditions, unmistakable.

"Brandy," said the district surgeons together.

"Ingested," added Myburgh, "as far as I can tell, just before death. I'll have the blood tested."

Strydom, with a return of his cagey expression, made no comment. He was, in a way, like a man suffering an attack of *déjà vu*, and his gaze turned blank for five drips of the blood into the bucket under the table.

"Come on now," Kramer urged, suddenly losing patience. "I know there's something weird on the go here. For a start, nobody's said anything about a brandy bottle being found."

"That's true," said Myburgh, who had gone back to sawing around the skull. "And I was there when Sergeant Arnot had the refuse bin—"

"All right, let's skip the brain for a moment, if you don't mind," Strydom requested him, but stayed where he was.

"Fine. I've been wanting to dive in at the back myself. Lieutenant? Could you give me a hand in getting the gent sunny side up?"

Erasmus, his face covered by a flap of scalp, was placed on his front, and Myburgh cut down to expose the spine.

"Third and fourth vertebrae," he reported. "Fracture-dislocation with the spinal cord ruptured a little over half its thickness."

"General state of surrounding tissues?"

"Good, considering. No severe tearing or other damage."

"Have you ever seen anything similar?"

"Only once," replied Myburgh, beginning to show some bewilderment over the way his senior was behaving. "When I was a medical student, and they let us in on a P.M. at Pretoria

31

Central. It was a study in the rate of digestion."

"Did they tell you anything about the length of the drop?"

"No, but I've read about it in *Taylor's*. The drop is usually six to seven feet, unquote."

"Dr. Myburgh, you'll forgive me if I speak as a man of experience?"

"Certainly. I welcomed your interest."

Strydom moved across to stand over the gleam of the neck bones and, after a quick check, said: "If this were the body of Constable Van Heerden, then I'd say it had been calculated to a nicety. A perfect job, in fact. But, gentlemen, I feel sure that a drop of six feet would have torn this man's head off."

Kramer quite forgot the match in his fingers until it burned him.

"I'm sorry, can I have that again?" asked Myburgh, doing a slow blink. "Erasmus is only about thirty pounds above average, and you're saying that could make such a difference?"

"In terms of striking force, because that is the crucial factor, nearly *half a ton* of difference," Strydom replied, taking out his notebook.

"Now, listen here, Doc—"

"Patience, Tromp. Try judging it for yourself. The optimum striking force has been standardized at twenty-four hundred weight, or 2,688 pounds. Any more or any less, and you could find yourself in trouble. And I'm not going into neck characteristics here, because both examples are good and sound, but very different."

"Twenty-four; I've got that."

"Which would suit Van Heerden exactly, and remember he's roughly ten pounds under average. However, give a six-foot drop to this bloke, and the striking force would be *thirty*-four hundred weights—or in the region of 1,120 pounds too many. I leave the rest to your imagination."

Myburgh actually seemed to shudder.

"Okay, Doc—so how much did he get?"

"Three feet."

"He couldn't have jumped from the fork in the tree."

"No."

"Or from the—"

"No."

This time the match made it to Kramer's Lucky, which trembled behind the cup of his hands.

"Then I don't see how he could have possibly done this by himself," Myburgh said softly, lifting off Erasmus's vault to look into his brain. "And yet..."

"Doc, what are you saying? That I've got a murder on my plate?"

Strydom shrugged. "You might have, Tromp. Only—and please don't laugh—it looks to me more like, well, a bloody state execution."

That was only the beginning. Kramer left the mortuary to ring Colonel Muller, and was immediately accosted by a self-satisfied Sergeant Arnot, bearing an object wrapped in a yellow silk scarf.

"Not so fast, sir! Take a look at this."

"From the car?"

The scarf was allowed to fall away, revealing a snub-nosed Colt Cobra .38 Special with walnut grips and six loaded chambers. The metal gleamed raw where the serial number had been filed off.

"Erasmus had it inside his driving door, where he could reach it through a slit he'd made in the leather."

"Nice work, Sarge. Label it up and I'll take it to Ballistics."

"And now the other hand," said Arnot, grinning like he was running a kids' party. "From under the seat on the passenger's side."

It was a second and much nastier weapon: a 9mm Browning Hi-Power automatic with external hammer, fixed sights, pearl grips, and chromed finish—also missing its serial number. The 13-shot magazine was full.

"Fantastic. Any brandy bottles?"

"Sir?"

"In the Ford, or at the site this morning?"

"None here, and no booze of any description, except for some old beer cans, down that way. Do you think this is the thirty-eight he tried to use on you?"

"Could be, if he was too scared to make contact for a new one, or too stupid to throw it away."

"Stupid's the word for it," agreed Arnot, pursing his broad upper lip. "Right here he had the means to bump himself off nineteen bloody times over, with none of that fooling about in the trees. Can you explain that to me, sir?"

Kramer, who didn't know the English word for *academic*, and who doubted if Cecil would recognize the Afrikaans term, which had been fairly recently introduced, settled for patting him on the shoulder.

And there was more to come. Back in the mortuary, with Colonel Muller's stunned silence still music in his ears, Kramer was informed of further discoveries by the team of Strydom and Myburgh, whose professional circumspection was having a hell of a time with their schoolboyish excitement.

"We have reason to believe," announced Myburgh, quite soberly, "that this isn't the same blinking rope!"

"No?"

"Which is why, Tromp, we'd like you to have a squint at the plaited impression on the cuticle of the neck—the weal, man. You see where it's starting to go brownish, like parchment? Your patient, Dr. Myburgh."

"Thank you, sir. Well, when I checked the pattern there, mainly to observe the ecchymosis, I noticed there was a sort of repetition—caused, I assumed, by the deceased's removal from the tree. Then it was suggested to me that we examine the upper points of the V mark, where the strain is lifting off the throat, and two dissimilar rope patterns were just discernible. Our conclusion was that the angle had changed marginally after the initial suspension, due in part to the two inches or so of stretch. We'd like to put all this under a microscope, of course."

"The uncanny thing," said Doc Strydom, as if that point needed to be made at all, "is that the second rope—or, as we see it, the first—shows identical characteristics to the officially favored variety: five-strand in three-quarter-inch thickness, covered in wash-leather. I saw more than seventy in my years, so I should know."

"Don't forget the bruise," Myburgh said generously.

"Oh, that. I hope you don't think we are unaware of the dangers of reading too much into the evidence, Tromp."

"Fire away, man. This is crazy enough to take it."

"Whoever did the estimate for the drop must have known that the knot of the noose, so to speak, must be placed at the angle of the left jaw—which allows for the quarter turn clockwise, snapping the head back. Put it the other side, and he just suffocates."

"Uhuh. You found a graze running round?"

"More than that: a bruise no rope could have made on its own. I would hazard a guess and say that a metal eye had been spliced into the end—again, in the approved fashion."

"Uhuh?"

"That's the very point I'm making: few people know what a proper noose is like—most think of the so-called hangman's knot the Yanks favor. They may be advanced in many respects, but as executioners they're terrible. A standard five-foot drop, for instance! The electric—"

"What," Kramer interrupted, "does this metal eye do, precisely?"

"It facilitates exact positioning and instantaneous, friction-free constriction, which means—ideally—as you can see here, the odontoid peg breaks the odontoid ligament and drives into the medulla, destroying the vital centers."

"An old wives'—" began Myburgh, then thought better of it.

"Same as a bullet, only you'd have to aim hell of a straight and it'd be messy. As well as that, there's . . ."

Van Heerden and some of the car-search party came tiptoeing in, hopeful of being allowed to share in the leftovers. They stopped at the foot of the table and nodded, with varying degrees of self-confidence, at Kramer.

"Got my plan yet, Van?" he asked.

"On Sarge Arnot's desk, Lieutenant. But your boy hadn't pitched up when we left, so I didn't bring him."

"Quick thinking," Kramer said, and turned back to the two district surgeons. "By the way, this lot found two firearms hidden in the deceased's car."

Strydom nudged Myburgh and half whispered, "Did you hear that? I told you this wouldn't have escaped you in the end!"

"I'm not so sure about that, but thanks, sir."

"Oh, Lieutenant, the sarge says he's got something for you on that number plate of yours," Van Heerden added, dragging his eyes from Erasmus's paunch fat, which was as thick as four fingers.

"I'll go and see him now. Well, gentlemen, anything more that's new?"

Myburgh looked into the sink. "Bladder had been voided, but we knew that already from the state of his pants. Fresh hair clippings in the ears. No, I don't think so."

"Me neither," concurred Strydom. "We'll get this little lot stuffed back in and stitched up, then I will be ready to leave when you are."

Kramer neglected to respond. Something Myburgh had just said—to do with either the pants or the hair—had sounded very wrong somehow. It was awakening obscure echoes of some previous investigation, and making him feel pretty certain that, right at the start, he'd overlooked an obvious incongruity.

With a grunt, he left for the main building, resigned to the fact that bad news must await him there. If it had been anything else, then the duty sergeant would doubtlessly have been across the yard in a great cloud of dung and dust.

5

THE BAD NEWS READ as follows:

> TO SAP DORINGBOOM: LICENSE PLATES STOLEN FM TRACTOR
> ON SMALLHOLDING MOUNTAIN OUTLOOK. LICENSEE RE-
> PORTS NO KNOWLEDGE THEFT AS TRACTOR ABANDONED IN
> FIELD AFTER TOTAL BREAKDOWN. THEFT CD HV OCCURRED
> ANYTIME SIX MONTH PERIOD. FORD SEDAN STOLEN FM JHB
> CAR HIRE FIRM YEAR AGO. ORIGINAL COLOR BLUE. BETTER
> LUCK NEXT TIME. ENDS.

"I must say I've always preferred a blue myself," said Strydom, folding the Telex message and handing it back. "But where would this bloke find mountains to stare at?".

"Probably the bloody mine dumps," answered Kramer, giving the Chev the gun as Doringboom petered out.

"You're a bit upset?"

Hearing it put this way, Kramer had to smile. "Ach, not really, Doc. At least it backs up what we collected on Tollie: he'd never have bought himself a motor that was warmer than a sodding Easter egg."

"I suppose it's over to Jo'burg now?"

"That side of it. Christ, it was lucky you were around today."

They covered a silent kilometer.

"No, I meant what I said to young Myburgh, Tromp; he'd not have missed the brandy, nor would he have left matters after the firearms find. He could have received the same help from several sources besides myself—Prinsloo, for instance. The basic trouble was our dependency, to a degree, on textbooks from England."

"Oh, ja?"

"The English are not, you see, taken on average, a very big race. Or at least this appears to be true of their criminal classes, and so these misunderstandings occur when generalizations are made. Now, don't mistake me; the English had hanging down to a fine art before they chickened out, but all that doesn't go into a forensic handbook. Myburgh reacted as I would have done under similar circumstances."

"All the same," said Kramer, accepting his light, "I still say it was one hell of a coincidence."

Strydom looked away. "Okay, so I admit it."

"What?"

"That this trip wasn't so coincidental. It didn't even have anything to do with Erasmus, except maybe indirectly. You could say it sort of triggered off an idea."

"I'm not with you, Doc."

"Er—this really ought to have come up naturally. You know? I just thought it would be a good opportunity for you and me to have a little chat. Man, you don't know how impossible it is normally to get you alone in one place for more than two minutes. However, you brought Zondi to do the driving and—"

"*Ach*, I see!"

"No, Tromp, I don't think so," Strydom replied grimly.

Kramer, whose thoughts had been trying to fit around the idea of an execution, which was harder than grabbing wet soap with boxing gloves on, realized abruptly what was being said. While he couldn't read the innuendo, some kind of trouble lay very plainly between the lines. This baffled him because, whatever they might say behind each other's back, he and Strydom got on well together, being always careful whom they said it to. And when it came down to sorting out a stiff, the Doc seldom let you down. Yet morgue work was only a single aspect of the DS's duties, Kramer remembered now, and felt himself tensing up. Strydom was also required to attend corporal punishment at the triangle, to investigate complaints by political detainees, to give yellow fever shots to air travelers, and to care for the health of all police personnel and their dependents, under the force's free medical scheme. Being rather dull by comparison, this latter function wasn't one that sprang readily to mind—as it certainly should have done.

"Doctor, what the hell are you trying to say?" Kramer demanded. "It's about Zondi, am I right?"

Strydom sighed, turning the sound into a low chuckle of respect. Then he took off his glasses to clean them—an old ploy of his when he wanted to appear defenseless—and began speaking again in an entirely different tone. At a guess, it was intended to be soothing, but its effect rivaled the scrape of fingernails down a whitewashed wall.

"I know you're a bit touchy in this regard," Strydom said. "You even proved as much this afternoon, by making him walk five kilometers just to impress me."

"Rubbish."

"You had no special need for the information at that stage, Tromp. I know it was my presence that influenced—"

"Ach, kak! You had nothing to do with it!"

"Then why did you, Tromp? Even Van Heerden looked a bit surprised."

"It was a job he could do best."

"So you might believe, but—"

"No, in *his* bloody opinion!" Kramer chopped across. "It was also his idea."

Strydom put his glasses back on and stared for a while.

"Can you explain that some more to me?"

This wasn't a topic Kramer liked in the least, and he wished he'd not responded at all, but the damage was done, and he had to go on.

"It would have been hard on the man to say no. Zondi has never done less than his best."

"Nobody's arguing. But you know that it's my duty to report

on the fitness of all CID staff, and that I depend on all senior officers for help with my assessments. Not once have I had anything from you, and that is making my position with Colonel Muller very difficult. I can't keep writing 'Progress as expected' week after week without him wondering when all this progress is going to stop, and he has an A-1 Bantu again. You do know that he insists on every member of CID being 100 percent fit, hey?"

"I heard it was 100 percent efficient."

With an uneasy laugh, Strydom said, "And I'd always understood that the two went together."

"So what do you want me to say? Chuck him on the scrap-pile?"

"We didn't say that when you got yourself shot up in that Portuguese café, Tromp. Please don't get unreasonable."

It was on the tip of Kramer's tongue to point out how unreasonable a comparison that was, and to do this very forcibly, when a much simpler solution occurred to him.

"Doc, just listen," he said gruffly, like a man baring his soul. "I've had that boy for how many years now? Do you know how many hours I've spent training him? You should know what slow learners some of them are, man, even if you've never had to work with them. But I tell you, and others would say exactly the same, that when you get a good boy, then you want to hold on to him. You must know as well as I do what could happen if mine was—"

"Say no more," Strydom interrupted. "I've got the same thing with Nxumalo down at my morgue. And besides, you sound like my wife, when the cookboy wants to give in his notice! But seeing as we are talking like friends again, the way we ought always to talk, then please take some friendly advice. Your noncooperation in this matter could have far-reaching effects, and I wouldn't want to be party to that."

"Up to you, Doc."

"Damn and blast, Tromp! You don't seem to appreciate what I'm trying to do for you off the record. Very well; I make out my next report on him this coming Monday. You send me a memo anytime before that you like. But if I don't get your memo, then you and the Colonel can argue the toss over what it is he requires. And I don't envy you trying to prove your version either!"

Kramer felt he'd gone some small way towards providing that proof when Zondi, looking very chipper, if in need of a good dry-clean, flagged them down at the picnic spot. He clearly had something useful to impart—which, as it turned out, far exceeded any expectations.

"Let's hear it," Kramer said, winding down his window.

"Two things, Lieutenant."

"Shoot."

"Number one, I have reason to believe," replied Zondi, who was such a flagrant mimic most of his subjects never noticed, "that the body of the deceased was brought to this place after his demise."

"What?" said Strydom, leaning across. "Did someone see this?"

"Not in as many words, Dr. Strydom, sir, but observations were indeed made. My witnesses stand over by the fence."

Two potbellied, small Zulu boys, possibly aged five and eight, dressed in a man's ragged shirt and a woman's torn summer shorts, respectively, peered at them from behind hands shyly raised.

"Part of the raiding party here today," Zondi explained, a smile flickering. "I thought it expedient to have them return with me, and to discuss exactly what they had seen upon arrival. They told me it is their custom to hide behind a tree while they ascertain whether the occupant of any parked vehicle—they had, of course, seen the deceased's car from a distance—will take exception to their presence."

"Uhuh, so they hide behind tree *A*—it's the farthest back," said Kramer, trying to speed this up.

"Correct, Lieutenant. Except when the sun comes out and the day grows hot, then they may wait by another one."

"Why?" asked Strydom.

"The ants, Doctor, sir."

"Oh, ja."

"This has some bearing?" Kramer grumbled. "Come on, I can

see you're enjoying this, but get to the bloody point."

"May I speak without reservation, sir?"

"You heard what I said, man!"

"Then I must confess shamefully that the children of my people have very crude natures," Zondi went on, and Strydom nodded. "Urination affords them many primitive delights. It gives them a true sense of power to see the creature upon which they have committed this act hop so swiftly away. Then there is the pleasure they take in seeing a man doing such a babyish thing as to wet down his trousers when he is drunk. For them to see a European—"

"Zondi! You're a bastard, aren't you?" Kramer laughed, his memory of an investigation in which ants had provided vital evidence, along with a caterpillar, suddenly restored. "History repeats itself?"

"Lieutenant?"

But Zondi hadn't recalled the case; his bewilderment was as great as that being shown by Doc Strydom, who was becoming very irritable, too.

"Just get on with it," Kramer sighed.

"Well, sir, all that happened was that these children expressed some surprise to find the ants still in their home beneath the place where the deceased was hanging. Ngidi had told me of the unfortunate condition of the trousers in question, and I could see what they were saying was true. It is common knowledge that ants will take away their eggs if someone makes water on them. But those ants are all happy—as you may come and see."

They did just that, to suppressed giggling from the far side of the fence, and Strydom finished up on his hands and knees, grinning down the ant hole.

"So who gets the Nobel this time?" he said over his shoulder to Kramer. "Yet those umfaans are quite right. These little chaps would have still been in there before eight, having their kip, and that's why none of this occurred to Sergeant Arnot—he was here too early."

"It also clinches your theory, Doc."

"Too right, it does!"

Kramer helped him back onto his feet, and checked to see what time it was: five on the dot, and getting pretty late, considering he and Zondi hadn't stopped in more than twenty-four hours.

"Now, what about the other thing you mentioned?" he asked, lighting a Lucky. "Let's hear it, then get the hell out of here."

Zondi lost some of his confidence, and pointed to the taller child.

"I am not so sure if this is important, Lieutenant, but that one picked up a bag near the stone this morning. He didn't tell Ngidi because the question put to him was had he taken from the deceased's car or person?"

Familiar with how literal the illiterate poor could be in their interpretations, Kramer found nothing remarkable in this, but he did wonder why Zondi was being so half-hearted. And he said so.

"It is a worthless cloth bag, sir. The only thing special is that it was not here yesterday, although I could not see a connection between—"

"Not perhaps a bank's bag?"

"Oh, no, Lieutenant—proper trash, and not strong enough to carry money, even notes. I will get it for you, as I left it in his possession."

The bag that Zondi brought back to them was black and made of a cheap cotton fabric, hand-stitched clumsily up the sides. There was no drawstring, nor any indication of what it might have been used for. Kramer looked down into it and saw, as Zondi must have done, that there wasn't even a little fluff at the bottom. Then, noticing the material was slightly stiffer at one point, he turned the thing inside out. The saliva stain wasn't all that became visible then—so did several blond hairs, fairly obviously from the head of Tollie Erasmus.

"God almighty," gasped Strydom. "It's a hood! A proper executioner's hood!"

"Boss?" said Zondi, startled into forgetting himself.

Very briefly, Kramer filled him in on the post-mortem results, and then, because this recital revived the initial impact of their bizarre discovery, stood in a brown study, his gaze fixed farther along the fence. When he focused again, he found himself looking at the desiccated forms of two finches, pinned onto the barbed wire by a shrike.

"If this bloke knows all about drops," he said quietly, "and wanted to fake a suicide, then he'd have easily found another tree with a platform the right height beneath it. But he didn't. He didn't even bother to find out where the hood had got to. Just stuck his kill up there for all the world to see, as if he couldn't give a bugger."

"Gives me the bloody creeps, Tromp. I get visions of a first-class scaffold, with provisions for half-inch adjustments and all the rest of it. Pit, steps going down. Hell."

This was too much for Kramer, and he snapped out of his reverie. "Ach, steady on, Doc! If you ask me, some bastards tried to screw the cash out of Tollie with a little homemade third degree, and it all went wrong. Must have been at least two of them involved, so that one could drive his Ford here."

"I disagree," Strydom said huffily.

"Well, something like that. Can't guess any better until we know where he's been the last three months. Probably got up the nose of a Jo'burg mob."

"I'm objecting to you treating this fracture as a fluke, Lieutenant. Hell, the flukes themselves are rare enough, without hoods and metal rings and God knows what else. Do you want me to prove that to you?"

The Colonel was scrutinizing his ceiling, where he had a favorite lizard that caught flies for him. But the hour was late and it had probably left the office.

"Just give me an outline to be going on with," he told Kramer, "as you're too bloody shagged out to talk any proper sense this evening. So let's stop psychoanalyzing Doc's little obsession and concentrate on what action you're taking."

"Firstly, sir, I don't want this getting to the press before we understand it better. You can see the effect it's had on a supposedly mature—"

"Consider that done."

"Ta. I've already handed the firearms over to Ballistics, and they're sending specifications to every gun squad from here to

Cape Town. Not much of a lead, I admit."

"Worth trying."

"The usual forensic checks are going ahead on Erasmus's clothing, vehicle, and so on. Also the hood we found."

"Good."

"We were too late to dust the car for fingerprints—Arnot's mob had already been through it. I get the Bible back in the morning—nothing on it so far, except Erasmus's own—and we'll see where that takes us."

"You never can tell."

"Lead kindly light, sir?"

"Trompie," admonished the Colonel, a full elder of the Dutch Reformed Church, who wore a black frock coat and white bow tie on Sundays, "you mustn't think being shagged out is any excuse for that kind of behavior! Now push off home, you hear?"

"One other thing: I've put out a description of Erasmus as a reminder to those in the big cities who didn't think this was a matter which concerned them. I bet you he was in Jo'burg the whole time, getting himself a nice tan at Zoo Lake, right under their bloody noses."

"Tomorrow, man. When you can also get all excited about what this same playboy was doing twenty kilometers south of Doringboom."

The man had a point there.

Kramer rose from the corner of the desk and started to leave.

"Oh, by the way, Tromp..."

"Colonel?"

"I believe you and the DS had a little chat together this afternoon."

"Did we, sir?" Kramer said, suddenly having had a stomachful of devious old bastards.

"I fully realize it was confidential," Colonel Muller added hastily, as though the last thing he'd think of would be to pry, "but I just wondered."

"Uhuh?"

"Well, how it had gone down."

"Like a glass of cold puke, sir."

It didn't seem possible that a final touch had still to be put to that day, but Kramer, who'd seen two sunsets and no sleep, should have known better.

He should also have been paying more attention to Zondi's droll account of the afternoon's adventures, because just after taking the turnoff to Kwela Village, he was aware of having missed a bit somewhere.

"Go back to not knowing how to catch them," he said, flicking away a half-smoked cigarette.

"That was easy, boss. You remember what I said about the excited state of these kids? All I had to do was to lie very still. Soon they came crawling to see what the matter is this time, and they come right up close to hear if I am breathing. Pah! Two hands, two kids! The rest run like—"

"You mean little sod. Thought you were too damn perky for a ten-kilometer round trip."

"They are happy, boss. By the way, twenty cents on expenses?"

"Fine."

"You know that bacon?"

"Don't tell me: Ngidi scoffed it."

"No, the sergeant"—Zondi laughed—"while Ngidi was chasing the kids."

This made a good note to end on. Kramer just added that he didn't want Zondi under his feet until at least the following afternoon, and then they drove in silence toward the smoky spread of the municipal township. Almost in the center of the serried rows of two-room dwellings, all as neatly placed as a thousand bureaucratic rubbers, the Chev stopped at one distinguished by a pathway edged in rusty cans. Zondi waved his thanks, and the Chev, which knew what to do, rumbled off down the corrugated dirt road and found the quickest way to Blue Haze.

Kramer had bought the old farmhouse, with its meter-thick shale walls and wraparound verandah, to put in his will. Pending the implementation of this will, he rented the property, at the cost of a Trekkersburg apartment, to the ultimate beneficiary, the Widow Fourie, and her family of young children. It was really a very uncomplicated arrangement, which allowed him to pursue his chosen career without any thought of irresponsibility, and to be able to sleep the odd night in the country when the mood took him. As it had, against his better judgment, done now.

But the children's lights were out by the time the Chev finally nosed into the driveway and came crunching to a stop outside the front door. And the Widow Fourie, whose ample mind and body had drawn Kramer there, came out alone to greet him, tying back her yellow hair.

"You caught me just going to wash it," she scolded, her kiss pleased and quick. "So what's been happening in the world I haven't heard about?"

"Ach, would you believe a state execution?"

"Big deal," said the Widow Fourie. "It's Tuesday, isn't it?"

6

THERE ARE DREAMS THAT can affect the whole of a man's working day. In the case of a very sweet dream, or of a positively terrible one, its influence can extend over a period far greater than that. Such a dream is, generally speaking, best not dreamed at all.

This had always been Kramer's belief, and it was why he was trying to get back to sleep again, the sooner to expunge all traces of the girl with long legs. Then again, to dream of one female, and to wake up in the bed of another, could leave a bloke feeling guilty for no good reason at all. But he remained dozing, remembering her now only in patches of sharp, scented detail: the neat knob of a wristbone, sweat pearled in the cup above her breastbone, the muss of honey wisps, a nipple swelling from pink raisin to grape, and the pinch of those long legs, straddling him, turning him over and over, and her laughter. So simple, so uncomplicated, so greedy it shocked him, made him greedy as well. Her crazy joy in him.

"Hey," said the Widow Fourie, whose warm back smoothed his belly, "what's the point, when Joanna will be in with the tea soon?"

He rolled away and looked down at the polished floorboards,

noticing where the original owner's great stinkwood bed had left the impression of a caster; what a hell of a nightly battering it must have withstood to do that. Then this gratuitous lewdness disgusted him, and he went to take a bath.

The Widow Fourie wandered in a few minutes later, carrying the tea tray, and bringing her cigarettes with her. Like Strydom, she often complained about getting in five minutes of proper conversation, and this had long been her little trick. She knew, of course, that the door would never be bolted.

"How are you this morning?" she asked, settling on the lavatory lid, which she'd prettified with blue lace. "You may not know this, but you were in a hell of a state all night. Worse than when the girls both had flu and I had them in with me."

Kramer, who liked to soak with only his nose, and as little else as possible, above water, shrugged a ripple down the bath.

"I've also been thinking about this hangman, though," she continued, clattering the cups, "and this I do know: he must be connected in some way with the prisons department. It's the only way of gaining the required knowledge—you can't tell me that the convicts really pick up anything but rumors. I remember reading once that a senior lecturer in criminology at the University of S.A. had to pretend he was a barber—actually his dad had been one—just to hear the inside story of Pretoria Central. You know how fussy they are about strangers in the jails? This prof or whatever used to cut the warders' hair across the road and ask them questions, just casually sort of. Are you taking this in?"

He raised his chin to say: "Fine, you've narrowed it down to an insider—but many warders do you think there are in this country? We've over two hundred and fifty jails, a hundred thousand locked up in them—"

"Ach, you know perfectly well what I mean! The expert knowledge has to come from somewhere, and at least we know roughly where that is. Your tea's poured."

Although voices carried well, he needed cues like this, especially when a tap was running.

"Ta, my girl. I can see the Doc's nonsense has really caught your imagination."

"Don't try to bluff me you aren't wondering a bit!"

"To tell you the truth," said Kramer, taking his cup. "I'm putting the who and why of this right out of my mind until we get a lead on Erasmus's last whereabouts. Switch that off, please."

She obliged, frowning slightly as if dissatisfied with his reply, but not actually querying it.

"Then you've got something else on your mind, Trompie, or you'd have tried out the new frigate Janie's made. He says it's to shoot General Amin with, for what he does to people, but I told him Uganda hasn't got any sea and besides—"

Kramer had submerged briefly, making quite a splash. He stepped out and took up his towel.

"Ja, ja, so maybe I have."

"Oh, that!" The Widow laughed, putting down her teacup. "That's the whole trouble with having servants."

"No, I—"

"Come on, why don't we, though?" she said with sudden mischief. "Jo's back in the kitchen and the kids aren't up."

She rose and slipped home the bolt slowly and suggestively, making a funny, erotic thing of it, watching his eyes. Then she began loosening the gown which covered her voluptuous maturity, her wealth of warmth and tenderness so enveloping. How detached the girl had been, how detached, he remembered; how free she had left him.

The Widow Fourie let go of the bow she had been undoing in her belt. "Is it Zondi again?" she asked solemnly. "There is definitely something; I can sense it."

Kramer began drying his hair.

"Now listen to me, Trompie. I've had an idea recently. If the worst comes to the worst, and his leg doesn't get any better, then why not start using some of the land round the back? Mickey could find—well—things to plant in it for us, turn it into a market garden. I know he grew up on a farm, so he's bound to be able to—you know."

"All he knows of farming is what it did to his dad."

"He could learn, though. You're the one who's always said how intelligent he is."

"Mickey's leg is mending nicely; you'll see."

"He should have gone on giving it rest after—"

"For him to decide."

51

"Oh, no," said the Widow Fourie, very firmly. "Chris Strydom says that you're the one who lets his hopes rise. Without you, he'd be treated like any other boy in the same situation, and it isn't right—"

"Behind my back, hey?"

"I just happened to see Chris in the street."

"Uhuh?"

"Tromp, you've got to realize this is for your sake as well! I wouldn't, normally. You know how I—"

"Then look at my back," he said, stalking out, "and try to remember it."

That made a lousy start to the morning. Admittedly, there was nothing rational in the tacit agreement over the leg, but Kramer knew where it mattered most to him—in his gut—that Zondi needed his backing all the way, whatever purpose he chose to put it to. And while the work still got done, sod them and their red tape; he just didn't want to know.

His punch knocked wide the door to Fingerprints, and he followed it through with a cheerful greeting.

"You can go out and start again," Lieutenant Dirk Gardiner advised him, rising stockily in his blue safari suit. "This isn't the place for what you're hoping."

"Nothing?"

"Nothing," affirmed Gardiner, handing over the Bible.

"You put the rays on it?"

"The lot. It's full of miracles, but none of them worked for you, my friend."

Gardiner was one of the few people Kramer knew who could crack jokes while their breath still smelled of breakfast. For once, however, this did nothing for him, and he had to force an appreciative groan before leaving.

So much for Fingerprints.

Ballistics didn't even try to soften the blow, but dispassionately delivered both barrels. The Colt .38 was not the same gun that had been used during the raid at Peacevale, nor was either of the recovered weapons described on the list of reported thefts. Kramer asked for more work to be done on the metal where the numbers had been filed off.

"It won't necessarily get us anywhere," murmured the ballistics man. "And we've got a lot on."

"Try it. Could be the owners were too scared to tell you their firearms had been taken, or maybe they don't even know yet."

"Hmmm."

"We'd have two addresses. I know it's a faint chance, but Erasmus could have stolen them himself."

The ballistics man made a sound like a silencer and went back into his lab.

So much for bloody science.

With the Bible in his right hand, and swearing quietly under his breath, Kramer took himself out onto the pavement. As chance would have it, an Anglican minister walked by on his way to the cathedral, pretending he didn't hear the row coming from Security on the first floor.

"Excuse me, Reverend," Kramer said on impulse, blocking his path, "but if you wanted to know about Bibles, where would you go?"

The minister responded warily, easing the dog collar around his plump throat, and clearing some phlegm there.

"Is this to do with television?" he asked, glancing about.

"No, sir; I'm from CID here, working on an investigation: This is the Bible we've got an interest in, you see, and we were hoping it'd give us a lead."

"Ah. Has it a bookshop label in it?"

"Been removed."

"Mmmm. Then one wouldn't really know where one should start. Not an authority on them myself, of course. Tell you what, though, there's always the Christian bookshop up the road a bit. You must know it?"

Having received his directions, Kramer set off at a brisk pace that gradually slowed down, adapting itself to a more sensible approach to a venture that held little promise. Quite soon he was half enjoying his walk, and the minor distractions it afforded him. The morning was muggy and warm, and the sky still the misty white of a bathroom mirror, which had brought out the housewives in their brightest of frocks. They darted from car to store-like tropical fish—some were just as ugly—and flicked away from the gray-skinned beggar crabbing his legless way down the gray paving stones. If you did catch their eye, they never blinked. More interesting were the gawpers, blacks for the most part, whose fixed stares made them blink a good deal, as they stood outside shopwindows watching the miracle of the SATV test card. Every other bloody shop seemed to be selling sets, Kramer noted, and this included a hairdressing salon and, so far, two respectable jewelers'. The gawpers were interesting because you had to work out which were honest idiots, and which were pickpockets and bag-snatchers responding intelligently to the advent of television. Then came Toll Street and the dividing line between bustling commercialism and the sort of shop assistants who kept a good book under the till. He crossed over against the lights, to hold himself in trim, and started along a wide sidewalk that had little eddies of confetti in its gutter. Just about every denomination known to Trekkersburg had its main church between that set of traffic lights and the next: Baptist, Dutch Reformed, Presbyterian, Methodist, Congregationalist, Mormon—and, at the far end, Lutheran, playing David and Goliath with the Bleeding Heart towering above it across the way. There was a funeral on there, and the undertakers were out having a smoke; Kramer gave old George Henry Abbot a wave, called out that he'd drop by soon, and took the next turning.

He immediately recognized the long, low façade of the yellow-brick bookshop, but excused himself his oversight on the grounds that, with its total lack of people appeal in the sign-writing of Larkin and Sons, Ltd., and its air of complacent prosperity, he had always thought the place sold veterinary supplies to stock breeders. That just showed how much you could miss from a car.

You could also miss quite a lot from the pavement. When Kramer went up the steps and into the showroom, he was astonished by what he saw there. Hell, never mind being Christian; Larkin's looked the biggest bloody bookshop in town. There were thousands of glossy volumes on the wall shelves and on the display units that covered the vast, carpeted floor, together with an unimaginable number of knickknacks— like the molded relief map of the Holy Land, or the Sunday school blackboard—and some pretty weird stuff near the cash desk. He browsed through this while the salesman wrapped up something in brown paper for a nun.

For twenty cents, you could buy a patch, presumably to sew on your jeans, that said *Jesus Never Lets Me Down*. At thirty cents, there was an American comic book called *God's Smuggler*, which told the true story of a young Dutchman who said things such as: "One Bible could buy a cow now in Russia!" and was rewarded by having a sexy wife with massive bosoms. But Kramer's chief delight was an American magazine entitled the *Moody Monthly*—in honor of some famous preacher, it seemed—which he very nearly bought for the Colonel's secretary.

Then the salesman, an old gentleman in rimless glasses tinted slightly blue, asked what he could do to be of service, and examined the Bible most meticulously.

"Jiminy," he said. "I'm afraid you couldn't have picked on a commoner sort. I might have sold it, I might not. This is also the line carried by the ordinary trade, and so there's no end of places it could have come from. I am sorry."

"Are you sure, sir?" Kramer persisted.

"In 1975, South Africa became the largest distributor of complete Bibles in the world," the salesman disclosed proudly. "I have in my office a United Bible Societies report. Would it help you in any way for your superiors to see it? Then I'm *sure* they'll understand that you've done for them all you can."

Kramer thanked him for his thoughtfulness, spurned the offer, and left, crumpling the free tract he'd been given. Bibles, next!—when the English-language press had already claimed that the Republic was a world leader in gun-owning, divorces, murders, assaults, road deaths, suicides, persons shot by the police, and of course, after all that, executions. The weight of statistics against his chances of success, even in the long term, was beginning to bear down intolerably, while luck, his only hope of relief, had clearly reneged on him. Like one other bitch he could mention.

Zondi had felt the younger children leave the bed they shared with him soon after their mother had done. When the smell of maize porridge began to drift in from the other room, he had heard the twins stir beneath the window, squabble in whispers over whose turn it was to stow away their mattress, and then go creeping out. For a long while following that, he'd heard and felt nothing, but had slept deep, where a man's spirit was restored.

Now he was awake and watching Miriam through the doorway, touching his wife's fine, straight-backed body with his eyes, and admiring the grace she brought to the humdrum tasks of the home. Once, however, she would have been humming softly—too softly to disturb him—and it was noticeable how silent she was. These were difficult times.

He yawned loudly, patting the sound as it came out, for a comical effect, and sat up.

Miriam smiled round at him. "I suppose you will be hungry now," she said. "There is mealie meal on the stove, and hot water, too."

"Hau! And I see my suit is neatly pressed. Is there a dress you have seen in some window?"

That made her laugh; it always did. Miriam had never thought to buy a new dress in her life, but she'd worked for a white family, where this catch phrase had originated. Her amusement was gone the next instant, when, unable to stop himself, Zondi flinched as he moved his leg and the rat woke up, too.

"Come, there is hot water," Miriam repeated brusquely. "I will also put on the kettle and my big pot."

He shuffled through to the other room, and found her zinc washing tub already positioned on some newspaper to protect the rammed-earth floor. With that grace he'd been watching, Miriam hefted an old paraffin tin off the stove and tipped four gallons of near-boiling water into the tub without spilling more than a drop. Then she carefully added a little cold from another tin, and nodded for him to get in. By wriggling about a bit, and by sticking his feet out straight, and leaning far back, Zondi found the right position again. He lapped the water over his thigh with his hand.

"It's good," he said.

Miriam went out to fill the kettle and pot at their tap next to the privy. While she was gone, Zondi gave his leg a ringing slap, to see what that might do, and thought it had worked for a moment. Then Mr. Rat recovered from his surprise and bit back.

"There is sweat on your lip," murmured Miriam, pumping the Primus for the kettle.

"A hot day, woman—don't you feel it?"

"Do you work this hot day?"

"Later."

He knew she'd sigh.

"But the boss Erasmus is dead. Can you not now—"

"No," said Zondi, who would debate this matter with no one—not even himself, come to think of it.

"You are always cross with the children," she went on. "You don't listen to why they think their education is not so good."

"You have heard what happened in Soweto? I am the one who knows how to work with authority! With children it is always the same; they are too impatient. And they must tell me if they hear of agitators, because those men are very foolish."

"Hau! You would talk of foolish men, is that so?"

The water was fast losing its warmth. Zondi soaped both his legs and cunningly massaged the right one. Then he sniffed, noted a strange aroma, and looked up to see what his wife was mixing in a cup.

"Yes, my husband," she said, "I have been to the street of the witch doctors, and there I have paid good money for what you told my mother was rubbish for old savages. Now drink!"

Zondi drank. He was, very secretly, desperate. And besides, his gentle wife had the kettle poised over his genitals.

The unbelievable breakthrough came at almost exactly the same hour that the new man from Fingerprints had walked up to Kramer the previous day. It owed nothing to luck, and had very little to do with statistics, but had been preordained by the system.

Kramer was slumped alone in his office, with his feet on the window sill and his brain on a shelf, when fatherly Warrant Officer Henk Wessels, from Records, looked in.

"I've just been talking to the station sergeant at Witklip," he said, taking Zondi's stool from behind its deal table. "Maybe you know him—Frikkie Jonkers?"

For a moment there, Kramer wasn't even sure that he knew where Witklip was, then he recalled a tiny dorp way up, practically in Zululand. On the other score he had to admit ignorance.

"Ach, Frikkie's all right," Wessels observed carelessly. "Got a chip on his shoulder, and isn't what you'd call a mass of intelligence, but I think the pace of Witklip just suits him. Three stock thefts, a beer party, and that's his week gone. Anyway, as I was saying, he gave me a tinkle."

"Uhuh?"

"Just on the off chance, Frikkie said. You know, he's got this big chum of his who runs a hotel there? Hotel? Christ, that's a bloody joke! The bastard cheats townies into booking it for their holidays by advertising horseback riding and all sorts. You've got to break the bloody horses in first! Him."

"You've been there?" asked Kramer, glad of the diversion, and already tasting the stolen vodka in this.

"My eldest did; nearly broke his heart, poor kiddie. On his honeymoon, too, it was. I wanted to sue. Anyway, seems they've had this bloke Tommy McKenzie staying there for quite some time, and then suddenly he vanishes. Two nights ago. So they look in his room and find his suitcase—a cheap job—and a few clothes—stuff nobody would worry about leaving behind. Not a large amount involved, Frikkie tells me, on the hotel bill, that is. And maybe he'll be coming back tonight, but to be on the safe side, he wanted a check. The name wasn't on our hotel-bilkers list, so I asked for a full description. Here, Lieutenant, old son—you take a look."

Kramer scanned the particulars and noted that they matched, in most respects, the particulars he had himself used to describe Tollie Erasmus. But what clinched the matter, on paper at any rate, was the green Ford with TJ number plates.

Then he shook his head. "Tollie? In Witklip? You talk about a townie, man! Hell, the idea of going to a place like this would never enter his head."

7

THE WHITE STONE to which Witklip owed its name was actually a giant boulder, balanced on top of a high, black hill overshadowing the settlement. It looked as though one push of a child's hand would bring the thing crashing down the fire-scorched slopes, and yet, by some miracle of brute inertia, it remained there.

This was very different countryside from that found around Doringboom. A dung beetle entering a field plowed by oxen would not have encountered a greater variety of gradients, obstacles, and ragged skylines than had the Chevrolet over the past fifty minutes. The red soil showed like infantile eczema through the wispy blond grass, and supported a wide range of aloes and other hardy succulents, as well as dustings of wild flowers in oranges and purples. The sky, too, had a vivid quality, a deep varicose blueness, and Kramer was pleased that he had brought his sunglasses.

They were making the final dusty descent of the journey, with loose stones rattling loudly off the underneath of the car, and Zondi dodging the biggest potholes whenever possible. Witklip now lay before them in its eleven or so distinct parts: four of these—a trading store, butcher's, garage-cum-smithy and another trading store, in that order—were lined up on the right; the small police station stood behind a hedge of Christ thorn on the left, its faded flag not quite at the top of the pole; and the rest of the buildings, all presumably residential, were visible as brush strokes of whitewash between the cool, dark-green daub of wattle trees up ahead. As for the hotel described by W/O Henk Wessels, it was represented by a large hoarding, nailed to a blue gum and streaked with bird droppings, that read: SPA-KLING WATERS—HAPPINESS RESORT—ONLY 800 METERS.

Kramer motioned for Zondi to ignore the arrow and to make the cop shop their first port of call. He had not, as he'd assured Wessels he would do, contacted Witklip about Erasmus after that little chat in his office. On second thought, it had occurred to him that too much hindsight on the sergeant's part might introduce too many red herrings, and so, in the interests of an open mind, a small lapse of memory had seemed perfectly in order. This did mean, of course, that Frikkie Jonkers wasn't expecting them.

The white constable on duty behind the charge office counter, who said his name was Boshoff and had a face like Elvis Presley's, tried a stall when asked where the station commander could be found. Then he contrived to elbow some stolen property to the floor—to wit, a trussed chicken—and its owner added her own squawks to the lament. For just a few seconds there, it was all very noisy. While Zondi brought the prisoner back from the verandah, Kramer followed Boshoff to a door, had it knocked for him, and then went into the small office alone.

Tubby Frikkie Jonkers rose at once from his chair behind the desk, where he had been apparently checking the station inventory, and responded to Kramer's introduction with jerky alertness. His smile, beneath a hairline mustache, was most welcoming, and the bright, wide-awake glint of his slightly poppy eyes impressive. What betrayed him was the impression of his tunic cuff button, as plain as a dimple, in his right cheek.

"Is this a social," he asked, as they sat down, "or are you here in some way we can help you?"

"I'm trying the whole area for information about a bloke we

found hanging from a tree. We can't get hold of the next of kin because he didn't leave any papers, and the car number plates are causing some problems. You know how it is these days with computers."

Jonkers laughed, holding up his fingers. "That's the only kind of computers we have got in Witklip, Lieutenant! For the really heavy stuff, we take off our socks as well."

"Have a look at this description anyway, and see if it means anything to you."

Kramer had heard somewhere that intelligence was curiosity mixed with an urge to join things together in patterns. If that was so, then Jonkers had just proved the other side of the argument, by grasping only what concerned him personally. It was fascinating to watch, but probably uneventful to live with.

"Almighty God," said Jonkers. "This is Tommy!"

"You know him?"

"Certainly! He's been staying at a pal of mine's place right nearby here. I tell you, this is a real shock to me. Only this morning I phoned Henk for a check because I was worried about him—which reminds me, he hasn't called back yet."

"Well, here's your answer," said Kramer. "Will you be able to furnish the necessary particulars?"

"Not really; his name, his home address from the register, which I haven't bothered to find out yet. He was a mercenary, you know."

"Uhuh?"

"Oh, ja; he could tell you all about it. Some of the things those coons do, you could hardly believe! He had memories that were terrible. I know because once there was a bloke in the room next to his, heard him whimper in his sleep at night—sort of like a dog that thinks someone is trying to catch it to beat it? Like that. My wife had the right word for him: she said he was haunted. But not according to Tommy; he laughed in that way of his, and asked if we'd never heard of malaria. He was always okay again after a few drinks."

"Boozed a lot?"

"Hell! I've never met a bloke who was better company in that department."

Then Tollie Erasmus must have been, Kramer reasoned to

himself, either very rash or very relaxed, and the more Jonkers had to say, the more it would appear to have been the latter.

"And you all liked him?"

"Man, you can't exactly say he was popular," Jonkers admitted, with the proper hesitation that goes with speaking ill of the dead, "but you can say that every man respected him. It takes quite a nerve to go and fight Commies in the bush, specially when you're working for bloody wogs who can't be trusted—and although there's good money in it, you can still see how all of us gain in the end."

"So he'd done all right?" Kramer said enviously, offering Jonkers one of his Luckies.

"Unlike some he could tell you about. But he still had to make his pile, he used to say, and he was hoping to get something quite soon."

"Angola hadn't put him off? The firing squad?"

Jonkers snorted and replied, "Tommy? That'll be the day! He was even trying to get me to go with him."

"Uhuh?"

"That's true," Jonkers confirmed with unconcealed pride, while studying the back of his bear's paw. "Said I would qualify for a top rank, maybe even colonel, at my age and with all my experience behind me. You know, the military training we get at college, and the attitudes I have formed. Could see I knew how to handle myself. Oh, ja, he really pestered me, Tommy did. You never know, it's possible if . . ."

How astute Erasmus had been in making the silly fat sod see himself as a gun-slinging glamor boy, and not as the plodding police sergeant he was paid to be. And of course, Jonkers had known all along that when it came to the crunch, he was going to say the wife wouldn't wear it.

"Do you think his experiences could have led to his death?" Kramer suggested, preparing to begin on another tack. "There was no farewell note."

"That's Tommy's style, all right. A hard man. You would have liked him."

"But I was really querying the reason for—"

"Ach, I see, sir; sorry. You know, I've been wondering about that myself. It comes so sudden. Difficult, too, when a bloke has only talked in a bar, where others can listen. What I mean is, Tommy was never actually *personal*, if you follow. The wife says there was probably a divorce somewhere in the background."

How right the good woman was; bigamy had also been one of Tollie's little failings.

"There's something that doesn't add up here," Kramer observed with polite curiosity. "How come he was thinking of joining up again, but had allowed himself to get so fat?"

"His leg," Jonkers said, as if this were self-evident.

"Hey?"

"He'd taken a hell of a fracturing of the thighbone—not quite a compound, he explained, but the muscles got all ripped up. That was the reason he came to Spa-kling Waters—for the treatment. He'd been advised by a specialist in Jo'burg, apparently, and wasn't to put too much weight on it till the insides had mended. There was nothing you could see on the outside, of course, even when he was in his swimming cozzy, and he didn't always limp."

The irony stunned Kramer. Then he rationalized, and saw that a fractured thigh would have been, after the story in the papers, the first injury to come to Erasmus's mind. A thinking mind that might also have gauged that a coincidence is the first thing most people dismiss.

Something in his expression must have cued Jonkers for a divergent response of his own: "Hey, that's it, isn't it, sir? The leg made him do it! I'd noticed he wasn't talking about it anymore— but it *wasn't* getting better, it was getting worse!"

Kramer could only grunt to that.

"You mean the big irony involved, Lieutenant?"

"Which one?" said Kramer, surprised by an abstract.

"The irony that in the end those bloody black Commies got Tommy," sighed Jonkers. "Oh, ja, it certainly makes a man think."

Which was as fine a red herring as ever there was, and in Kramer's opinion, his complete vindication.

The hotel was positioned on a wooden shelf in a steep-sided valley, all of one kilometer down a rutted track that expanded into a nothing designated FREE CAR PARK. Some black children squatted there, hoping to pit their strength against any incoming suitcases. A four-wheel-drive vehicle could continue on around the corner, go through an assault course, and end up near the kitchen entrance, trailing oddments of vegetation behind it. The hotelier's own Land-Rover had a good-sized branch wilting on its roof rack, and a flat front tire.

Kramer followed Frikkie Jonkers along a crazy-paving path and out onto the scrubby lawn, further designated THE TERRACE. He was fast learning that if you found it difficult to believe your eyes at Spa-kling Waters, then a reassuring notice was bound to pop up. A deep verandah ran the full width of the farmhouse—it could never have been anything else—with access to both private and public rooms being provided by narrow French windows. The concrete pillars that held up the verandah's molting thatch had been painted various fairground colors, and the rafters had been strung with colored electric light bulbs— which weren't working, because at least one in the series had fallen out. On the verandah itself was an assortment of cane furniture, repainted so often the weave had almost been obscured, and in this cane furniture sat an assortment of guests.

Kramer felt pity prick his hide; plainly, for many of them, the place could be safely renamed the last resort. They were the not-so-rich sick, making do with frayed collars and goiters, crudely-made hospital boots and clubfeet, and daring him, with their eyes, to insult them with a stranger's compassion.

"Good afternoon," said an old duck with her legs in bandages. "Hasn't it been nice today?"

"Good afternoon," they all said.

"Hell," said Kramer, looking hard at her legs, "you seem okay to me, lady—but what did you do to the poor bloody horse?"

How she laughed—they all did—and he was able to escape gratefully into the reception hall. There he barged straight into Piet Ferreira, the manager, and Jonkers made the introductions. Ferreira was, surprisingly, only a little over thirty, and meatily plump; he wore sunglasses in his overlong hair, a bleached shirt, dirty white shorts, slip-slop sandals, and carried a huge jangle of keys, mostly for small padlocks.

"Bar doesn't open till six," he said, "but if you'd—"

"No, hang on a tick—we're here on business about Tommy," Jonkers interrupted, very importantly. "This officer has informed me that his body has been found murdered."

"Christ!"

"And so you see I was right and you were wrong, hey? But we'll consider the matter dropped."

"What's this?" asked Kramer, all innocence.

"Nothing, sir. Now, if you'd like to see that register and the—"

"Later, Sarge; once me and Mr. Ferreira have had a little talk. Here, you take his keys. I'm sure you know which one it is. It's on me."

There was not much Frikkie Jonkers could do, except go off to the bar, and the swiftness of the transfer of the key ring had left Ferreira looking quite amenable himself. They went into his office, which was prettier with unpaid bills than the pillars outside, and Kramer invited him to sit down. A short, thoughtful pause followed, and then the man was about ready.

"I detected a conflict of opinion over Tommy, Mr. Ferreira."

"Oh? Well, not exactly."

"That he perhaps had tried to bilk you? And you had grounds for suspicions of this nature?"

"I—I wasn't too sure."

"Uhuh?"

"Just a casual check was a question of favors, really. I do Frikkie quite a few off and on, and when the occasion arises—"

"Forget that side of it. How long did Tommy McKenzie stay here?"

Ferreira relaxed a little, and took up a rubber band to play with. "He came just under three months ago. He'd been told by a Jo'burg specialist to rest up and find a hot spring for his leg—someone recommended us. He had this leg trouble; did Frikkie tell you? Got hammered when a land mine blew up his jeep in Biafra or Angola or some such place. I was never much interested."

"Did he limp all the time?" Kramer asked.

"Most of the time," Ferreira replied, with a faint smile just hinted. "Obviously, some days his leg was a lot better."

"Come on, man! You didn't say that like you meant it."

"Well, I wasn't too worried, put it that way. Frikkie said he was okay, and I'd had a mercenary here before, back in the days when the spa wasn't developed. One of those organizers hiding from the others because the kaffirs hadn't paid up what they'd promised."

"And you thought Tommy might be one himself?"

"Sort of. The organizers never leave themselves short, and—well—I wasn't really worried, like I say. He paid monthly in advance."

"So what did worry you, finally?"

"The way he vanished, to begin with. But if you say he's—"

"No; please explain your side first," Kramer interrupted. "All of a sudden he was gone?"

"Ja, gone. Normally he never went out much, and when he did, he'd always have something to say about it. Then I looked in his room and found just a few cheap clothes and a case not worth taking. That's when I began to wonder. He'd been putting a lot on tick in the bar recently, plus he'd been making long-distance calls from my office here, also on account."

"Which he'd have to settle when paying his next month in advance? Due this coming Monday?"

"Exactly. It was nearly triple the amount before. Frikkie argued with me, said I was being too suspicious, but I said he'd left the clothes to make me—"

"These calls—do you have the numbers?"

"No, but it's a farm line, so the exchange in Brandspruit—"

"I'll contact them. Did he get any mail?"

"Never. Said he had no family, and that all his friends were either dead or in England and the States."

Kramer offered Ferreira a Lucky Strike while thinking that little lot over. It vexed him to realize that he'd never know whether Erasmus had consciously exploited the acceptable shadiness of a soldier of fortune; whatever the intention, it had been a stroke of genius. The hotel manager had been able to quash his own doubts quite happily, much encouraged, of course, by a half-witted policeman and the demands of assorted creditors. Yet this perfect plan had obviously come unstuck somewhere down the line.

"Do you think the other mercs could have got him?" Ferreira asked, supplying their light. "From the stories he told us, they sounded a real bunch of madmen. He even admitted once shooting up a school of kaffir kids to teach them a lesson—he thought they were helping the rebels, but it was a mistake. Killed forty of them, he said. If he was holding out on his mates, they might not show much mercy. What do you think?"

Just for an instant, Kramer almost fell for Erasmus's cover story himself. "Ach, no; I'm not sure this is connected," he said. "But talking of other people, did he ever have visitors?"

"None I know of, and—like I told you—he hardly ever left the place, except to go to the bank. Our terms are strictly cash, of course."

"Uhuh. What about guests?"

"Always kept clear of them. You could see he didn't much like getting in the same pool as the cripples."

"And the locals? Was there anyone he was particularly friendly with?"

"Apart from Frikkie?"

Kramer nodded.

"No, nobody special. The farmers all knew him from the bar, naturally, and a few of them liked his stories. They sort of respected Tommy, but they didn't invite him out or anything, if that's what you mean. He wasn't all that social himself. We hold a barbecue here every Saturday night; he came to the first one, but didn't really show for the rest. I can't remember seeing him, anyway. Everybody around here comes, sort of a tradition, and—"

"What about women?" Kramer cut in. "From our knowledge of this man, he had to have it twice a day, practically."

Ferreira shot the rubber band at his calendar. "Unless he was taking his chances with black velvet, not a hope—not around here."

"Sure?"

"I should know! If it isn't a bloody granny, then it isn't white. Period. You must have been in this kind of country before? The young ones can't wait to get out of it, get themselves off to varsity or training college and stay there."

"Best take a weekend off and come to Trekkersburg to collect yourself a wife," Kramer half joked, having sensed something false in the man's locker-room bravado.

"I was married," replied Ferreira, his face a blank, "but she died."

That could have led to an awkward pause, to all sorts of imaginings about what had led to this poor sod's burying himself alive in the backveld, yet Kramer handled it smoothly, he thought, by saying: "Register."

"It's by your elbow. His address is 'care of' the YMCA, Hillbrow, Johannesburg."

"Then I'll not bother to look. Just a couple more questions."

"Ja?" said Ferreira, trying to find his rubber band again among all the papers. "Keep talking."

"I need to know if anyone contacted Tommy here on Monday. You say he didn't get any mail, but what about phone calls?"

"None I know of, and I was working here in the office almost all day. He vanished while I was still in here, doing the bar receipts."

"Any strangers in the bar that night?"

"No; I've already asked to see if they knew where he went. Just the usual crowd."

"And has anyone been here since Monday? Any new guests?"

"Nobody."

Kramer took a look at the register after all, noted the number of Erasmus's room, and got to his feet.

"I'd like to see 14," he said.

"Seems a bit pointless," objected Ferreira, scratching under his sunglasses. "If you want his things, the boy will put them in your Land-Rover. Frikkie and I were in there this morning."

"All the same, I'd better."

It was true that Kramer hadn't any idea of what he might be looking for. But then again, it was equally true that Ferreira and Jonkers had been expecting to find very little—and that men who found what they expected seldom looked further.

8

THERE WAS A DECIDED contrast between the weekly tariff pinned behind the door of Room 14 and the standard of amenities to be found therein. The floor was red concrete, softened and warmed over one square yard by locally made grass matting, and the four unevenly plastered walls were sloshed over with lime that came off on your hand. The plumbing to and from the cracked washbasin was the gray plastic stuff trained baboons can screw together, and both taps said COLD on the top. The wardrobe and dressing table were so flimsy they moved bodily toward you at the tug of a knob, and the bed, a knee-high divan, seemed to have prolapse problems. Without question, the only furniture worth a second glance—not excluding the two blotchy mirrors—was an armchair of vast proportions in front of the French windows.

These windows, Kramer discovered, opened into an enclosed courtyard once used as a KIDDIES KORNER. He turned away with a slight shudder and applied himself to searching the room very thoroughly, scoring a great big fat zero. So he began on the armchair again, and Ferreira lost interest, mumbled something, and went off to have the leper's bell rung for tea, leaving him alone.

Zondi slunk in then, raised an eyebrow, and said, "The very object of my intentions, boss."

"This chair? Why? Have you picked up something?"

"Maybe. The bedroom boy has been telling me what a strange boss this was. He says that every morning, when he came to do the room, Boss McKenzie would be sitting in the big chair and wouldn't move. This made his task very difficult, and so he reported it to Boss Ferreira, but he said it didn't matter."

"How about that?" Kramer said, tipping the chair back.

"There was another strange thing about him as well— he would wash his underwear instead of leaving it for the girls to do."

"Uhuh? Or are you pulling my leg?"

Grinning, Zondi went on: "Honest to God, boss. He would leave it in the basin to soak, then hang it up in that courtyard out there. The bedroom boy was very cross about this because it meant he had to go into the next room to damp his cleaning cloth."

Kramer laughed and tried the chair for comfort. "He just sat like this? How? Like a dummy?"

"Reading a book or a newspaper, the bedroom boy says. Never has he known another person in this place to behave in such a fashion."

Back went the chair again. "Come on, you've got the skinny arms," Kramer ordered. "Let's see what you can bloody find."

They spent twenty minutes on the stuffed armchair in Room 14, littered the floor with tufts of horsehair, and found nothing but a mouse's nest, long vacated.

"Bugger," said Kramer. "I'm damned sure he must have been up to something—agreed? But if he wasn't sitting tight on it, what was he doing?"

"Perhaps just watching the boy, boss."

"Do what?"

Zondi opened the French windows. "When the boy had gone, he would come out here to hang up his washing."

"Hmmm. Doesn't grab me. How many other doors open onto it?"

"Three."

"We'll take a look, anyway," Kramer suggested, following

him out. "You have a go at that sandpit, while I poke around the toys."

What was left of the toys, to be pedantic, because the hotel must once have catered to a particularly destructive bunch of little bastards—just the sort, in fact, who'd have parents capable of breaking in wild mustangs. The rocking horse was legless, rockerless, and eyeless, the pedal car was a write-off, and the playhouse had been trampled flat; only a few items in stout plastic and a scattering of big wooden blocks had survived intact, or almost.

"Nothing buried here," Zondi said presently, dusting off his hands.

"See what you make of this, then."

Kramer had just come across a blue hula hoop with a longish piece missing from it; one end had separated at the join, but the other seemed to have been severed by a sharp penknife or razor blade. The cut marks were fairly recent, too.

"Ah, there is the rest," said Zondi, going over to where he'd spotted a length of blue tubing sticking out of a small plastic watering can with lamb decals on it. "Hau, it is very clean."

"Ja, that's true," Kramer murmured, taking the tube from him to examine. "What the hell can you do with a thing like this?" He tried a bugle call.

Zondi shook the can and listened.

"Hear anything?"

"Rain water."

"Time you got that job in the lab, man. That's brilliant."

"Huh! You do not believe me?" snorted Zondi, spilling a little into his left palm and licking it. "Correction, boss. Soapy water."

He grimaced and wiped his mouth on his sleeve.

"This way!" Kramer said, plunging back into Room 14 and confronting the washbasin. "He always had his underpants in there, right? So we put in the plug. We add water, soap, and...?"

"We put the pipe in...."

There seemed no point to that. Zondi lifted out the tube and held it vertically, bringing the watering can up underneath it. He began lowering the two things together.

The idea struck them simultaneously.

"Siphon!"

"So the water will not—"

"—go down the outlet pipe!" Kramer rounded off, bending to sniff at the plug hole.

"Drugs, boss?"

"Drains. Push the chair back, and let's pull this whole bloody thing apart."

The hotel manager and his friendly neighborhood police chief returned to the room at that moment, but went totally ignored. Very sensibly, they said nothing.

A blank was drawn with the U-tube, although it was bone dry, and the same went for the first short section down to the elbow joint. But when the main length of plastic piping was eased away from the wall, improvised stoppers could be seen protruding slightly at either end. One of these was tugged out, the piping held upright, and the best part of twenty thousand rand, bound tightly in fat cylinders of used bank notes, bounced on the grass matting and rolled under the bed.

Piet Ferreira looked as sick as any man might who discovers a little too late that, by simply turning on one of his own cold-water taps, he could have struck oil. As for Frikkie Jonkers, he just gaped.

"This is a security matter," Kramer stated briskly, recovering to break the prolonged silence. "It would be unwise for either of you to ask any questions, or to mention this to anyone."

He saw Zondi blink.

"What—er—what do I say if someone here asks?" Ferreira asked anxiously, his avarice having died of frostbite. "Asks where Tommy is, I mean."

"Just say that he ought to be back soon. Any problems on your side, Sergeant?"

"None, sir!" replied Jonkers, coming to attention.

"Then let me give you one. This guest was making long-distance telephone calls recently; I want you to contact the Brandspruit exchange and tell them I need those numbers chop chop."

"Immediately, sir. Anything else?"

"Ja, your friend here can see if he's got a nice metal strongbox for me to stash this stuff in. Go."

Both men hurried from the room, closing the door very gently behind them. Zondi's low, puzzled laugh followed as the thud of their footfalls died away.

"Boss? There are times when you do things I do not fully understand."

Kramer grinned. "If you knew how I'd been misleading them this afternoon, maybe you'd appreciate how much explaining I've just saved myself. Besides, it's nice to see a bit of action."

"So you do not suspect—"

"Ach, of course not! Which isn't to say this case has got any less peculiar. What's your view?"

"Hau, hau, hau," sighed Zondi, kneeling on the mat. "This money was not my expectation."

They began to gather up the rolls.

"Could be that we fell into the old trap of presuming too much," Kramer said, sitting back on his heels, "because, from one angle, it still being here does make sense."

"How is that?"

"Well, everything they've told me makes Monday night sound as if it came as a nasty shock to him. He had his bum in the butter and could easily have stayed another three months, I reckon. Out he goes, expecting to be so short a time he doesn't bother to make his usual lying excuses to Ferreira, and they nail the bastard. He won't tell them where the moola is, takes the drop, and they're left scratching their arses. Now all you've got to do is explain why, if they knew where to contact him, they didn't come here and turn the place over."

Zondi pursed his lips.

"What's the problem?"

"I am a kick-start kaffir, boss, as you well know."

"Oh, ja?"

"I would first like to hear about these telephone numbers."

"Can't help you there, man," Kramer said, smiling as he recognized the same pattern of thought that had him in a tangle. "But I do know one thing: whoever was on the receiving end would know from the operator where the call originated, even if he didn't tell them himself. 'We've got Witklip on the line,' and all that. He'd know this, too, and the chances are that only persons he really trusted would—"

"A big mistake?" Zondi broke across. "He chose unwisely?"

"Either that or one of his contacts was got at. The timing of all this does suggest nobody knew where he was until he began the calls."

"Hmmm."

"Tollie would recognize the risks himself?"

"Yebo, and this does not tell us why the telephone became necessary to him."

"Boredom? He'd begun to hit the bottle a lot harder. Might have been checking to see if we were still so interested. Then we start the other permutations: Why should he be worrying about anyone except us? Wasn't it natural for him to keep in touch? Et cetera."

"We could go mad."

"True. Is that the last one?"

Zondi flipped the roll over. "There is no necessity for us to consider this matter, boss. What you said just now is the important thing: If we can find one person who was aware of the whereabouts of this man, then we have a lead."

"Let's hope so. Those numbers could all be for public phone boxes."

"In Zambia," added Zondi, and enjoyed his joke hugely until Jonkers came tiptoeing in.

"Hell, I haven't got such good news for you, Lieutenant," he said nervously. "The exchange says finding your information isn't going to be all that simple, although the night shift may be able to get it for you by the morning."

Kramer had, however, been expecting a cloddish reversal of this kind, and refused to allow it to spoil his mood of mild jubilation. With a maturity he very much admired, he waved aside the apology.

"We've got to get the tom back, anyway," he said, taking the strongbox Jonkers was carrying. "Ring them again and say they'll find me working under Murder and Robbery in Trekkersburg."

And so it was, not a quarter of an hour later, that they bowled out of Witklip, feeling justly pleased with their day but somehow unable to reconcile themselves to the idea it had ended.

"We might look in on the exchange on our way through," Kramer suggested.

"Can do, boss."

"So tell me when we hit Brandspruit."

"Okay."

Zondi seemed about to add something. Kramer waited in case he did, then settled down comfortably, with his knees against the dashboard, to ruminate and even to doze a little. Very soon he was forcing his eyelids open for just long enough to see—and instantly forget—any onrushing obstacle. This was no more than a reflex response to a slight change in his center of gravity, caused by Zondi's easing up momentarily on the throttle; the donkey carts, ox sledges, and wobbling cyclists were in themselves very dull. A farm truck appeared, heeling over against the sunset, dark and menacing, and gave them a long, angry blast on its horn, before scraping by with a broadside of loose stones.

"Jesus!" said Kramer, sitting bolt upright.

This amused Zondi.

But Kramer's smile never made it. About nine kilometers from Witklip, on a road leading nowhere else he knew of, he'd just seen an enormous man with a beard at the wheel of a farm truck. And—in what had been like a remembered glimpse of a dream, so vivid it had made his loins leap—he had seen, on the far side of this man, a beautiful girl with honey hair and blue eyes and a mouth like a whore. She had laughed at him.

"Fluke!" muttered Strydom, putting down his favorite work, *The Essentials of Forensic Medicine* by Cyril John Polson, who was a barrister as well as a pathologist, and could be depended upon for a very dry wit.

"You're not still moaning about what Trompie said," grumbled his wife, Anneline, as she came in from watching the neighbors' television set. "It was lovely, Chris; you really missed out. And do you remember *The World at War* you saw last week? Well, tonight Maria's husband told us that those Nazi concentration camps were all faked by the Jews afterwards."

"Rubbish," said Strydom, who was still wrapped up in his own problems of conscience.

"I told him you'd say that, and he lent me this clipping from the Jo'burg *Star*. It's a letter from a Mr. G. Rico, who states that the figures were grossly exaggerated. 'Furthermore, any such casualties as did exist were not victims of any premeditated act.' So what do you say now, before I have to give this back?"

"The chances of the drop being a fluke are a million to one," began Strydom, then realized that these odds were greatly exaggerated.

"Ach, you're impossible, Chris! You mustn't let Trompie prey on your mind like this—and if it isn't him, it's that damned boy of his with the leg."

"I've got to make certain, Anneline. I could be wasting everybody's time."

"Like mine, for instance?"

"Sorry, my poppie," he soothed, getting up to hug her plump warmth. "I'll leave this till tomorrow, when I can get at some old P.M. reports and study the incidence."

"Tomorrow night the TV's in Afrikaans," she said, keeping hold of his hand, and they went automatically through to the kitchen for their coffee. "They've invited us again, so can you come over?"

"What's on?"

"An Australian baritone singing translations from real Italian opera. I'm going."

That, thought Strydom, was exactly what the old Minister of Posts and Telegraphs had warned about when describing television as the Devil's instrument. Not once that week had they sat down together as man and wife and talked over his more interesting cases.

Zondi had hitched a lift home in a patrol van by the time Colonel Muller and the bank officials had released Kramer from their small private celebration. There was a note to this effect propped against the water carafe in their office.

Kramer looked at his watch and was disappointed to find that he could still focus: ten minutes to midnight. The whole object of drinking so much bad wine had been to take the edge off his sensibilities; in a deep and disturbing way, he was still feeling the tantalizing impact of that encounter. This was, of course, ridiculous.

He sat down at his desk and put a hand on the telephone. As it happened, he had a perfect right to ring Ferreira and ask him what the hell he'd meant by saying there were no women about—a statement which had been clearly contradicted. Arseholes to the fact it was the middle of the night: this was a murder investigation! And the girl could have been a casual visitor....

The telephone rang under his hand and startled him.

"Can I speak to Lieutenant Kramer?" asked someone who spoke slowly and distinctly. "Or perhaps leave a message for him?"

Kramer frowned; he knew that voice, a very recent addition to his collection. Then it clicked: he was being addressed by the chief telephonist at Brandspruit exchange, who had ears that stuck out at right angles until he slipped on his headset.

"Speaking," he said, grabbing up a ballpoint. "You've got something for me?"

"We've been through every log going back until the date you gave us, Lieutenant."

"Uhuh?"

"It would appear that the caller invariably asked for the same number—and it's a Trekkersburg one, too, you may be glad to hear."

"Shoot, man."

"Trekkersburg 49590. The subscriber's name is Miss Petronella Mulder, of 33 Palm Grove Mansions."

"Never!"

"So you know the lady, I gather?"

"Ach, anybody can," replied Kramer, "providing you fork out ten rand and don't mind injections. Thanks a lot, hey? I must be going."

And, after a short stop at the coffee machine, he went.

The small block of flats was up near the railway station and seemed a little like an extension of the marshaling yard. Puffing couples in drab coats were forever shunting their shabby trunks and packing cases along its mean balconies, either on their way in or on their way out, for few ever stayed there very long, despite the low rent. The snag was that the pock-necked little runt who owned the place gave nobody more than an hour's grace to pay up, and this was a deadline many found impossible to meet in a lean week. It never worried Miss Mulder, however, whose delivery time was reputedly under seven squalid minutes.

Kramer raised his knuckles to the door of Number 33 with the expression of a man about to crack a rotten egg.

"Who-zit?" came the challenge from within.

"Vice Squad."

The welcoming smile soured the instant she recognized him, but by then Kramer had his foot in the doorway and crushing down on her instep. While she blanched, gasped, and hopped about, he opened up properly and went in. The room was its usual shambles, and looked like a flying cosmetics display that'd hit a concrete mountain. The pity of it was that the smell didn't match.

He kicked ajar the bathroom door. Nothing. No well-known city Rugby players in the kitchenette either.

"Alone at last," said Kramer, turning to face her. "And how is my pretty tonight?"

Cleo de Leo, as she preferred her clientele to call her, was sitting on the edge of her tumbled bed holding her foot. The black wig was askew, one eyelash had come adrift, and her limbs, which had the shiny pneumatic look of a bus seat, were inelegantly positioned. The crumpled kimono gaped, exposing such gifts as she had to bestow: a sag of breasts as pendulous as two grapefruit in a pair of Christmas stockings, a navel like a novelty pencil sharpener, and a rusty pot-scourer. For lips, under a faint mustache, she had hemmorhoids.

"You stinking pig bastard!"

"Ach, no, be fair," Kramer protested mildly, "because if you're what you say you are, then I'm an amateur photographer."

"You call that a lens?" she sneered, snuffling into a tissue.

"I get results."

"Oh, really? You must try and show me sometime."

"Now, if you like."

She reached for her menthols. "For free? You must be joking! Just because you're big and pissed doesn't entitle you to anything."

"For free," said Kramer, handing over the mortuary photograph of Tollie Erasmus with a rope around his neck.

It made an impression.

"No!"

"We found him yesterday, near Doringboom."

"But Tollie wouldn't—"

"He didn't. He was murdered."

"Hey?"

Her surprise was so complete that she turned into a human being. The eyes which knew it all suddenly knew nothing, and at the drop of her jaw, the hard little face shattered, showing the soul-sick slack underneath.

Kramer took back the picture and said nothing. He watched her close her gown, drag off her wig, and bring her knees up to hug them. He stood there while she began rocking to and fro, her gaze fixed on the floor. Then he poured her a stiff gin and a straight lime and water for himself.

"You bastard," she whispered, thanking him with a nod as she lifted the glass.

"Give me a chance next time, Cleo, and things will be different. Who else knew he was at Witklip?"

"Where?"

He straddled a chair opposite her, folding his arms over the back of it. "Don't be that way," he coaxed, and then pursued the most perverse line possible: "Even if you deny setting up Tollie, I've still got you cold as accessory after the fact and harboring a known criminal."

Cleo's head jerked. "Setting him . . . ?"

"Ja, his murder. Mind you, I think that one will stick."

"*Me?* Are you crazy?"

"Logical, Miss Mulder. We have proof from the post office that he was in contact with you here on 49590, from which it follows that they must have worked through you to—"

"I told-told nobody!" she stammered.

Kramer sighed.

"No, that's the God's truth. I swear it!"

"Uhuh? Maybe the judge will believe you. Personally—"

"Just you listen! All right?"

Fear, shock, and gin soon had the facts tumbling out, and Kramer was kept busy rearranging them in chronological order. Erasmus had apparently found her number scrawled in a phone box on the day of the raid, and had asked her if she was willing to perform a "special" for R100 cash. Once inside her flat, he had offered another R100 a day for nothing but the use of her telephone and somewhere to lie up. He had been no trouble. Then on the fourth day he had made a further offer: R200 down and a lump payment of R500 later if she agreed to act as "middle man" in a transaction. All she had to do was relay on any messages she might take from a man called Max, who would be ringing her sometime in the near future. Max was, in fact, helping him to get out of the country, but there were complications caused by the number of black states now surrounding South Africa. This Max had rung her twice, both times to say it would take a little longer, and recently Erasmus had been becoming very restless and nervous. Instead of his weekly call on a Saturday night, he'd been in touch almost every other day. And that's all there was to it, as Cleo de Leo saw no percentage in moral side issues.

"Max knew he was at Witklip?"

"Tollie said I shouldn't tell him and he never asked," she replied, putting her glass down. "How many more times? *Nobody* knew except me; it was meant to be secret. Tollie said Max was a good guy, but the fewer who knew made him safer."

Kramer stood up and paced about a bit. The trollop was telling the truth, he felt sure of it, and yet this wasn't making things any easier.

He snapped his fingers and spun round. "Why Witklip? What the hell put that into his head?"

"Oh, it was an old idea one of his friends once had. I can't remember exactly. When he was in Steenhuis Reformatory and they used to talk after lights out. This bloke had been to it once with his folks, and said the store there didn't even get a newspaper. Tollie checked while he was here and found it was still such a dump. They used to tease this guy—Robert? Ja,

Robert or Roberts; that's a name I remember. Nothing else, though."

Then Cleo stiffened.

"You're right!" said Kramer. "It wasn't such a bloody secret after all, was it?"

9

Someone had left a fresh memo pad on his desk that rainy Thursday morning. Someone else had written the Widow Fourie's home number on it, underlining the word *Urgent* five times. The next someone to poke his head into the office was liable to have it bitten off.

Kramer had spent a surprisingly bad night in the austere room he rented as, his landlady insisted on calling him, a paying guest. Presumably, he had slept. If asked to describe his night, however, he would have compared it to a bout of malarial fever, while being cynically aware of how unimaginative that sounded. His impatience to trace the man Robert or Roberts had been a primary cause of his restlessness, and had meant that, at first light of dawn, he had risen, taken a shower, and gone for a long walk. But even on this walk, which had led him down to the muddy sloth of the Umgungundhlovu River, his mind had never freed itself from a garish, sunset glimpse of the girl with honey hair.

"Why not?" he muttered, dialing the Widow's number. "I heard you wanted me? The kids all right?"

"Term ended yesterday, so you can guess for yourself! How's the case going?"

"Progressing."

"I had an idea, Trompie. You know this business of the hangman knowing all the skills? I suddenly remembered my copy of *The Vontsteen Case* by that young chappie who was clerk of the court at the Palace of Justice. That had some details in it."

"Nonsense; the law prohibits the publication of any matters pertaining to prisons unless—"

"Just listen, hey?" the Widow Fourie interrupted him. "Here's the mention on page three which tells how they do it: 'They are brought to the gallows at a quick trot, the measured rope is round the neck in a second, and at a push of the lever the floor opens beneath them. They tie a white cloth over the mouth because the blood tends to gush out.'"

Kramer lit a Lucky.

"Hello—are you still there?"

"You mean that's all? It doesn't tell you anything special—and that blood part sounds rubbishy to me. There wasn't any blood coming out of Tollie."

"I just wanted to help if—" she said, her voice catching. "Look, I want to talk to you about what I said about Mickey."

"Hearsay," said Kramer.

"Pardon?"

"That's just something the writer picked up somewhere: The kind of information Doc's all excited about would never be published in this country, and I can tell you that for a fact."

There was a silence.

The Widow Fourie gave an uncertain laugh. "Man, to hear us you'd think we were an old married couple having a row!"

"Maybe that's our problem," Kramer remarked unkindly, surprising himself with his curious indifference. "So if there's nothing else, I'd better get on, hey?"

She hung up on him.

The memo pad went into the wastebin and the interdepartmental directory came out of its drawer. After a start like that, Kramer expected nothing to go right for the rest of the day. However, once he had convinced Steenhuis Reformatory that he wasn't reporting an absconder, but inquiring after an inmate who must have taken his lawful leave some twelve or so years earlier, things began to happen. According to the records, there had been nobody in Erasmus's dormitory called Robert, yet he had shared with one Peter David Roberts, whose last known address was 4D Rasnop Court, Dewey Street, Durban. Kramer thanked the clerk, rang off, and, encouraged by such luck, took a whimsical look in the ordinary telephone directory.

"Man, oh, man," he said, stopping his finger at the same name, initials, and address.

Zondi came in at that precise moment, his expression strangely sullen, and wished him good morning.

"Don't just stand there, old son—can't you see the keys?" Kramer asked. "We're taking a quickie to Durbs."

"A lead?"

"Uhuh, and a good one. Brandspruit came through with the number of Erasmus's contact, and she was right here in Trekkersburg. I'll explain on the way."

The keys were picked up off the desk and held in a clenched fist.

"What's the matter, Mickey? I've just cut us a few corners, so let's not hang around. Or have you something better to do?"

"No, boss."

"Let's go, then."

Kramer noticed a puffiness under the eyes, as they were going down the stairs together, and concluded that he hadn't been the only one thrashing about in the night. This hollowed his belly a little, and he eased the pace on reaching the sidewalk.

Zondi paused while unlocking the car door, and said, "Lieutenant, is it all right to ask you?"

"Ask me what?"

"Your meaning when you said I should go and find a job in the laboratory."

"Hell, who's getting sensitive?" Kramer replied, very relieved to discover the pain had only been mental. "You know we don't allow you thick kaffirs in there."

And with that they left for Durban.

Dr. Strydom was standing where he'd least expected to be that morning: in the showroom of a brand-new store that specialized in the sale of television sets.

His presence there owed nothing to rash impulse, however, but was the result of a long night spent worrying about poor Anneline and the time she was having to waste in front of the neighbors' screen. As a study of the programs printed in the paper showed all too clearly, only seventy minutes of air time could possibly be of any interest to her on any one evening, and yet, having been asked over, she could hardly get up and leave, at the start of another documentary on Bushmen, without implying a severe, almost theological criticism of their investment. It wasn't right that she should sacrifice so many precious hours in this way, simply because she had the manners of a true lady, and so he had finally found a solution to this problem—which was, of course, to invest in a set himself, while applying certain sensible rules concerning its usage. In fact, according to his calculations, fifty minutes a night would probably be more than she could happily assimilate.

But now he was finding he had other sums to do.

"That's a price and a half!" he exclaimed.

"May I inquire, sir," asked the pleasantly-spoken young salesman, "your profession? You certainly give the *impression* of a professional man, sir, if you don't mind my saying."

"I'm a surgeon," said Strydom, wagging his stethoscope even more vigorously at the color set before him. "But that doesn't mean I can't express an opinion about highway robbery! It hasn't even got proper legs for a thing that size."

"I knew it, Doctor! I've always said that you can't bamboozle a professional man into buying the first thing you show him, whether it's a TV set or a swimming bath or a little runabout for his good lady. It isn't the cost that matters to a man such as yourself, it's the—"

"Legs," snapped Strydom. "Do you seriously call those spindly things 'legs'?"

The salesman smiled foolishly.

Strydom stared at the next set along and an idea occurred to him that put everything into a different perspective. If you pretended that the price tag was on a small car, just supposing that Anneline had learned to drive, then the cost came to about the same and seemed far less of a shock. Warming to this business of high-level decision-making, he decided on a sly compromise.

"How much is a black-and-white?" he asked.

"Ah, a black-and-white," the salesman repeated. "A monochrome? I could have one brought up from the back, if you like. Monochromes do tend to be more a specialty of our nonwhite customers, so I'm afraid we..."

He turned to call someone, but Strydom caught his sleeve.

"Just the price for comparison, hey? The wife said to ask—it's her who likes to see the flowers."

"There's a coincidence for you, Doctor," said the salesman, losing his look of embarrassment at being caught out. "Only yesterday we had a judge's wife in here, and she wanted a panochrome for flowers, too! Let me see... the monos are about 50 percent cheaper, depending on this and that."

"Interesting. Now, what about aerials and so forth?"

"We see to everything, and it's same-day delivery, all-inclusive. Oops, that's the volume control—no need to apologize. Would you like to be left to take your time browsing?"

"Ach, no," Strydom replied casually, digging for his checkbook. "I've got a lot on this morning, and a television set is just a television set after all. Personally, I couldn't care less if the Americans had never invented it!"

A feeling of heady well-being, puffed up by a sudden pride of ownership, and given an edge by the dread that always went with spending more than ten rand of his money at a time, then took Strydom round to the court records office with a decided optimism. It was exactly the moment to check on the incidence of neck fractures in hanging, and to prove how right he'd been in his original assessment.

"I want to look up suicides," he said. "White, colored, Asiatic, and black."

Being in Durban, the country's major port and the playground of a nation, did nothing for Kramer. From the shark nets protecting the bathers off its whites-only beaches, to the suburban anthill of the Berea, its humid and lush sprawl caused him an unease that could be remedied solely by getting the hell out again, as quickly as possible. The snag was that he'd only just arrived.

Durban seemed soft to him, somehow alien; this wasn't

simply because there were so many Indians about or so much English spoken—Trekkersburg had, on a reduced scale, similar drawbacks. No, it had to do with the sea, and with the way you were exposed on the brink, facing God knows what insanities beyond the horizon. Any one of the waves, for example, could have creamed from the bows of a Chink battle cruiser to come all the way across to splash over a man's kids. Just like the waves that had thrown up other people's rubbish along the shoreline, all those Miami apartment blocks and English beach hotels and Spanish ranch houses. If you flew high enough, Kramer had noticed, then Durban looked like a high-water mark, with all sorts of tiny, nasty things crawling about among the pastel shells and the glitter.

Zondi liked Durban—it went with his sophisticated taste in neckties—and he murmured appreciatively as a bikini passed by, accentuating a fine, wide pelvis. If the girl had been topless, he wouldn't have noticed.

"You're not a detective; you're a bloody obstetrician," grumbled Kramer, who had taken the wheel and was searching the beachfront for the right side street.

"I'm also a damn fine navigator, boss."

"Watch it."

"Two blocks more."

"Ask that churra over there."

The Indian streetcleaner directed them two blocks north, one block west, and Kramer double-parked outside Rasnop Court soon afterward. By the look of it, the four-story building had just weathered a bad crossing from Singapore, but at least it was now in a white-zoned area.

"A few words?" Zondi suggested.

"Ideal. Don't know a bloody thing about this bloke."

So Zondi got out and went over to a pair of servant girls in grubby uniforms, who were gossiping at the entrance to the block. He flashed his shoulder holster at them. His jacket closed, their eyes opened wide, and none of those few words were wasted. He came back with his report.

"These females do not know of a Boss Roberts, but they say there is an old missus by that name. She stays on the top floor, flat number 4D, and her shopping time is eleven."

Kramer checked his watch; ten forty-six. "Just make it. You

talk nicely to the traffic cops, but don't move if you can help it."

Zondi caught the keys and took his place behind the wheel, tipping his hat forward for a short nap.

The lift was out of order, and as there wasn't another for nonwhites, Kramer had to take the stairs. Some junior Michelangelo, living on or about the third floor, was all set to have an obscenities charge slapped on him for his murals. Kramer quite enjoyed the one depicting the depravities of kangaroos, though, and wondered what the old lady thought of them, as she came whizzing down the banisters each day at eleven.

Mrs. Wilfreda Roberts didn't turn out to be that sort of old lady at all.

When she opened the door of 4D just a crack, it wasn't really to hide behind—you could see practically all of her. She was so thin and so frail that her earlobes looked fat, and her pallor was like candle grease. But her empty eyes, much the same freckled gray as her dress and most tombstones, said she hadn't been ill: it was just that life had sunk in its fangs and had a good suck.

"Lieutenant Kramer from the CID, madam," he announced in English, smiling cheerfully.

She noticed this and became excited.

"Peter?" she asked. "You've come about my son?"

As she spoke the name, color came to her hollow cheeks, and she stepped back, drawing the door wide in invitation.

"Come in, please—do come in! But don't say a word until I'm sitting down. Gracious, how sudden! You just can't begin to imagine what this means to me!"

Kramer, who was in complete agreement with her, followed Mrs. Roberts with sudden reluctance across the small hallway, and then into a dim living room that was stifling with birds. There seemed close to fifty of them—parakeets, budgies, canaries, finches, and a parrot—in a dozen or so cages set on pedestals against the curtained windows. Even in the gloom, their plumage had a startling brilliance, and they immediately began a shrill clamor, as they fluttered against their silver bars, that was fairly startling in itself. Although the parrot, a molting African gray, merely blinked a bland eye at him, and went on picking its beak.

"Shoosh!" said Mrs. Roberts, and added, "Please excuse me

for a moment while I get some lettuce."

He glanced about to note what else she had managed to squeeze between the four cream walls. There was a fold-up writing desk, a drop-leaf dining table, a glass-fronted display cabinet, a small table supporting a radio, and two easy chairs. One of these had a darning needle stuck in an arm, where she must have left it to answer the door. On the foam-rubber seat of the other chair, a modern affair in light wood, lay a copy of that morning's newspaper, a carton of American toasted cigarettes, a six-pack of Lion lager, a can of peanuts, and a ten-rand note twisted into the shape of a flower. Maternal goodies, it could be assumed, for the flashy young bastard whose portrait adorned the display cabinet in a thin silver frame.

Craaaaaaak! said the parrot.

"Who's a pretty boy?" Kramer leered amiably.

That really set it off. Only its diction was terrible, and he felt sure the daft bugger kept saying *Where's a pretty boy?* instead.

The task Strydom had set himself in a dusty corner of the court records office was fast getting out of hand.

Theoretically, it shouldn't have been difficult to pick out a fair sample of death-by-hanging cases from which to extract his statistics, but in practice it was like juggling fresh-caught flatfish. The papers from each inquest hearing were clipped together in an unwieldy, slithery mass—autopsy report, magistrate's transcript, maps, plans, documentary exhibits, photographs—and stacked so that one clumsy move brought at least half a dozen flip-flopping out to spread over the floor.

And if this wasn't enough to content with, he had just discovered a fracture dislocation of the neck that didn't make sense.

The deceased, a railway foreman with a history of violence and aberrant behavior, had been found four years earlier hanging in a gangers' portable rest cabin near a level crossing miles from anywhere. "Freakish misadventure sustained in pursuit of orgasmic enhancement," the district surgeon had recorded, having noted the classic presence of lewd pinups on the wall and the corpse's erection. He had also satisfied himself that there had been a perfectly good platform for the man to have stepped from: to wit, a large wooden box used for storing shovels and pickaxes. But this was textbook thinking; an erection was common to all forms of hanging, whereas, for a man of Strydom's experience, there could be no ambiguity about the fact that the ceiling of the cabin was far too low to have afforded the right drop.

This meant, of course, that the case did make sense—provided he was prepared to accept *positive* evidence in support of his hangman theory, when all any sane man could have anticipated was *negative* proof that fracture dislocations never occurred without precisely the right circumstances.

Cautious and sweating slightly, but with his fine mind whetted, Strydom wondered whether to pack it in temporarily, or to demand that he be given some assistance. He was given, because of the flu going round, which had incapacitated the records office like a tea break, a Zulu messenger called Alfred.

Just for a minute or two of speechless indignation, Strydom despaired. Alfred's literacy ran to identifying public notices that affected his life directly, telling him where to go or where not to sit, and to matching the letters on a package against the letters on a solicitor's brass plate—when he wasn't delivering by ear, that was. Asking Alfred to pick out the words *suicide by hanging*, especially when most magistrates' writing is so dreadful, was tantamount to having him write the key phrase himself.

Then Alfred, embarrassed by the delay in receiving his orders, twisted his head round to admire the picture on the front of the television-set brochure that Strydom had left lying about.

"You buy, master?"

"I buy."

"Hau, plenty good picture, that one. I see by the shop."

Strydom placed an avuncular arm across the man's khaki-uniformed shoulders and led him to the huge pile of nonwhite inquest papers. There he showed him what sort of photographs he was interested in, reinforced this with some mime, and told him to get going. In fact, it was such an expedient idea that he used it himself.

"So arrest me," said Kramer, getting back into the Chev outside the block of flats where he had just finished his interview with Mrs. Roberts.

Zondi made a show of awakening slowly. He tipped his hat back, blinked, and turned toward him. "On what charge, boss?" he asked.

"Indecent exposure. I got caught with my pants down."

"How was that?"

"She thought I'd come to say, Bring on the dancing girls, lady—your naughty little boy is back."

"You are talking about the old lady?" Zondi queried.

"That's right. Ma Roberts—but she hasn't bloody seen him for five years!"

"Hau!"

"I tell you, it was rough, hey. You should have seen the look of disappointment on her face."

Zondi shrugged. "But why should you blame yourself for this, Lieutenant? You only—"

"I could have checked with Henk Wessels first, and saved a lot of bloody time. What if I say that her son was better known as Ringo?"

Zondi frowned, searching that near-photographic memory of his, a legacy from his years in a mission school where the one textbook for each subject had to be shared. Then his face registered a hit.

"Hau, but that was long ago, boss! The Vasari case?"

"Not bad, my son. I couldn't even get the wop's name."

"Anthony Michael Vasari," Zondi said slowly, "who was convicted for killing a pensioner he robbed on the Bluff. Ringo was his accomplice, but he turned state evidence after first pleading not guilty at the preliminary examination. But why didn't Cleo tell us this?"

"Probably didn't make the connection either. Ringo's a Beatle name, came along much later than when they were in Steenhuis, and so Erasmus—ach, that isn't a point that's important. Our problem is where we're going to find the bastard."

"Can his mother not give any clues?"

"Take a look at this," Kramer said by way of an answer.

He slipped a hand into his jacket and produced a mimeo copy of PLEASE HAVE YOU SEEN MY ONE AND ONLY SON? It gave a full physical description of Peter David Roberts, also known as

Peterkins, and then listed his endearing habits, considerable gifts, and sophisticated tastes in food, drink, and clothing, as only a mother could know them. At the end it implored: "Amnesia (Forgetting One's Memory) Can Happen to Anyone—Help Peter and Me (Widow & Pensioner) Like You would Want to Help YOURSELF."

"Mangalisayo," murmured Zondi, skimming through it. "This is very sad, boss. The woman has a great heart."

"Whenever she can save up enough, she gets a few more run off and posts them to shipping offices, new dam projects, hospitals, loony bins, et cetera."

"But what is your own reading? That this small-time fellow went to try for big time in Jo'burg?"

"Could've done," Kramer agreed, but his heart wasn't in it; there was more, which he'd been trying not to think about. "On the other hand, his ma alleges he was a changed character after the trial, having nearly taken a one-way to Pretoria. He got himself a job in an electrical-goods store, worked hard there, and found himself a steady girlfriend, whose brother was going to let him have a share in a ski boat. All set up. Got a phone put in, started saving for an MG—next thing he was gone."

"Like—?" Zondi flipped a hand.

"Uhuh. One Saturday afternoon he walked out, saying he was going swimming, and never came back. Underneath all this, you can see she thinks a shark might have got him. He always said the beach was too crowded where the nets were; liked to go to deserted areas."

"Then maybe she is right, boss. He took no case or anything?"

"Just a towel," said Kramer, and felt as flat as he sounded.

Zondi started the car up. "So this is why you think we waste time, Lieutenant? Yet Ringo could have planned for a fresh start more cleverly than she suspected."

"Ja. I'd better check with the locals—but let's get some grub first."

The Chev moved off slowly.

"Oh, and another thing," Kramer added, finally facing the futility of his morning. "Ma Roberts had never heard of bloody Witklip."

10

DR. STRYDOM WAS BY now in something of a state. No fewer than four inquests, each indicating an excusable error of judgment, had come to light—and this wasn't counting the observations he himself had made at Doringboom, of course.

His feelings of conflict were very natural. It seemed incredibile that he should, within so short a time, and with the ungainly means at his disposal, pick out this number of cases for reappraisal. But then again, there just weren't that many white suicides by hanging in Natal each year, and Alfred had obeyed his direction to ignore any obviously narrow ligatures; between them, they had called a halt in the late '60s before three o'clock. It also seemed incredible that one of these likely oversights appeared to have been his own.

Incredible, but not impossible, because this time round he had known what to look for, and had not presumed a thing. The remains in question had been those of a white adult male, aged somewhere between twenty-five and thirty, discovered in a skeletal condition at the foot of a small krantz or ravine. One end of a rotten rope had been found around the neck—of which very little remained, due to decomposition and rodent life—and the other end had been tied to a broken branch. It had not taken him long, on that wet and chilly afternoon, to agree with the police that the branch, which came from an overhanging tree, told the whole story. The deceased had secured the rope to it, allowing himself virtually no slack because of the length involved, and had stepped over the cliff's edge. The sudden weight had been just enough to snap the branch and send him plunging to his death—a death that could have been attributed to several causes, among them exposure brought on by the paralysis of a broken neck. Strydom's only comfort was that he'd not been dogmatic in his summation, because, when looked at from another viewpoint, that broken branch could have come as a surprise only to the hangman, hurriedly ridding himself of a night's work.

Having gone over it again in his mind briefly, he could see that his first assessment had probably been correct, but there were the two others. One was the product of slapdash, lamentably perfunctory work on the part of a district surgeon known for his high output and habit of dribbling cigarette ash into things: he had simply not made any real effort to ascertain anything about the white male, suspected of being a tramp, who'd committed suicide by hanging in an empty barn. Not even the hyoid bone had been examined. This was in direct contrast to the fourth DS involved, whose punctilious treatment of a witch doctor's death deserved the highest praise. "An interesting case," he had written, "in which the deceased did as neat a job as any state executioner. Note the low tree stump used as a platform, but the weight of animal skins, etc., he was wearing would presumably contribute to producing the minimal force necessary. Taylor reports one fracture-dislocation in 52 cases—this is my first in 109." The man's lack of experience had, however, led him to overlook a couple of things which Strydom spotted as soon as he saw the photographs. They showed a small contusion on the left jawline and the knot at the occiput—or back of the head—where all it would have achieved was mere strangulation.

"Alfred," said Strydom, as the messenger returned with a wrapped sandwich for him, "we've got something really weird on the go here."

"No cheese-n-tomato, master. I bring ee-ham."

"Different DS, different magisterial district each time—have you noticed? There could be method in that."

"Uh-uh," corrected Alfred, with a firm shake of his wooden earplugs. "Ee-ham."

Pursuing the Roberts angle with obtuse Detective Sergeant Prins in the Durban Murder and Robbery Squad office that afternoon was definitely a mistake, Kramer told himself, and wished he had gone straight up to the records section instead. Not only was Prins being as condescending as he dared about an out-of-town inquiry, but he kept breaking off to shout abuse at a suspect crouched in the corner, and several times he had got up to kick him.

"Where was I?" Prins asked.

"In your chair," Kramer replied wearily, having lost the thread of the conversation once again.

Prins grinned—a quick show of very white, very narrow teeth in a deeply tanned face that seemed made up entirely of straight lines, like a brown paper bag still showing its packing folds. "And so, with Ringo being of age, and us having no warrant out for him," he said, sitting down again, "the fact that—stay still, bliksem!—he went off into the wild blue yonder was of no bloody consequence to us. Adult persons can go where they like—correct? As I said to that crazy old woman myself, she'd best forget the bastard and start enjoying life. But no—still!— she has to go on and on. Even wanted us to make whites carry proper passes as well, so we would know their whereabouts at any given—stop that noise, you hear? Last time I really lost my rag and warned her—*quite still!*—er, and now she does the same to you. Man, I'm sorry about that, hey?"

"No consequence to you? What she says about him going straight is—"

"Ja, we scared the poop out of him that time, I can tell you. And if he had been in any more trouble, I'd have been among the first to know."

"You weren't suspicious about him going like that?"

Prins dragged his attention back from the corner. "In the first place, she didn't report him missing for nearly a week in case he was mixed up in something. And in the second, Ringo was a nothing, Lieutenant; I'm even surprised Erasmus ever remembered them."

"Them? Vasari was at Steenhuis, too?"

"*Ach*, of course! They started early together on the bag snatch."

Kramer pulled out his notebook. "Did Vasari have a brother or anything?"

"Two sisters. But they're not around here anymore."

"Gone far?"

"Italy."

"Uhuh?"

"Buried the bastard and went. The whole family."

Prins began to fidget impatiently with an ebony ruler, rolling it between his lean, carefully kept hands.

"Ringo had no other known associates?"

"None," Prins stated categorically, getting to his feet. "Looks like you've picked a lulu, hey, sir? No other leads you can try? I can't see that yellow shit as your man in a million years, if I can be honest—it was him who panicked out there on the Bluff. Why not drop him and see who in that dorm was talking about Witklip?"

"Thanks," grunted Kramer, knowing a dead end when he saw one, without needing to have it pointed out.

But he went on sitting there, doing his own bit of fiddling with the old woman's pathetic circular, and wondering if he shouldn't make at least some attempt to trace Roberts; a quick glance through the list of unidentified whites males, kept in the inquest place back in Trekkersburg, might well be all the time it would take. The whole thing had that feeling to it. There was the backwash as well as sharks, and hands didn't last long in the Indian Ocean—but with an approximate date and a description of stature and clothing, he just could save her the cost of the printing. He watched the ruler arc into the corner, and the man go to fetch it.

"Just a sec!" exclaimed Prins, twisting round with a squeak of his rubber heel. "I've seen a way to work this."

"Oh, ja? With a pencil and paper, you mean?"

Prins laughed. "That comes later. No, this Witklip hideout

idea, Lieutenant: would it be Tollie's style to tell the female where he got it from exactly? He could never say anything without a bloody twist to it."

"So what? Roberts has already proved wrong."

"But before you go looking for the rest of them, Tollie was sure it was a big secret, right? Who keeps the best secrets? Doesn't tell tales? Do you get it?"

"Vasari," said Kramer, but did not thank him.

Instead he got the hell out of Durban.

Colonel Muller passed the sugar bowl to Doc Strydom, then popped two self-righteous small tablets into his own coffee with all the blatant stealth of a stage poisoner. He stirred, tapped his spoon on the lip of the cup, and placed it in its saucer.

Kramer, who had come straight up to the office from the car park, in response to a tip-off from Henk Wessels that something funny was going on, watched all this with one eyebrow raised. While he had expected some sort of reaction to his investigations in Durban, this prolonged and rather smug silence was baffling him.

"And so, Tromp," the Colonel said at last, "so far as you are concerned, the reason for Erasmus choosing Witklip has now been satisfactorily explained away. Is that correct?"

"Right, sir. We're back at square one again."

"My grandma," murmured the Colonel, dunking a Marie biscuit and winking at Strydom, "used to have a saying, you know."

"Oh, ja?"

"When I was a little boy, she would tell me that whenever one door closed, then another would open."

"Colonel?"

"Are you prepared to accept that?"

Kramer shrugged. "What's the game?" he asked irritably.

"I'm trying to clear your mind, Tromp. I'm trying to get you ready for a little shock that still has me shaking. In fact, now I've heard your story, too, I'm shaking even harder."

Then he handed Kramer a file which contained inquest papers relating to the discovery of a body at the foot of a krantz.

The only shock Kramer experienced was that of having been

preempted. "Who the hell thought of looking for this?" he said softly. "Did Mickey get in touch with you?"

Strydom shook his head.

"How well do those particulars match the ones on that form thing of yours?" the Colonel asked.

Kramer had no need to read Mrs. Roberts's appeal again—it was part of him. "The date is almost spot on, sir; the hair coloring and length is the same as Ringo's, allowing for sun-bleaching; five-foot nine is the right height. Does it say here one blue eye was found? That would be correct as well."

"No; better disregard that for now," Strydom said cautiously. "Eyes have been known to regress to blue after death."

"Where's the list of clothing, Doc?"

"That investigating officer will be getting his arse kicked," the Colonel growled, making a note. "It'd rotted off, but he should have recorded buttons, zips, footwear. No fingerprints of course, as you can see from the picture."

Then Kramer felt the shock pass and his natural distrust of the fortuitous take its place. "These four common factors don't actually count for much, not when you see them against a fair percentage of the white male population, do they? How about these five extractions and two temporary fillings? I've got nothing on the teeth, but you must have sent round the dental chart."

"No takers," Strydom disclosed. "The fillings were on the crude side, like you'd get on a ship or any army camp—not done by a dentist, I'm pretty sure of it."

"Ringo was never on a ship or in the army," the Colonel added. "How do you feel about it now, Tromp?"

"Inconclusive. But what made you look at this suicide in the first place? I can see it's one of Doc's, only—"

They told him.

Then added the three other inquest files to make a chronologically arranged row across the Colonel's desk, while Strydom provided a thumbnail sketch of each one as it was laid down.

"Have you gone mad?"

"I hoped you'd say that, Tromp. Those were my exact words when Chris first came rushing in here. It shows there was no ill will on my part, hey?"

Kramer sat down, stunned and unable to control the seethe of implications filling his head.

"Chris?" prompted the Colonel.

Strydom did a very old-fashioned thing and mopped his brow. "Perhaps I should explain a little. You see, most DS's are busy family doctors with no special interest in forensic work per se, and they don't—um—come into contact with each—"

"I meant the facts, man! That's what Tromp wants to hear about," Muller said.

"It's a fact that Natal's bigger than a lot of tin-pot countries," Strydom dared defensively. "Instead of blaming us, you might see that in dotting them around, his executions are—"

"*Murders* are," snapped Colonel Muller.

"Query murders," corrected Kramer, recognizing an urgent need in himself to treat the situation as routinely as possible. "Tollie's is the only one we're sure of." Having said that, a calm settled on him, just as it might on a drunk who decides that the only important thing in his whirling world is to soberly select the right key for the right keyhole.

His quiet observation seemed to steady the others as well— God knew what wild imaginings they'd been through before his arrival.

Colonel Muller cleared his throat. "The period, gentlemen, would appear to be one of five years, with one hanging occurring each year. But not, you will notice, in any particular month or season, so the timing may be more random than it seems."

"How many years were looked through in all?" Kramer asked, lighting up a Lucky.

"Alfred and me did another five before that."

"And?"

"Three fracture dislocations, none of them arousing suspicion of any kind. One involving a fall on a ladder."

"Uhuh. And how many of these are really borderline?"

Strydom mopped again. He was beginning to look like a man who'd cast his bread upon the waters and had forgotten to let go.

"If you're having a few doubts now," the Colonel said slightly sarcastically, "then which of these cases, not counting Tollie's, are you quite certain of?"

"The railway foreman couldn't have died under the given circumstances in the manner indicated."

"And the others? What order of certainty would you place them in?" Kramer asked, noting this down.

"On the scanty information I have?"

"Whichever way you like."

"The witch doctor I'm 80 percent sure of; the tramp, about 65. Make the krantz case 50."

"Fifty-fifty? Why's that?"

"Well, there were more variables involved in that one."

"Like yourself, for instance?"

That got its laugh and the tension eased, placing the discussion on a more objective level. Kramer made the routine check for a pattern.

"No real pattern," he said, "although it could be significant that there's only one black, that there's three unknown persons out of five, and that the other two had police records."

"The hangman is more likely white, then," Strydom suggested, with a logic that wasn't altogether sound if you thought about how certain blacks felt.

"I don't think we should waste time on surmising until we've more information," the Colonel said firmly. "Nor do we need to worry about anything under 100 percent—again, on the same basis."

"Or what about treating them as separate cases, each on its own merits?" Kramer put forward, aware that his conflicts arose from trying to relate such disparate individuals. "If, by some bloody miracle, they start linking up, then we'll rethink our approach."

"I like it, Tromp. Two murder inquiries and three suspicious deaths?"

"That's right, sir. Zondi can take the witch doctor and Marais can see what he can get out of the other two."

"But," said Strydom.

"Ja, Chris?" Muller replied.

"What about the hangman and his—"

"Look, man! I told you how many times? That's a dangerous fixation you've got, and I don't like the words you use. They only confuse the issue, which is bad enough as it is."

Strydom reddened. "Would you like a second opinion, Hans? I could take these down to Gordon in Durban."

"God in heaven! Nobody must hear about this until at least I've had time to talk to the brigadier. Of course I trust your judgment, Chris; it's just you must leave the investigation side to us, hey?"

Kramer went over to the door, wary of what more talk might do to the brittle simplicity of his present outlook.

"I'll get the sergeants going," he said, "and seeing as the Erasmus case has reached a blank wall, I might as well have a crack at railwayman Rossouw."

"Fine," replied Colonel Muller. "Is it okay for us to share your biscuit?"

Zondi took the photograph of the unidentified umthakathi down to the street of the witch doctors in the lower part of town.

Several of them there had wholesale departments, stocked with everything from bulk packets of aphrodisiacs to entire desiccated baboons, and also supplied the fur trappings a black man was no longer permitted to hunt for himself. He went from store to store, from fancy glass counter to self-service emporium, from holes in the wall to sinister back rooms, and from one end of the street to the other.

None of the fat cats he questioned had any recollection of the face cupped in his hand, nor were they much interested. Yet the effort involved wasn't entirely wasted: the dead man, they said, sniffing, was plainly an ignorant old peasant. Anyone with a smattering of the art would have secured his release with a handful of the right seeds—not that they sold them personally, of course. This confirmed in Zondi's mind what had seemed a rather strange paradox.

He hijacked a pirate taxi for a lift back to headquarters, put in a requisition for a dozen more copies of the photograph, and went to the Lieutenant's office to await their delivery. It was difficult to think of what else he might do.

After pushing pins into the wall map, to represent where the five bodies had been found, he sat down on his stool near the door and propped his leg on the table. The rat released its grip, wriggled a little, then lay comfortably on its belly.

Then Sergeant Klip Marais came in, yellow mustache bristling and gray eyes aglint, and barely nodded as Zondi stood up. He dumped some files on the Lieutenant's desk, retrieved a memo pad from the wastebin, and gave the telephone a dirty look.

"Did your boss ring this number?" he asked.

"I do not know, Sergeant."

"Huh! As if a bloke hasn't enough to do. What the hell are you doing here, by the way? You got your orders."

Zondi explained where he had been, and that there would be at least an hour's delay before he could have his photographs for distribution.

Marais, who never talked to him in the ordinary way of things, but was always happy to grumble, said: "Trust you to get off so lightly. The witch doctor is an easy one; me, I've been landed with the real bastards."

"They have no fathers?"

"Hey? Not bastards—ach, forget it. There's nothing on this tramp, and there never was. When I rang up the local station, they didn't even know what I was talking about for the first few bloody minutes."

"Hau!" Zondi sympathized.

"And Pa Henk couldn't assist either."

"Hau, hau!"

"And since then," Marais went on, taking the Lieutenant's chair, "it's got worse. Look at this."

Zondi examined the dental chart that had been sent spinning through the air for him to catch. Five extractions and two fillings; a wisdom tooth impacted.

"That's a thing to show the teeth in the krantz case—the teeth in the skull, understand? The two black dots are where fillings had been put not so long before, and the crosses are teeth that had been pulled out. I got straight on to the old—to a Mrs. Roberts, and asked her what her son's dentist's name had been. Guess?"

"I could not do such a thing, Sergeant."

"I'm not bloody surprised! He hadn't got one! She said he'd always been poop-scared of dentists, and she had given up trying to get him to go to one. His teeth stayed perfect? Oh, dear me, no; some had been neglected so badly they'd had to be pulled out. Which ones? How many? Peterkins hadn't told her—he'd just sneaked off and had it done. Fillings? She starts up all over again about how nervous and sensitive her little boysie was, and always left his poor teeth until they were completely buggered. You see what I mean?"

"Too difficult, this one."

"So I start ringing round all the dentists she could think of"—Marais sighed, rising wearily—"but the receptionists all say the same thing. They say they don't keep records of casual emergencies, if that's what I'm talking about. Cheeky bitches."

Zondi had been staring down at the chart and thinking, with some wry amusement, how like his own mouth it looked; not that fear kept him from the doctors who took turns at being the dentist down at the black clinic, but because they did only extractions, whatever shape the tooth was in. His gaze shifted to the black dots.

"A filling is plenty painful, Sergeant?" he inquired, with genuine curiosity.

"I don't mind them—but my brother does. Hates the drill. It scares a lot of people."

"Hau! Then maybe this skeleton boss was forced to have this filling done to him."

"What?"

"He was forced," Zondi repeated respectfully. "This treatment was not a matter of his own free will."

Marais turned in the doorway, laughed, and said: "Forced? Trust a coon to think of that! Nobody forces you to do things with your teeth you don't like, man! Have some bloody sense."

Zondi laughed, too, then put his leg back on the table. He was sure he had something there, somewhere.

11

THE BEST PERSON TO see about the unlamented railway foreman, everybody said, was good old Joep Terblanche. He'd hated the bastard. Hated him right down to his little blue socks, and then some. If, in fact, the good Lord hadn't finally made Rossouw do the decent thing, then Joep would have seen him off personally. It had been as bad as that. And nobody could blame him.

Dear God, thought Kramer.

To find Joep, you had to try the bowls club, the jukskei pitch, the tennis club, and the fishing club's stretch of trout water. Having run through all the amenities of the dorp of Olifantsvlei by then, there was just a chance he might be at home.

It started to rain heavily, so Kramer drove straight round.

The former station sergeant of Olifantsvlei, retired these three years on full pension, was living modestly in a tin-roofed bungalow overhung by tall pawpaw trees and their overripe fruit. The broad leaves shed by the Chinese fig tree lay undisturbed on the garden bench, and a pair of secateurs were rusting, forgotten, on a homemade sundial in the middle of the small, unkept lawn. It was also significant that the tracks down the clay driveway stopped at a point nearest to the front verandah, and that the garage, some ten yards farther on, had weed growing high against its dull green doors. Good old Joep, all this suggested, was a widower—and a fairly recent one at that, who hadn't grown accustomed to his solitude.

Kramer made a dash for the verandah, and reached it with his hair plastered down. He gave the front door a rap. Something inside, either a ghost or a cat, set a dish clattering.

Then a battered Land-Rover chugged in at the gate and the whole feel of the place changed. Big and beaming, broad enough to wear a barrel without needing braces, Joep Terblanche came doubling across; two fish dangled from his left hand, and in his right he carried a six-pack.

"Caught in the act!" he said, tossing the fish aside onto a verandah table. "Lieutenant Kramer, here on business—am I right?"

The bush telegraph in Olifantsvlei was obviously not to be sniffed at. Kramer shook the outstretched hand, approved the firm grip, and told himself to come off guard. The man had a simple and tangible goodness as pronounced as freshly baked bread.

"I'm here to ask a few questions about one of your old cases," he said.

"Ja, so I hear. Man, it's a pity my sister has passed on, or she could really tell you a thing or two about Toons Rossouw! Like to come inside?"

They went through into a kitchen that had a strong undersmell of cockroach powder and very few signs of food. When Terblanche opened the cupboard to remove two glasses, only breakfast cereal packets were exposed, and it was reasonable to suppose that he now took his main meals with some family living nearby.

A sodden crash resounded loudly on the tin roof overhead, making Kramer glance up.

"Pawpaw." Terblanche grinned. "The rain knocks them down."

"Christ, I thought a bloody maternity stork had dropped its load."

Terblanche frowned slightly, as though disapproving of that kind of humor—or perhaps it was that he just didn't understand it. Then he smiled again, handing Kramer his beer and inviting him to be seated.

"Naturally, I'm curious to know why the interest in Toons Rossouw all of a sudden, Lieutenant."

"You're well rid of us now, man, so let's make that 'Tromp.'"

"I prefer 'Joep' myself."

"Fine," said Kramer, still stalling; his instincts were insisting that he play this one very cool. "Ever heard of Witklip?"

"Certainly. It's that little place north of—y'know."

"I'm involved in a murder inquiry there, and Rossouw's name has cropped up in some of the past history. We don't know exactly what it's got to do with anything, so we hoped—by trying our luck this end—we might find out."

"Witklip?" murmured Terblanche, twisting the tips of his graying moustache between thumb and finger. "I can't see any connection either. Male or female involved?"

"Would you like to guess?"

"Huh! A woman, of course. But the railway doesn't go anywhere near the place, and Toons stuck very much to this dorp, as far back as I can remember."

"What was the story about him, Joep?"

"One you've heard before, that I'm sure of. He was a drunk, a fighter, a thief—when he got the chance—and a proper bad bastard all around. So who should agree to marry him? A little girlie he could crush the ribs of in one hand. Personally—and my sister Lettie also shared this opinion—the marriage was the minister's fault."

"Shotgun?"

"Hell, no!" said Terblanche, quite shocked. "Stefina came of a good family; poor like kaffirs, but good. He most probably thought she would reform him."

This was indeed the old, old story. They clinked glasses and drank.

"Nobody can say that little girl didn't try," Terblanche went on. "Others in the community tried for them also. Oom Dawid let Toons rent a shack on his property, and Lettie went round collecting up old curtains and suchlike. The place wasn't much, yet Stefina made it look as pretty as a picture from the catalogue. You could stop by there anytime, I'm telling you. The little black stove would be shining, there would be coffee in the pot, and always wild flowers in a jam bottle on the table given by the minister himself. I think you call it a card table, with folding legs; anyhow, it wasn't fitting for his position.".

"And they lived miserably ever after?" Kramer asked.

"Ever after," sighed his host, "until, of course, what happened came to pass. He was clever that one—oh, ja. The first time he took his belt to her, he was lucky and one of my men let him off with a warning. After that, when he came back drunk, or from his womanizing, he'd find ways of never leaving a mark. 'Stefina,' I would say—because Oom Dawid would always call me when he heard the screams—'Stefina, you just make a charge and the doctor is sure to find marks.' But she would shake her head. Not an ugly girl, you understand, although, in the eyes of some folk, a little on the plain side. It was her bones, man—bones like a little bird. To think of him beating her took you in the stomach. I tell you, when I got a chance, and had to have Toons in my lockup for the night, then he went in there off all four walls and the bloody ceiling. Mind you, like him, I had to be careful."

Kramer drank to the irony of that.

"I wanted to slap charges on him—any bloody charges, so long as he'd be put away inside. But Lettie asked what would happen to Stefina then, out in the shack alone, with kaffirs all around, and the magistrate followed a similar line, giving him long lectures. They all wanted this dream of theirs—*ach*, I don't know what to call it—to work out as it was planned and make them all happy. Never mind Stefina in the meantime! I watched her turning to a shadow of the happy kid I had known. The round cheeks and big dimples and—hell, it was terrible. She'd sit in the church on Sunday, reading her Bible like it would put blood back in her veins. Then she became pregnant."

"He resented the . . . ?"

"No; for once he settled down. That was actually when the railway job came up—you know how they look after poor whites—and the first was born. A girl."

"Ah," said Kramer.

"And the second, also a girl. The third, Stefina told us, was a miscarriage."

At this point, Terblanche rose and went off to fetch his fish from the front verandah. The rain drubbed harder on the roof and two more pawpaws burst and slid. Kramer switched on the kitchen light when he saw his host take out a gutting knife.

"There was a nagmaal," the old man continued, talking now as much to himself as to anyone. "Folk came from every direction, from places you never even heard of. When we hold communion in Olifantsvlei, the minister likes to make a big thing of it—bigger than most ministers do, and I'm not sure it's right. Anyhow, there were hundreds camping here, around the church and down by the river. You can imagine how many kids that added up to! They were the ones who began the talk."

His knife slid into the fish's belly rather too deep. He drew it out a little way and tried again, slitting up toward the head. He scraped the innards away.

"They told their parents and soon everyone was whispering and pointing behind Stefina's back. Naturally, it wasn't long before the story reached my ears, and when it did, I went straight to her. 'Stefina, I want you to charge him,' I said. 'Your children are saying that their pa kneed their ma in the stomach, and this made her sit on the potty and do a baby there. Stefina,' I said, 'they think it was a joke, Stefina.' 'Leave my man alone,' was all she said. I caught Toons not two minutes later, and he said, 'That's not true—why not ask my wife?' So I looked for the kids, but Stefina had taken them away. Not a word would they say when I finally had them to myself. Nothing! You have never seen kids—or a woman—so terrified. And what could I do about it? Also nothing! Not with the minister and the magistrate and every other bugger on the opposite side!"

The fish had begun to bleed.

"They didn't mean any harm, Tromp. They said it just couldn't be, they didn't believe it. Not after Toons had been making such wonderful progress! But us bloody old sinners weren't nearly so certain, and we made sure he knew it. We told Toons to his face. We said he was lucky it was nagmaal. Huh! So life goes. Don't tell me you haven't heard the rest?"

"How much later was he found in the gangers' hut?"

"About a fortnight. The magistrate kept all this out of the inquest for Stefina's sake; he said it wasn't material."

"Suicide, Joep?" murmured Kramer, emptying the last of his beer can into the glass before him.

Terblanche crossed over to the sink and carelessly inspected the cut in his palm. The tainted water eddied pink round the plug hole, not becoming any lighter.

"Now you're asking, my friend. When she got over the shock, Lettie always used to put it best, I think. She used to say that no man is ever safe from the higher law, and this was what Toons Rossouw had forgotten."

"Divine justice?"

"Call it what you like," replied Joep Terblanche. "The man was a murderer."

The color-control knob on Dr. Strydom's new television set had his primitive employees in fits of laughter in the living room that evening. This was as well, because the cookboy, the gardener, and the maid had slightly annoyed him by taking his magnificent acquisition almost for granted, and by being less than astounded when the screen first lit up. It had been as disappointing as showing a conjuring trick to very small children, who simply accepted the magic as genuine and failed to appreciate the human ingenuity which lay behind it. Then it had occurred to him that they were probably unaware of the skill involved in getting a lifelike picture, and he'd given the knob a twist to the right. And now, as he exercised his power to transform the news reader from flesh pink to almost any shade of the rainbow, he was being rewarded by delighted giggles and guffaws that signified a proper degree of amazement.

"Didn't you hear the phone?" Anneline said a little crossly, coming in with her knitting. "Gracious me, why's that man gone green?"

"Er—a small teething trouble, I think. There, that's fine now. The phone, you say?"

"He's too flushed; looks like an immigrant."

"Better?"

"Yellowy, like a Cape Colored."

"Sorry. Try this."

"Mmmm. But his tie was never so shiny as that. It was the Colonel."

The servants took their leave then, thanking Strydom for his kindness and the demonstration, and he waved them out impatiently, eager to hear what else his wife had to say.

"What was Hans's problem this time?"

"You don't have to ring back; he just thought you'd be interested to know that one of your hanged bodies had been identified."

"No! Really?"

Anneline paused to hear an item of interest to her, and then went on: "The krantz case—is that right? He says that Sergeant Marais had an inspiration and got in touch with the prison doctor where someone called Ringo had been kept during remand. This prison doctor remembered noticing two holes in the man's mouth during the routine checkup, and having put some fillings in so there wouldn't be any problems during the trial. Oh, a whole lot more, but that is the main gist of it. Can you do something about the sound?"

Strydom did do something—he wasn't sure quite what—and then sat back on the sofa beside her, very content with the world and, in particular, with the way his day had been spent. As soon as the news was over, he and his huggable old helpmeet would certainly have a great deal to discuss.

The front doorbell rang.

"Oh, good," said Anneline, elbowing him in the ribs. "That'll be Hester and her mother from over the road. Go and welcome them in, Chris—this will be the first time they've seen it, poor things."

Kramer returned from Olifantsvlei with a very definite idea of what he was up against; an idea that—as he'd been telling himself in the car—made the mind bloody boggle. It wasn't so much a murderer they were looking for, but an avenger.

He chanced across Colonel Muller in the vehicle yard of police headquarters, just as the old bugger was sneaking off home after a long day, and they sat on the mounting step of a handy troop carrier for a quick debriefing.

"But I don't see what you've established this afternoon," the Colonel said, when each had given the other his news. "If the minister at Olifantsvlei claims there must have been folk from the Witklip district at his nagmaal, then surely that doesn't in itself begin to clinch anything? What about all the other people from all the other places? Any of them could be equally suspect."

"Sir?" muttered Kramer, replacing the notes on the positive identification of Ringo Roberts in the Colonel's briefcase—and blocking an impulse to be distracted by them. "Oh, I just threw that in for good measure. It was the interview before that which clinched it—the one I had with Joep Terblanche, the ex-sergeant who eats his meals with the foreman's widow."

"Terblanche couldn't see a Witklip connection. Haven't you just told me that?"

"Please, sir, disregard Witklip entirely. In Terblanche's mind, Rossouw had committed a capital offense—murder."

"Ja, I understand that. Quite natural."

"Then take the three hangings we know something about. Rossouw was, to all intents and purposes, a murderer—agreed? But weren't Ringo and Tollie *also* involved in capital offenses?"

"Er—in a manner of speaking."

This hesitancy really annoyed Kramer and goaded him into sarcasm. "It may be a fact that only one white rapist gets hanged for every hundred bloody ntombi shaggers," he said, "but you're not denying that even attempted robbery can, strictly speaking, get you the noose?"

The Colonel frowned. "Now you've lost me, man. Tollie's wasn't just attempted; it was a case of armed—and he took a shot at you! That wasn't what I was getting at, but you just carry on. My dinner likes to get cold."

"Then—"

"And what's rape got to do with it?"

"It could," replied Kramer, improvising swiftly, and rather wishing he'd left all this till the morning, "it could be the capital crime for which the tramp was executed."

"Hey?"

"The same could apply to the witch doctor. There are nine different headings we can choose from, but those political ones seem a bit far out."

"Unless," said the Colonel dryly, "he had been putting evil spells on the government dipping inspector. I'm beginning to see where you're going, and I must caution you not to slip into a trap."

"Which is?"

"Coming back from Terblanche and using the word *executed*. So far, you and me have successfully avoided thinking about all this like some trashy newspaper, and that is the proper professional attitude. Stick to the correct terms, please."

"But, Colonel, *is it* murder to kill a murderer?"

"Hey? If you're speaking about doing it in cold blood, as part of a premeditated act and not where innocent lives are in any immediate danger, then obviously the crime is one of—"

"When you use a noose on a rope?"

During the clap of silence that followed, Kramer took out his Lucky Strikes, lit one, and flicked his match at the yard cat.

"The state," began Colonel Muller, then seemed to lose the thread of what he was about to say.

"Is the embodiment of the people," Kramer continued for him, "each being required to act in its interests. But let's keep it simple."

The Colonel humphed. "By all means, Tromp! By all means! What you're going to say to me now is that this hangman bloke is just doing our job for us. And who are we to complain when he does it so nicely?"

"Not us, sir—the state."

"My apologies."

"I'd not actually taken it that far, though," said Kramer. "I was looking at it in very practical terms, and just trying to see why he ever thought this was necessary. Never mind for the moment how he learned the tricks of his trade, or where he's got his gallows; that can all come later."

"Certainly! Who's in a rush?"

"In each of the cases we know something about," Kramer persisted, wanting himself to hear how it sounded, "the law—or the state—was not in a position to exact its due penalty. Rossouw's is a prime example of the spirit of the law being defeated by the letter."

"Hmmm. And what about the two cases we've nothing on? Do we conveniently overlook them meantime?"

"Hell, no! They give us all the more reason to believe that the state couldn't act—simply because, ipso facto, it has remained in ignorance of the offenses committed!"

"Aha," said the Colonel, bending to tickle the yard cat under her chin. "How are things with you, Ilahle, my girlie?"

"Look, sir—how many times have you known for an absolute fact that some bugger is guilty, only you haven't been able to produce one bit of evidence to prove it?"

"Hoo!"

Evidently, the point Kramer was making had at last been handsomely conceded, and he sat back to await a more intelligent response, picking up the yard cat's kitten as he did so. This was presumably Little Ilahle, as it too looked like a shiny lump of coal. They rubbed noses.

"I fully appreciate," grunted Colonel Muller, "the importance of trying to form some idea of what's going on, but you're forcing things to fit. Do you see what I mean?"

By puffing air out of alternate corners of his mouth, Kramer—who otherwise felt undeflatable—made the kitten blink and shake its head.

"Ach, no, Tromp! I'm being serious, man! In what way would the state have been thwarted if this bloke of yours had reported Tollie's whereabouts to us? We'd have nailed the bastard without any further assistance—correct?"

"But that's presuming my 'bloke' did him for the bank job. Like I said yesterday, when we found the money, it might have been some other aspect of his past catching up. Christ, we'd had him in on suspicion often enough! Remember that unsolved shooting at the Wartburg garage?"

For a while, only the yard cat said anything. Then Kramer, who had talked his way into a clarity of thought, found himself becoming impatient with the Colonel's apparent failure to grasp the situation. It wasn't as if much imagination was required: the gallows provided, as it were, a ready-made and familiar framework of logic into which, sooner or later, everything must surely fit. You could no more dismiss the inherent premise of crime and punishment than you could try and call the bloody thing a weapon; it just wouldn't work.

"I was wondering," murmured Colonel Muller, "why Ringo had turned state evidence."

"Hey?"

"When those two first appeared for remand, they stood every

chance of acquittal: the prosecution's case had holes in it a mile wide. I thought Ringo must have changed his mind in order to pass the buck on to Vasari, just on the off chance that things went wrong, but that doesn't make sense anymore—not since I've read through the docket you brought up from Durban. That's the trouble with these petty cases that are over quick—the newspapers don't give you enough details. Did you yourself follow it at the time?"

"Only headlines and the first couple of paragraphs. Prins says Ringo was putty soft, so maybe his conscience pricked him."

"In my book, conscience begins at home," said the Colonel with a vague smile, fully aware he was being got at. "They were old friends, him and Vasari, and they'd always pleaded the same way together before. Huh! Here, let me have that fine little fellow."

The kitten was passed over and its mother climbed into the Colonel's lap. A huddle of manacled prisoners, being escorted across the yard by Security Branch plainclothesmen, looked at them curiously.

"Well, Colonel?"

The yard cat's proud purring was like a row of dots.

"Well, Tromp, you just carry on, man. Let's see where this theory of yours gets us. Personally, I find this case one big mess of assumption, presumption, names that link, names that don't, and a bit of a nightmare into the bargain. But what else can one do? Blast away with your shotgun at anything that moves and you're bound to hit something, I suppose."

"Thanks, sir. It's certainly reached that stage now."

Colonel Muller yawned. "Only wish we'd managed one positive achievement today, that's all."

"Ach, we have," replied Kramer, giving mother and son a last chuck under the chin. "I'd best go and give Ma Roberts a bell."

12

BUT WHEN KRAMER HEARD that the parrot had taken ill, he hadn't the stomach to add to Mrs. Roberts's troubles. So instead he asked her whether she knew why her son had turned state evidence. It was the first thing that entered his head.

"So many people have asked that," Mrs. Roberts replied in a voice twittering with revived indignation, "and it really isn't at all fair. Especially as Tony made him do it, made him do what he'd never have done otherwise, the loyal little mite. If it hadn't been for that kind Sergeant Prins, the Lord knows where he might have ended up! And to think that Tony could try a trick like that on his friend—that came as a terrible, terrible shock to us."

Kramer winked at Zondi, who had just walked in with some photographs, and then tried to extract some sense from that bewildering outburst.

"Tony? You're saying Tony Vasari—"

"Where they got the money from we'll never know, of course." Mrs. Roberts steamed straight on. "I mean, they lived only around the corner from here, in some flats not nearly as nice, and his father wore the greasiest overalls you've ever seen.

So where did it all come from? I certainly couldn't tell you. Not from their pockets, you can be sure, because when it came to sending them back where they belonged, that was only possible through the generosity of others—or so I was told."

Kramer gave a bemused grunt, and found it instantly mistaken for one of disapproval.

"Not that you must think for one moment there were any sour grapes on our part, Lieutenant Kramer—well, certainly not to begin with. In fact, when we heard Tony was getting Mr. Colgate, our feelings were quite the reverse. It wasn't until Sergeant Prins—"

"Cecil Colgate?" Kramer interrupted to ask, realizing just how little notice he'd taken of the case at the time. "Do you mean Vasari was represented by the advocate himself? Or by the son who's just started?"

"*The* Mr. Colgate."

"Hell."

"Now you see what I meant about the money! Of course, I was a proper dunce about these matters then, and thought that anything which helped Tony was bound to help Peterkins as well; I just wouldn't have suspected for one moment what was really going on. Then, thank goodness, Sergeant Prins came of his own accord to explain it all. What an eye-opener that was!"

"Uhuh?"

"Surely you don't need me—"

"Please, I'm interested."

Zondi slipped him a note to say Jonkers had rung, and would be ringing again soon.

"Well," said Mrs. Roberts, "when you have two people accused of something, Sergeant Prins said, and they both come up in court together, then it isn't just the prosecutor who comes after them with his long knife. Oh, no; each person has to watch out for the other one's lawyer, who'll try to push the blame on him as quick as a flash, especially if they're being paid lots to do it! And all my Peterkins had was the free lawyer, who wouldn't be free if he was much good. Do you see?"

Kramer saw, all right. Prins had offered Ringo the immunity of turning state evidence as his only hope of escaping the rope. The irony being that Colgate would never have risked attacking

Ringo if he'd stayed in the dock; he would have simply secured an acquittal for both accused by using his cross-examination to corroborate Vasari's evidence. As tricks went, this one ranked dirtier than pricking holes in condoms, especially as it'd had the opposite effect.

"Hello—are you still there, Lieutenant?"

"Still here, ma'am."

"Then you do understand, don't you? Tony Vasari was only thinking of himself. Trust an Italian! Sergeant Prins said they were often very funny people, and not just because they're Catholics. Very cowardly, I believe, and Mr. Kleint, who lives below and fought against them up north, says they aren't clean either, not in their personal habits. Was Peter expected to stick his neck out for one of these? 'Heavens,' I said to Sergeant Prins, such a fair-minded man, 'I must talk to my son immediately.' And before I knew it, he'd got me special permission to go to the prison right then and there. Peterkins was horrified."

"I bet," said Kramer.

"Being the sweet boy he is, I still had to talk to him for rather a long time—and so did Sergeant Prins and some other kind men—before he'd stop his nonsense about telling tales on Tony. It made me feel a little awful, and I had to keep reminding myself of what those dreadful people were trying to do. What it came down to, of course, was that we simply hadn't any choice in the matter."

"Uhuh."

"And then, as you know," Mrs. Roberts said, sighing almost contentedly, "it all happened just as Sergeant Prins had told us it would, but my Peterkins was quite safe. Oh, you should have heard some of the things that Mr. Colgate accused him of! It was wicked. I had a good mind to write to his wife and tell her what I thought about her husband and how they'd made their money. All that swank and posh! The late Mr. Roberts may have been only a—"

"Are you sure," Kramer cut in, circling an estimated R16,000 on his memo pad, "that Mr. Colgate wasn't appearing *pro deo*? For nothing, in other words? He does do that sometimes."

"No, he wasn't," she said firmly.

"And how would you—"

"Our own lawyer told me. In fact, he said he believed there was something *very mysterious* about the money—and I'll leave you to decide what to make of that!"

Kramer changed the receiver over to his other ear, and took the cigarette Zondi was offering him.

"They couldn't have sold some property, Mrs. Roberts?"

"What property? They were renting, the same as us. Mind you, they always found enough for all those trips up to Pretoria, but they didn't think to save anything for later. Typical! The funeral was a disgrace."

"Oh, ja? You went?"

"Hardly! Mrs. Kleint did—she's ever so religious—and she swears she's never seen anything cheaper or plainer. Isn't that awful? You'd have thought they would care more about what they did with their own flesh and blood. I know my Peterkins won't even dream of skimping on my arrangements, bless him, when the time comes!"

"You're damn right, lady," said Kramer, then found an excuse to ring off. "Jesus . . ."

Zondi shifted uncomfortably under his blank stare.

"I've just learned something, old son."

"Boss?"

"It's the ones with the empty eyes who do the bloody sucking, not the other way round."

Then Kramer listlessly repeated what else he'd learned, before wandering off along the balcony to the lavatories, fully intending to stay there until the world was a better place. But he was recalled almost immediately by the promise of some comic relief.

"Witklip on the line," said Zondi, handing him the receiver.

"Get the dictation set on," Kramer whispered, and waited until he was plugged in. "Hello, Frikkie? What is it, man?"

"Sorry to trouble you, Lieutenant, but you did say if I had any information I should—"

"Hold it! I'll put this on scramble."

Kramer clattered a pencil in his mouthpiece, gave the dial a slight twist, and saw, out of the corner of his eye, Zondi gag himself.

"All clear. You can speak freely now, my friend."

"Well, sir"—Jonkers began faltering—"I don't know if this means anything to you, but I think I know why Tommy chose to come here."

"Uhuh?"

"I've heard, shall we say, that he once had a friend who stayed here with a rich uncle. A long time ago, but it'd made an impression—such an impression that Tommy had always wanted to see it for himself. I think that's right. He also used to boast he was a really bad boy when he was younger. Errol Flynn the Second, he described himself as. Not in the criminal sense of bad; just a bit wild—five or six girls chasing him all the time. Is that what you want?"

"What do you mean, you've 'heard, shall we say'? What's your source?"

"Well—er—"

"Security must—"

"Yirra, I'm not arguing, hey?" said Jonkers hastily, lapsing into a long, sweaty pause which ended in compulsive fluency. "He apparently made this statement to one of the farmers at the hotel bar, Lieutenant. Everyone was talking away about him last night, wondering where he was, and fortunately I caught the words, but owing to a coon waiter getting in the way, I'm sorry to say my view was obscured. I thought it best, in the light of the warning you gave us, not to draw too much attention by asking for the person's name who made this report, and I'm sure you'll feel I acted correctly under the circumstances."

What a bloody dreadful prevaricator he was. Even Erasmus, with his pathological need to lie his arse off, would never have tried that level of crap on a grown man, let alone a Witklip mealie strangler. At the very least, he would have required a half-witted woman and a degree of cozy intimacy before letting loose that little lot—two things that, everyone seemed to agree, Witklip had denied him. Then Kramer had a sudden, diabolical inspiration.

"On another matter entirely, Frikkie," he said matily, "your lady wife does haircuts—am I right?"

If pink sound were a possibility, that was all that came down the line for nearly half a minute.

Kramer did his chuckle. "No need to fear the Commies when we're around, hey? Tell her I might be calling soon for one of her creations. And, Frikkie, thanks for the other stuff, man; it has cleared up one small point very nicely. Bye now."

He replaced the receiver, opened the Erasmus docket, and put a tick beside the note about hair clippings being found in the deceased's ears. Then he looked up to see that Zondi had missed the joke.

"Can't you see? He chucks in all this bulldust about Errol Flynn and that, which is some gossip his wife told him, hoping to make himself sound like a big agent, and gets caught up in his own—I give up. The only thing that makes you kaffirs laugh is a Rhodesian."

"I think, boss," Zondi said solemnly, "that Sergeant Jonkers accidentally told us more than he realized."

"And that isn't funny? I lay you ten rand Mrs. Jonkers hasn't been to a barbecue for twelve weeks either—never mind what that randy bastard organized with her during the rest of the time. Where's my jacket?"

Zondi helped him into it, allowing himself a small, pinched smile at Kramer's expense.

"Okay, Mickey," Kramer challenged, "you tell me what makes kaffirs laugh, then."

"I will tell you two words to which we are sensitive."

"Watch it! Kill the light; I'll do the door."

Together, and rather slowly, they started along the balcony to the staircase leading down to the hall and the street.

"Those two words," said Zondi, stopping on the top step, "were 'rich uncle.'"

"That was the Tollie Twist that he always—Christ!"

"Whoa, boss! There are many rich men in this country, and that case is only fifty-fifty— Boss?"

"Come on, man! It's not midnight yet," Kramer called back from the hall, and went out into the dark, clutching at a straw he hoped to make bricks with.

Kramer found the eminent Mr. Cecil Colgate robed in his less than judicial dressing gown. "I confess that I do prefer," Colgate rumbled, "to have my failures decently forgotten, and to rest—

particularly at this hour of the night—upon my laurels."

Kramer made his appreciative smile double as an apology.

"I certainly won't offer you coffee, Lieutenant, as you obviously don't get enough sleep—but I dare say a brandy would do?"

"Very kind of you, sir."

While his host poured the drinks, Kramer took a polite look at the photograph hanging above the study fireplace, and was surprised to see a Rugby team with several nonwhite players among it.

"I was a Dark Blue," Colgate murmured modestly.

"Uhuh?"

"But you've intrigued me, old chap, so let's not become sidetracked. Here, sit."

They sat down in a pair of leather-upholstered armchairs and stretched out their feet to the dusty fire logs. The brandy was as smooth as spit: sheer perfection.

"Cheers," said Kramer, belatedly remembering his manners.

"Your health! We were discussing the Vasari case, and you'd just sailed rather close to the wind by implying I'd profited by ill-gotten gains. Criminal slander."

"Hell, I'd done that, sir?" replied Kramer, knowing the sly twister of old. "So okay; let me sail all the way and ask you for the truth of the matter."

"Can't do it."

"But I thought we'd agreed that if I didn't—"

"You see, if you wanted to know *exactly* where that money came from, then I'll say again I can't oblige. Can't, not won't."

"Sir?"

"But I can tell you something of the background—which I insisted on knowing before I accepted the brief."

When Colgate's chin trebled and his hooded eyes closed to slits beneath the white mustaches he had for eyebrows, there was never any need for anyone to beg him to continue. Kramer merely cocked an ear.

"Dear me, yes; that brief. As it happened, I'd already turned it down flat, being a trifle chary of the situation, when Mrs. Vasari came alone and unbidden to my chambers to have me repent my decision. By Jove, what a scene that was! I'd never set

eyes on the good woman before, of course—had just had a few
words with young Willerby, her solicitor, over a game of pills at
the club. Didn't care for the sound of it at all; extremely
dubious."

"In what way, Mr. Colgate?"

"Willerby said he'd had a telephone call from an 'anonymous
well-wisher' offering to meet, on Vasari's behalf, the fees of—as
he put it—the best at the bar. One does get this sort of thing now
and again, especially when a young defendant is involved, and
these cranks can be a terrible bore. Willerby tried to knock it on
the head by quoting my usual remuneration, and then had to do
a spot of humoring when, to his disgust, this individual asked for
a week or so in which to arrange payment."

"This 'well-wisher' stayed anonymous?"

"Oh, absolutely! Willerby was only too happy with the
notion that no names would embrace no pack drill, and he was
responsible enough to make no mention of this to the family.
But the next go-off was that Mr. Vasari received an anonymous
call at his place of business a week later. On this occasion, the
well-wisher merely gave my name and stated that the money
would arrive shortly. And so, by God, it did! Willerby's
secretary found it in a brown paper parcel, left lying on her desk
and marked very clearly. He had the family in that morning, as
you can imagine, and asked them if they had any way of
accounting for this munificent gift. After the first spot of
excitement, Mr. Vasari could only suggest with fervor that it was
all thanks to the Virgin Mary."

Kramer gave an amused snort. "And the scene in your
office?"

Colgate fetched over the brandy bottle to replenish their
glasses. "She came walloping in, was fended off by my clerk,
then by a junior—and ended up chucking the money about.
Better than a grand opera! I had to have her into my room, if
only to place the money in the safe, and despite my maidenly
protestations, she insisted on pleading her case."

"Uhuh? I mean, yes?"

"Say when. Here's where I break my professional confi-
dences, I'm afraid."

"When."

"Bit of background first," Colgate said, sitting back and warming the brandy between his huge pink hands. "In '42, Signor Vasari was interned by Smuts, having left Italy four years previously because of an intense dislike of fascism. Often wondered if he was aware that the illustrious Field Marshal, architect of the UN and all that, had once had a native village bombed for not paying its dog tax—but that's by the by. Off he went with the other Italian chappies, and the little woman was left to fend for herself. Not a bright prospect, when your English is still wonky and your Afrikaans is *non est*, so she did the only sensible thing: she took in lodgers. Plenty of youngsters were after digs in Durban at the time, having been seconded from the backveld to take over jobs left behind by men in the armed forces, and she experienced no difficulty in soon establishing herself. They got used to spaghetti and she learned to speak Afrikaans; dreadfully lonely, many of those youngsters were, of course, and quite unable to feel at ease among the lower sophisticates of the post office sorting room. On one occasion, when she was sitting in the parlor alone with one of them, she burst into tears over hearing that her home town had been razed by the Yanks—they were listening to the nine o'clock news—and was mortified when her guest, while attempting to comfort her, burst into tears himself. But I seem to be wandering rather from the point, except it is pertinent to understand she had a true *mamma mia's* heart. Those young men all loved her, as I heard subsequently from other sources. Now I shall attempt to remove your glazed look by coming to the nub of the matter: Signora Vasari was unmistakably Italian, a comely wench with dark eyes and a gorgeous accent, and this—"

"Nub?" Kramer said, in his most Afrikaans accent.

Colgate toasted him with his glass. "Oh, very well, you unromantic son of the earth, I'll come to it. An Italian POW escaped from the camp at Hay Paddock just before the end of the war and sought sanctuary with her; he'd been in some scrape with a homosexual guard or other—I'm afraid that's a big vague now. Rather stupidly, although one can understand her compassion, she took him in. The police were round like a shot, but were so taken with her Afrikaans that their search was most perfunctory. Her lodgers were beginning to drift back to the country again by now, and she managed to keep this chap hidden for several months without detection. On the eve of the internees' being released, she supplied him with clothing and a little money, and he was able to slip away. Just how he managed after that, she hadn't any idea—quite a number of POW's stayed on, so he may have just swapped identities—but years later he popped up again in a letter. He'd done very well for himself and wanted to repay her."

"Two and two makes four," Kramer said, placing his glass on the mantel shelf, "but why the anonymous voice? I don't follow that, hey?"

"Then you weren't listening, as I thought!" Colgate snapped irritably. "Why did Vasari leave Italy? What sort of man had his wife been harboring?"

"He felt that strong about fascists? This bloke mightn't—"

"If you'd met Signor Vasari, you would be left in no doubt that it could well have ended their marriage. He was a man of such stern principle that I'm certain he was really to blame for his son's delinquency, far too overbearing. Those two daughters they later adopted must be leading a devil of a life among all the temptations of Europe. Ironically, he also loved that boy deeply—perhaps he wished too much of him. It doesn't take a mathematical mind to see that Anthony Michael was the blessing of their reunion, give or take a few weeks."

"So the father never—"

"God knows, I did the best I could!" Anger uncurled in Cogate's deep voice, and he rose, standing with his back to the cold fireplace. "I'll never understand what possessed Roberts! I'd only just agreed to take him under my wing with Vasari— who insisted I should do so—when I found out we were too late. That *wasn't a murder* until that damned little renegade started lying!"

Kramer waited and then said, "So the father never got to hear about this man? She kept it to herself?"

"Wouldn't you have done? Sorry about that—er—little outburst."

"And she never actually saw him again?"

"As a matter of fact, I think she did. Yes, took the family to see him without the old man being any the wiser—which is how this chappie knew about the son, one presumes."

"It was also in the papers. Did she tell you his name?"

"For my part," Colgate answered him, frosting slightly, "I was satisfied that the 'well-wisher' had a most admirable reason for not intruding, and saw no reason to press the matter. The poor woman was distressed enough by having to entrust her secret to me—it ultimately destroyed her, you know. Ghastly business. And furthermore, I'd like to remind you, I was being paid in cash."

Colgate always slipped them in at the end, using laughter like some kind of antacid.

Without letting his smile fade, Kramer pressed harder: "No idea of his occupation?"

"None. Came originally from farming stock; that's the best I can do, but that's true of so many Italians. Your questions are beginning to interest—"

"Did she say—imply, even—when this get-together took place?"

"A 'chance' encounter on the beach seems most likely, wouldn't you say?"

"What about at Witklip?" suggested Kramer.

And saw Mr. Cecil Colgate, S.C., M.A. (Cantab), slap a hand to his forehead in a courtroom gesture of sudden, very decided comprehension.

"Witklip was where Vasari wanted to be buried, old son," Kramer disclosed some thirty minutes later.

The Chevrolet was wending its own way to Kwela Village; he and Zondi had just lit their last cigarettes of the day, and the smoke was tasting stale and unpleasant.

"Hau, boss! Everything goes click."

"A lot does—or seems to," said Kramer, "but we shouldn't try to generalize. Keeping what I've found out just to Ringo, let me fill you in on the rest of what old Colgate had to say first."

"Yebo?"

"Witklip came up in conversation just the once, directly after sentence of death had been passed. Colgate had gone down to the cell to shake hands and say an appeal would be useless. The kid took it calmly, like they often do, and Colgate asked him if there was any request he'd like to make. Vasari wanted to know if it would be possible for his burial to be at Witklip."

Zondi clucked his tongue.

"Ja, it put him in a hell of a position. He hadn't any means of knowing whether the Commissioner of Prisons would be giving the body back, nor did he know what sort of funeral might be permitted. He asked if there was some special reason, not having ever heard of the place himself. Not really, Vasari said; it was just a place he'd always liked. A long time before, when he was still a kid, he and his folks had stayed there with an uncle over a long weekend. He'd gone horseback riding and swimming, and there'd been a party at the farm one night. But best of all he'd liked walking in the veld and being so far away from people. The only other time he had been in the country was at Steenhuis Reformatory, and being there had made him talk about Witklip until his pals teased him. In the end, if anything went wrong for one of them, the catch phrase was: '*Ach*, it'll be okay when we get to Witklip—hey, Vasari?' He talked a lot in the cell, making jokes like that, but Colgate could see it meant something to him. Then they took him away to catch the train."

"No church there, boss."

"Aikona—no bloody graveyard either. Colgate found that much out and never mentioned it to anyone."

The rutted dirt of Kwela Village juddered beneath them, breaking off the long ash on Zondi's Lucky. He took a hand off the wheel to dust himself off and stub out the rest. Then he gave a long, low whistle and said: "Are you thinking what I am thinking, boss? About this uncle?"

"Could be. He's a bloke who must definitely have felt very bitter over what happened."

"Had he not provided money for Advocate Colgate, then—"

"He'd never think like that, Mickey!" objected Kramer, having not allowed himself the thought either. "Or at least, God help him if he did! No, he couldn't have, man; he stayed too far in the background to know exactly what went on."

"Then what, boss?"

"Something simpler. He evened up the score and the hell with the legal niceties. Paid his debt in full."

"Ah, the spirit of the law!" said Zondi, drawing up at the end of the pathway to his house and stepping out. "Thanks for the lift, Lieutenant."

"See you. We make an early start, hey?"

"For Witklip?"

"Where else? Let's just hope Sergeant Jonkers and that dozy constable of his are getting a good night's rest! With any luck, we should really have their work cut out for them tomorrow."

But it was already tomorrow, so without further ado the Chevrolet moved on.

13

CONSTABLE WILLIE BOSHOFF, once known to his tormentors at the police college as Elvis, reined in under the great white rock above Witklip and wished he could believe that Friday was going to be exciting and drastically different.

His shoulders slumped. There had been a time, of course, a couple of years back when he was only seventeen, when all he had asked of life was a horse and a gun. A time when he would leap into his saddle and gallop off at the slightest excuse, even if it was only a Bantu female reporting attempted rape at a beer party. These sorties into the reserve had seldom come to anything—inevitably the party would have been disbanded before his arrival on the scene—but it had been showing a police presence that mattered, and the Bantu had appreciated this. On about as many occasions, they had tried to force roasted mealies and other small gifts on him, and, to a man, they had always praised his fine horsemanship. The bugger of it was, however, that every time Willie had gone off like this, in one direction, then something far more serious would have to happen in another direction, and he'd return to find Sergeant Jonkers climbing the wall of the charge office. And so, except for his early-morning exercise, Willie had cut right down on horse-riding, and had been bored almost to tears by a coincidental drop in the crime rate during the weekends he was on duty.

"Bastard," he muttered, having reminded himself that Jonkers had suddenly fixed up an extra-long weekend off, starting the night before. "Lazy, selfish bloody bastard. What's he want in Durban?"

The horse clopped forward a few paces, nibbling neatly on the new stalks of grass that stuck out of the burned stubble like green knitting needles. Its warm rub against his inner thighs had a pleasant yet aggravating effect.

That was another thing: after fiddling almost every weekend for himself, Jonkers still expected Willie to create some form of love life in the nearest town, fifty kilometers away. Very funny, if not hilarious. Brandspruit's only bioscope wasn't even a building, but a battered 16mm projector owned by the chemist and set up for viewing on Saturday nights in the meeting hall; the bars were—like every bar in the country—for men only, yet neither hotel had ever heard of a ladies' lounge; and the nearest thing to a milk bar was run for and by bloody coolies. Overrun, you might say, if the matter weren't so serious. Because if you didn't own a car, this left you with nowhere to sit with a shy young girl, let alone sweep her off her feet, from Monday to Friday.

Willie sighed.

He knew damn well he was just making excuses. His landlord, Mr. Haagner, the Witklip butcher, had offered him the use of the van any evening he liked. And the lads stationed at Brandspruit had promised him a little goose any night he had to stop over for a court hearing. Even if he was pressed for time, they said, there was a red-haired nympho in the Bantu Affairs office who made short work of anyone in uniform. It was, in fact, just this sort of talk, which excited him and scared him all at the same time, that kept him well away from town except on urgent business. As to why this was, he still wasn't sure.

With a harumph, the horse raised its head and listened, tipping forward its ears.

Willie looked across the valley to where the road from the south came through a notch in the far ridge; all he saw was a plume of dust left by some vehicle that had already dropped out of sight behind a fold of barren hillside. Then, almost stealthily, he allowed his eyes to sink to the farm that lay almost below that point, and he felt his loins leap. To think that she'd still be in bed, for it was not even eight yet, and that, in a perfect world, he could be in bed with her, coaxing a new awareness. Bringing her slowly, gently into the new day, urging her with small, exquisite thrusts of his body; while in each hand, cupped from behind, those sweet marshmallow breasts would be stirring. Then she would laugh, break free, and come back at him her way, shameless and inquisitive and eager, so hard here, there so soft....

"Hey," said Willie, checking himself with a chuckle, and being sure to banish the dangerous fantasy completely.

He clapped the horse on the shoulder and ruffled its mane. His mood had perked up suddenly, and the prospect of a whole weekend without Sergeant Jonkers hovering in the background, over at the hotel, took on a different look. He might even drop in on Ferreira himself for a change—or better still, attend the weekly barbecue, leaving Luthuli to give him a bell if there was trouble. Without Ma Jonkers getting her talc all over you every time she asked for a dance, and without his lordship making you grill his chops for him, a bloke could probably have a very nice time. And if Tommy the merc had returned, there might well be a chance of hearing his gruesome stories at first hand for once.

Again the horse harumphed.

Without his being particularly aware of it, Willie's gaze had been following a car far below him; a car that had approached swiftly from the south, and was about to enter the last coils of the dirt road into Witklip.

Away in a corner of his mind, he now recognized the vehicle as the orange Chevrolet belonging to the tough CID lieutenant from Trekkersburg; the one whose boy had a limp, yet could strike at a fleeing chicken thief like a bloody black mamba. In an adjacent corner of his mind, he realized that, as acting station commander, he'd better giddy-up and get down there.

But Willie Boshoff just sat and stared, preoccupied by an idle fancy born of height and distance. Like a spark eating up a fuse, the glimmer of the car was turning the road behind it into billowing dust, into powder smoke, as it advanced through each twist and turn, hastening for the wattle-dark village.

"I've seen the Lone Ranger," said Kramer, "but where the hell is his boss?"

Startled by this sudden inquiry, which had been made without warning or preamble, Bantu Constable Goodluck Luthuli placed his eye to the star-shaped hole in the privy door and peered out at him.

"Hau!" said Luthuli.

"Well?" Kramer demanded. "You've seen me before, so out with it! I haven't got all bloody day! Christ, now where has this one got to?"

The eye had vanished.

"Luthuli is saluting the officer, sir," translated Zondi, after some mumbled Zulu from within. "At attention."

For an instant, Kramer's high hopes for the day sagged, then he managed to say quite calmly: "For God's sake tell him I salute him back—and to stand at ease as quickly as possible. Plus, repeat my question."

Zondi did that.

"He not here, suh," Luthuli replied in kitchen English. "He go last night on holiday all time to Tuesday next week."

"The sod!" Kramer snapped.

And the eye, which had returned to the hole, gave a little twinkle.

"Maybe it will be easier like this," murmured Zondi, showing more tact in his use of Afrikaans than in his suggestion. "Remember what you said about the red herrings last time."

"Rubbish! I want a few facts on the locals for a quick elimination job, and I reckon he'd have known them off pat. I wonder who he cleared this leave with?"

"We have not informed headquarters of our—"

"Look, man—stop being so bloody reasonable, okay?"

Kramer started back up the path through the weeds to the station house, walking with his hands thrust deep into his trouser pockets. The sudden departure of the Jonkers couple sounded very like the consequence of a domestic crisis, and he had only himself to thank for that—however, as Zondi said, it wasn't all that much of a catastrophe, and the day was still young. A comic thought dashed through his mind.

"Who are you smiling at, boss?" asked Zondi, catching up.

"Me," said Kramer. "Has it occurred to you that Sarge Jonkers might have really got the wind up after our little conversation? That he might be part of all this?"

"Of course."

They laughed and walked on.

"What shall I do this morning, boss? You will be working in the office, not so?"

"What you like, Mickey. Catch up on some sleep."

"You will give me a shout?"

"I shouldn't think it'd be before lunchtime."

"Okay."

Tossing him the car keys, Kramer turned and went indoors. It was the work of a minute to sweep everything irrelevant off the office desk into one of the drawers, and another ten seconds saw the cat in the Out tray on its way. In the same time again, he had put a call through to Trekkersburg.

"Morning, Doc," Kramer said, taking the telephone over to the barred window. "It's Tromp here. I'm in Witklip, looking for a gallows setup such as you started to describe the other day on the way back from Doringboom. Something about half-inch adjustments? A vertical space at least twenty feet high? Just give me all the details and procedure notes and have them Telex it up to Brandspruit. Thanks, hey? Bye."

"I suppose you'd like specifications for the hangman as well?" Strydom asked caustically. "It wouldn't be any trouble. Or are you coping all right in that direction?"

"I'm doing fine, only I'm in a bit of a hurry right now. Anything you can let me have will be much appreciated." Kramer killed the line. "Luthuli!" he yelled.

The tiptoeing in the charge office became the businesslike clumping of size-twelve boots, there was a knock, and the door opened. It wasn't Luthuli but a Bantu constable still in his teens, flat-featured and bright-looking.

"Mamabola, sir," he said, introducing himself.

"Lieutenant Kramer, Trekkersburg CID. I've taken over while the sergeant is away. Understood?"

"I understand, sir," Mamabola said in Afrikaans.

"Can you drive?"

"Yes, sir."

"Take the Land-Rover to Brandspruit and wait there for a Telex I'm expecting. I want that Telex before it arrives."

Mamabola smiled, saluted, and withdrew in his size eights.

"Cheeky sod," Kramer said, enjoying the joke. "And now for his lordship."

But it was a little too early to catch Colonel Muller in his office. Kramer compromised by leaving a message to say where he was, and that he'd be calling back later in the day, with any luck. Then he heard a horse come clattering into the yard behind him.

It must have done that by itself, because its rider arrived at the office door almost simultaneously, tugging a trouser crease out of his backside, and otherwise trying to assume the dignity of an acting station commander. The face was much as remembered, although the frown seemed more a matter of short-sightedness than personality, and the rest—with the exception of the strong, thick wrists—was nondescript.

"What do they call you?"

"Willie, sir. I mean—"

"Sit. Explain the absence of Sergeant Jonkers."

"Um—well, it was his weekend off. He's gone down to Durban—ja—because his mother or some relative was sick."

"Do you know his address there?"

"He didn't leave one, sir."

Willie plainly didn't believe the story he was giving any more than Kramer did, but there was nothing to be gained from dwelling on the matter. "Make me a list, commander, of the names of every farmer around Witklip, starting in the north."

On the bank of a river about one kilometer south of Witklip, Zondi was giving Mr. Rat a nice long rest in the shade of some willow trees while he waited for the local girls to begin flirting with him. They were still at the giggle-and-peep stage, very conscious of the well-dressed stranger above them, yet wholly intent—or so they'd have the world believe—on the clothes they were washing in the silt-soupy water.

He had made the steep walk down from the village because he was after gossip, and this was where most gossiping was done. Then again, while his city bearing had an intimidating effect on male rustics, such as those to be found hanging about the general store, it invariably excited curiosity among their wives and daughters, making them very ready to strike up a conversation. And of course, as it always took time to win the confidence of strangers, Zondi liked to think that not a moment need be entirely wasted.

With unflagging pleasure, he watched the washing being slapped down on the flat rocks and rubbed so hard that breasts bounced and bracelets jingled. He laughed softly when someone knocked their packet of soap powder into the current and had to wade hastily after it; he clucked his tongue when a buxom maiden lost her footing, soaked herself through, and rose in a shift dress that had become skin tight and revealing.

"Have you no shame?" the others teased her.

"She would surely need no shame," observed a coarse-faced woman, grinning up at him, "if all she desired was to be mounted by a lame dog—what do you say, stranger?"

"Hau, mother, that is true! But would not a dog prefer to mate with a bitch?"

Shrieks of delight followed as Zondi beckoned to the woman and patted the grass in front of him. Then the banter began, with the womenfolk speculating loudly and pessimistically on his worth as a lover, and, in return, being treated to the best repartee he could offer. The coarse-faced one enjoyed all this hugely, although she still managed to get through more work than any of the rest.

"Now, if I were seeking a wife," Zondi hinted craftily, nodding at the clean washing she had been tossing up near him, "then I would wish to know your name, my mother."

"My name you could have for nothing! But would you have enough cattle for ilobola? My husband gave my father twenty head of perfect stock for me!"

"And how long was it before he stole them back?"

Little by little, Zondi won her confidence, and when that was done, the rest of them felt free to join them under the willow trees. How they giggled.

"You are a wicked woman," he whispered, giving Mama Coarse-face a nudge. "Can you not see how your lustful talk has put ideas into the minds of the young ones?"

"Is a fire to be blamed for what cooks in a pot?" she answered, nudging him back in matronly glee.

There was a pause. Toes wriggled, and river clay was poked from between them with stalks of grass; the rat also wriggled, annoyed by the elbow that had bumped against the leg. Zondi slipped a hand into his inside jacket pocket and felt for the picture of the white tramp.

"And now to a serious matter," he said, pleased with the progress he was making.

Kramer was standing at the window of the station commander's office, gripping the bars very tightly and trying to get an equally strong grip on his temper. After all, he'd not asked for much, simply a list of farmers, which any half-wit should have been able to provide in a twinkling, but Boshoff was still stuck on the seventh name thirty minutes later.

"This is too bloody much, man!" Kramer snapped, spinning round and thumping his fist down on the desk. "How long have you been here at Witklip? Since police college?"

"Twenty-six months and three weeks, sir," replied the abject acting station commander.

"And you can't do better than this? Christ, Witklip's a place for getting away with murder, all right!"

Then Kramer realized how precise that count had been and, despite himself, he had to smile; obviously, Willie Boshoff wished that the duration of his stay had been a great deal shorter.

Encouraged by the smile, the youth said, "I just never get many jobs outside the reserve, Lieutenant. If a farmer has a complaint, then he sees Sarge at Spa-kling, or if he phones, then I've got to fetch Sarge to speak to him. They don't really know me, you see—and someone has to look after the Bantu."

"They don't have Bantu on their farms? What else have they got to complain about?"

"Ach, what I mean is that I've never got on a personal level, if you understand, sir. Naturally, I raid the compounds from time to time, but nobody wants me to go banging on their front doors to tell them about it! They're all friends of Sarge's and so—"

"Hold it, Willie."

"Well, he likes to do favors, sir."

"Shut up."

Kramer was searching for an alternative, and in no mood to have his shoulder wept upon.

"Favors? What about Ferreira? Don't they all use his bar and come to the barbecue!"

"That's brilliant, sir! He must know them at least as well as Sarge does. Shall I go and ask him to come?"

"No, Willie," Kramer said patiently. "Unless you want to be in Witklip all your life, you will go and *tell* him to come."

He began to root in the filing cabinet, just on the off chance of finding something interesting. What he did find was an accident report on Mr. and Mrs. P. W. J. Ferreira and their daughter-in-law, Mrs. P. E. Ferreira, who had all been fatally injured in a level-crossing collision near Brandspruit some six years back. The report gave their home address as *Rest Haven, formerly Happy Valley Hotel, Witklip*, and said that their son, Pieter Eugene Ferreira, had been at the wheel. No charge was going to be preferred, Jonkers had added in his own handwriting.

"Tea or coffee, sir?" asked Luthuli, hovering in the doorway.

"Coffee, I think—for three."

"Tree? You want girl make rocky bun for visitor?"

Somebody, it seemed, had taught the man to regard himself. as a bloody butler. "No, thanks. Plain coffee—that's all."

"Hau!"

"Three spoons of Nescafé, three cups—you've got the picture? Have yourself a quiet day."

"Hau!" Luthuli exclaimed again, and disappeared mumbling.

Then Ferreira arrived with Willie, looking far less sloppy than he'd done the time before, and without those idiotic sunglasses. His smile lingered like the damp feel of his handshake.

"I'm told you want a list of everyone," he said, taking the chair pointed out to him. "Is this some development regarding Tommy? Willie didn't seem to know."

Kramer saw no reason to start explaining anything at this stage either, and settled for what was immediately important. "I can tell you both this much, hey? I'm engaged in trying to trace where a certain woman and her young son stayed for a long weekend on a farm in this district about twenty-five years ago. That isn't as impossible as it sounds, and when I get the answer, I'll be a long way towards solving a serious case."

"Of...? Please, sir," said Willie.

"Call it suspected murder," Kramer replied, being careful to keep within the framework he'd laid down for himself. "How many farmers do you reckon there are?"

Ferreira needed a second longer to function again. "Around two dozen. Taking those nearest, we've got Peter Crowe, George van der Heever, Gysbert Swanepoel, Karl de Bruin, Mr. Jackson—"

"Write neatly," ordered Kramer, sliding the sheet of foolscap across. "Full names, farm names, home language, approximate ages, any comments."

The list was returned to him twenty minutes later.

"I wasn't too sure what you meant about comments," Ferreira admitted, having failed to make any. "Newcomers I've left out."

"Thirty-two!" said Willie. "Phew!"

Kramer looked down the names with equanimity. Compared with some elimination jobs he'd done—like when one of 1,400 black workers had stitched up a bullying foreman in a boot factory—this was a walkover. Of those thirty-two names, none was foreign, but he had been expecting that. Twenty-seven of them had Afrikaans as their home language, and the rest English; he'd been expecting that, too. The five English-speakers would be his prime target.

"Not that I see how you'll pinpoint this bloke," Ferreira murmured deferentially, having had time to think. "Not if he's mixed up in any way—which I can't imagine for a start. I mean, he's not likely to say, 'Oh, ja; I was the bloke who had them to stay.'"

"There was a party," explained Kramer.

Willie waited, then said, "And, sir?"

"Ach, I'm relying on people who were at this party to

remember those two. When they do that, then we'll know who the host was—and take it from there. From these figures I would conclude that if one of the English-speakers gave a party, he'd have to have Afrikaners among his guests, too, to make up the numbers."

"Jackson's the only stuck-up redneck in the district," said Ferreira. "The rest of us—man, you wouldn't know the difference. Was this party specifically for these people?"

"I don't reckon so. But—"

"Then you'll excuse me saying, Lieutenant, that having folk for the weekend is quite common out in the country, and twenty-five years is a long time to forget one little party."

"I was thinking the same," said Willie.

"Not if she was tempted to do her party trick," Kramer told them, a smile quirking his lips. "The lady concerned was an Italian *mamma mia* who could speak some Afrikaans. That should jog a few memories—or do you get them here pretty often?"

Ferreira grinned his defeat and sat back. "Okay, you win. The only wops we've ever had here could only speaka da English."

"'We've'?"

"You know, at the hotel when I was a kid."

Perversely, Kramer's mind skipped sideways to investigate why he had always presumed that the Ferreira family were late on the scene and hardly an established part of it. Then he recalled the farmhouse-like architecture of the hotel—which wasn't an uncommon feature in itself, of course—and tried to reconcile this with the fact that the building wasn't very old. You surely didn't design something one way to convert it almost in the next breath.

"Spa-kling Waters," Willie said helpfully, in response to the uncomprehending silence.

"No, not then," Ferreira contradicted him. "It was still Tobruk Guest Farm; my dad called it that when he made a mess of trying to be a farmer after the war. He'd dreamed too much in the desert."

An unlucky family, mused Kramer, seeking distraction in the three changes of name for the grotty place he'd come across. A family of losers struggling to find the right words for the sign writer; the right spell, if you liked, to fend off their fate. None had worked so far, and yet here was the surviving son still mixing self-deception and bad magic, still trying to prove a point nobody else cared about.

"Right, Mr. Ferreira," he said, rising in sudden restlessness. "Tell me all about the wops at your hotel."

"What I remember best was my dad kicking up hell over having them to stay—I mean, he'd been sticking bayonets in their backsides not so long before—but my mum liked the lady and really put her foot down."

"She had a son?"

Ferreira glanced at Willie, then went on: "Ja, and a husband. I played with the boy quite a bit, showed him round—y'know? He wasn't bad for a banana boy; quite daring, in fact. Usually the kids we got were skits of horses and all that, y'know? And Jesus, could he swear! Which is why I nearly peed myself at the barbecue that Saturday night—when him and his uncle started singing."

"Really?" said Kramer, sitting down again. "His uncle, you say? What was so funny?" He'd said nothing about an uncle to either of them.

"You had to be there, man! You know how soft these bloody farmers get? I mean, they all took it so seriously some even got tears on their cheeks; first stood as if they were in church on Sunday, then they started swaying—like this. I had to run with the coons to the peach tree by the barn or they'd have seen us laughing. Naturally, it was in Italian, being opera or something, and there these old fools were saying he was just like a little angel and pretending they knew the words. It was Ava-something— can't remember, although I've heard it on the radio. *Him* a little—"

"Italian?"

"Of course," said Ferreira, looking puzzled. "I mentioned they were wops at the beginning. This bloke off a ship, his sister, the husband, and the kid. There's always a sing song once the party gets warmed up."

Kramer nodded. "I see. Is it possible to say why they'd chosen Witklip of all places?"

"That's what my dad kept on asking!" said Ferreira with a fond laugh. "While my mum kept on telling him it was the uncle—him and his sister looked like twins, hey?—who wanted to give the family a treat, show the kid what the country was like and all that. My mum said if you put adverts in all the papers, you had to take what you got—especially if you were just starting up and trying to make a go of it."

"Off one of those Itie ships that used to go up the coast to Egypt?" Willie wanted to know. "Did he work on it?"

But Kramer cut across: "So you're saying it was simply a matter of chance that they came here?"

"Sorry, Lieutenant?" Ferreira glanced again at Willie, who shrugged. "Isn't that how they all come, one way or the other? Even if it's only a friend making a personal recommendation?"

"True," said Kramer, after a pause. "How very, very true." He felt sick.

And saw nothing to laugh at when Goodluck Luthuli, in all seriousness, placed three spoons of Nescafé and three empty cups before them. That seemed to sum it all up.

14

DESPITE ALL ZONDI'S ATTEMPTS to jog the memories of the women by the river, the white tramp had remained a total mystery. The witch doctor, however, had been immediately identified from his photograph with some cries of amazement. He was that old rogue Msusengi Shezi, the women had said, better known by his nickname of Izimu—and it had been years since anyone had last seen him.

From that moment on, Zondi had felt certain he was earning his keep: Izimu was Zulu for "cannibal." Dozens of slanderous stories had then been told to him about Izimu, but he'd begged off after hearing one about a child who had gone missing, and now, in order to have the same story from a more reliable source, he was making for the kraal of the local headman. The upward path was steep, and loose pebbles caused it to be slippery in parts.

"Hau, rat," he said vindictively, correcting a stumble. "This is not going to be a good day for you, which gives me much pleasure."

Then he turned his attention to the cattle being herded on the slopes above him, picked out the finest beast, and memorized its characteristics. Higher up, the young herdboys were practicing two-stick fighting, prancing about with a fine show of aggression, yet pulling their head blows rather clumsily; soon someone would get more than a bump to rub if they weren't more careful. The pasture was fair to poor, he noticed.

Absalom Mkuzi proved to be a headman of the old school. Although none too well off, to judge by the patched raincoat he wore without a shirt, his hospitality was as carefully observed as the dignity of his position. After an exchange of compliments lasting several minutes, he summoned his wives to the squatting place outside his hut and ordered them to bring refreshments for the visitor. The sour milk was excellent, having curdled to just the right thickness, and Zondi was most grateful for it after his walk.

By way of getting down to business, a certain brindle cow was mentioned. Zondi confessed to having never seen a finer animal, and—so that the headman would be able to seek it out for his own eye's delight—he went into the finer detail of its haunches, its horns, its broad belly, and its left foreleg, which was marvelously marked. And when the headman admitted, with all due modesty, his ownership of the beast, Zondi gasped enviously. This rigmarole, in which the deceit involved was understood by both sides and welcomed for its civility, brought the inviting pause that begged the visitor to speak his mind.

"I have heard it said, my father," Zondi began, taking a little snuff from the proffered gramophone-needle tin, "that there was once a witch doctor in these parts known to your people as Izimu. It is also said that he stole children to take their fat. These are matters which concern me."

Mkuzi's rheumy eyes narrowed as they tried to see him better. "You are police?"

Zondi said nothing. He sniffed up his snuff.

"They come and they shout at me," Mkuzi said angrily. "They pull open my door, they grab my youngest wife. They say they will shoot my dog if it does not cease barking. *Hau!* And what is the reason?"

After a moment's thought, Zondi still said nothing.

"The reason is that they want me to report any stranger to them. There has been a farmhouse broken into, they say, and the white boss is very angry. Is this a thing to come and tell me in the middle of the night?"

Mkuzi took the sour milk and drank deeply from the pot.

"Luthuli and two Xhosa baboons from Brandspruit did this to me," he added, wiping his lips. "They gave me these orders."

A smugness sweetened the old man's wrinkled face, and Zondi knew that had six Zulu regiments been discovered lurking about Witklip and the reserve, not a word of this would have reached the appropriate authorities.

"You ask about Izimu," said Mkuzi, settling down comfortably on his haunches again, and passing the pot back. "He was a fool, that one. He could not give you a medicine to take without making false claims about it—or, if they were not false, then he was encouraging you to imagine terrible things about himself. I, of course, would never use his medicines; instead I have always gone to the nuns' clinic and to Jafini Bhengu, a very fine witch doctor to the south."

"Was it child's fat that he spoke of?" Zondi inquired.

"Never *spoke*, young man; with Izimu it was always the words he did not say—they rang loudest in the ear. He would lead you to form these words on your own lips, as when an old crone is becoming tedious with her tales and you know, when she stammers, what is to come next. But with a name such as the people gave him, need I say more? How proud he was of it, too, for it undoubtedly gave him more power and influence among the stupider types. Then came the time when he wished to be known as Izimu no longer."

"This is of great interest, my father."

"There was a woman living in these parts who was called Mama Buza. A widow woman, whose husband had been killed in the mines, who had five small children. One day the youngest of these children, a boy of some six months, was taken from his sleeping place during the afternoon. Mama Buza had gone to borrow from a neighbor some article—I cannot remember what. For a long time, she thought that maybe the older children were playing a trick on her, and so she waited and listened for its cries. The neighbor came and was told of this curious happening, yet still nobody could believe that a baby had been taken, like a pumpkin from the hut roof. It must also be said that Mama Buza was not a very good mother to her children, and jokes were whispered that she had left him lying somewhere, perhaps beside the river. I know that many people were surprised by how very distressed she became."

"Did you, my father, play a part in this?" Zondi prompted, shifting his weight off his heels as a cramp threatened.

"I was asked to take charge very soon after that. We began a search of every hut and granary and chicken house around there. When the sun started to grow red, I went to the village and spoke to Mr. Botha, the good man in the trading store. Then Mr. Botha told Police Chief Jonkers and a big, big search began. All the white bosses said to us, 'Not to worry.'"

Zondi chuckled at this unexpected mimicry.

"Do you know, my son, for four days we looked for that child? But long before this, the rumors concerning Izimu were already on everyone's lips. On the fifth day, God came to help us."

"Hau! You found the child?"

"Dorothy Jele was led to it. She is the chief servant girl up at Mr. Jackson's farm, which is on a hill with many trees around it. These trees come close up behind the servants' quarters, right near to her room—or so those who have worked there say. This was the fifth morning, as I have told you, and these were the trees where we were going to look that day. Mr. Jackson was very kind, and said we may cross his whole farm, look anywhere we liked. It was not necessary because, just after the dawn, Dorothy heard the cry of a baby. She is a brave woman, that! She took up the wood ax and went towards the trees. For just a short moment, Dorothy says, she saw a figure running away, and that it looked very like Izimu to her from behind. The baby was wrapped up in an old sack and so dirty and hungry she washed it straight away. She also gave it food and a small blanket, then she woke Mrs. Jackson to tell her."

"Izimu had become frightened of the police search, not thinking Mama Buza would worry to tell them, and he'd left the baby to be found?"

Mkuzi nodded, and fondled his yellow dog's tattered ear. "Such is my belief," he said, "but others think Izimu was attempting to escape that way when Dorothy Jele gave him a fright. The trouble was that she is a true Christian woman: she told the police she could not swear by God's holy name it was definitely the witch doctor she had seen."

"And what about Izimu himself, my father?"

"Oh, they did not trouble with him long," sighed Mkuzi. "How could it be proved? He said he had been far away collecting herbs that day. We beat him also, three or four times, yet he stayed just as stubborn. Then, when his mother died of shame, and his wife fled to Nongoma, he suddenly went from us overnight, saying no farewells. I cannot tell you where he is now, although it is probably a great distance from here!" Then Mkuzi added politely: "Do you know, perhaps?"

"I know. It is a very, very great distance."

"That is good. Have I told you what you wish to hear?"

"Indeed you have, my father! Believe me when I say that your words have brought great joy to my heart," said Zondi, rising confident in the knowledge that the Lieutenant would feel the same way about the theft of Mama Buza's baby.

Alone in the gloom of the station commander's office, which was darkened by the approach of the four o'clock thunderstorm, Kramer sat hunched over the desk and glowered at some jottings he had made on the case. Only with an effort did he drag his mind back from worrying about what had become of Zondi— who was now several hours overdue—to the present state of the investigation.

The night before everything had been there, slotting together as snugly as anyone could wish: farm—party—uncle— hangman. But now, like alkalis added to acids, the words *guest* farm and *barbecue* party and *Italian* uncle had neutralized the whole process of deduction.

"Buggeration," he said, losing concentration. "Come on, Mick! Let's get out of here, man!" There was anxiety in his voice as well.

He doodled a noose and wrote *Erasmus* underneath it. He drew another to go above *Ringo*. The ballpoint dithered, trying to find a way of connecting them. The telephone rang.

"Tromp?" said Colonel Muller. "How goes it, man?"

"I'm getting Ferreira disease," Kramer replied with a crooked grin, pathetically pleased to hear the old bastard's voice. "I'm sure there's a couple of—"

"The lead wasn't any good?"

Mamabola looked in, holding out a large brown envelope. "Hold on a sec, please, Colonel."

Kramer opened the envelope and unfolded a huge wad of Telex. The DS had gone to town with a vangeance: it looked as though the screeds of figures might even include the hangman's inside leg after all. Such a mass of mumbo jumbo was strangely comforting, if only as something to grasp onto when all else had gone to pot, and Kramer thought for a moment of the Bible in Tollie's dead hand.

"The lead was fine," he said, "but it led us nowhere, as I'll explain." Very briefly, he went over the main points.

"This uncle could have been—" the Colonel began to say.

"Looked like his sister, plus he had a passport. And wouldn't old man Vasari have known a blood relative?"

"You made other checks, just in case?"

"Put it this way, sir: I'm quite satisfied there's no bloody Italian anywhere near this place. All we've done is double-prove what we knew already. I don't see this ex-POW as a suspect any longer either: paying the money was one thing, but carrying out a murder a whole year later doesn't sound right anymore. A man like that wouldn't take such a high risk, not in his position."

The Colonel said carefully, "Now—er—what if I suggested we brought in some more men on the job, and made sure you were right on that last—er—business? I hear you told Marais he could get back on the scissors case, which leaves only you and your Bantu."

"If you like," Kramer sighed, leafing through the folios of Strydom's message. Then he froze. On the last page was a postscript:

> PLSE DNT FORGET MEMO REQD
> B/SGT M. ZONDI MONDAY. C.S

"But what's the matter, sir? Have you lost faith in the efficiency of your subordinates? We sweat our guts out and—"

"It's not—"

"Jesus, that's what it sounds like!" Kramer snapped, goading the old sod, yet knowing he'd have to give in afterward.

There was a shocked silence, then Colonel Muller spoke sternly and very coldly: "You do realize, Lieutenant Kramer, that your attitude is not necessarily in the best interests of the department?"

"Uhuh," acknowledged Kramer, making the most of this while it lasted, and remembering Strydom's exact words. "It could have far-reaching effects."

"First you agree to a full-scale operation, and now you're behaving like this? What's going on, hey? You tell me!"

"Ach, something's just come in to change my mind."

"You bastard!" Colonel Muller laughed, with a warmth that surprised Kramer. "You bloody devious old bastard! For a while you were really giving me a bad time there; I thought you'd cracked. One day I'll get you back, hey? That's a promise! But you'd best get weaving now. Good luck!"

And the line went dead, dropping a weight of trust on Kramer's shoulders that made it impossible for him to lift the receiver again and call his own bluff.

"Oh, Jesus," he said.

The light from outside became dimmer. He went over to the door to thumb the switch, nearly asked after Zondi, but returned to the desk and picked up the Telex. A subheading caught his eye: JUDICIAL HANGING AS SUICIDE.

He slumped down and began to skim the annoying capitals.

FM T NEW YORK TIMES O 6TH APRIL 1926. T ROOM WAS ABT 35FT HIGH, 25FT LONG AND 25FT WIDE. T WALLS WR PAINTED A LT GREEN. TWO HIGH-POWERED ELECTRIC LIGHTS WR SUSPENDED FM T CEILING AND ANOTHER BRILLIANT LT WAS ON T WALL. IN T FAR CORNER STOOD WARDEN SCOTT. BENEATH HIS FOOT WAS A PLUNGER SIMILAR TO THOSE ATTACHED TO GONGS ON T FRONT PLATFORMS O STREETCARS. (MISS A BIT. C.S.) IMMEDIATELY ON HIS RIGHT AS HE ENTERED IS A CLOSET WH CONTAINS T DEATH MECHANISM USED BY T STATE O CONNECTICUT IN HER EXECUTIONS. TO ONE END O T 50FT ROPE, WH GOES UP THRU A HOLE IN T CEILING, IS A WT CAREFULLY BALANCED, IN THIS

CASE, AGST T 135LB O CHAPMAN'S FRAIL BODY. ON T OTHER END, INSIDE T DEATH CHAMBER, WAS T NOOSE, WH WAS HELD BY A HOOK IN T WALL AND, AS IT WAS BEHIND CHAPMAN AS HE ENTERED THE ROOM, IT WAS PROBABLY NOT SEEN BY HIM. T WT IS HELD 3FT ABOVE T FLOOR LEVEL (VARIES O COURSE. C.S.) AND IS CONNECTED BY A STEEL ROD TO T PLUNGER AT T POINT WHERE T WARDEN STANDS.

WHEN IT WAS FIRST INSTALLED T CONDEMNED MAN UPON ENTERING T CHAMBER STOOD UPON A SMALL TRAP IN T FLOOR. HIS WT RELEASED A QUANTITY OF BUCKSHOT WH ROLLED SLOWLY DOWN A SLIGHT INCLINE UNTIL THEIR WT RELEASED T TRIGGER WH HELD T WEIGHT. IT WAS DECIDED, HOWEVER, TT THIS METHOD O EXECUTION WAS ILLEGAL, AS IT VIRTUALLY COMPELLED T PRISONER TO COMMIT SUICIDE, AND IT WAS ABANDONED FOR T PRESENT APA APPARATUS. FIFTEEN SECONDS AFTER CHAPMAN ENTERED T ROOM THERE WAS A SUDDEN CLICK AS T TRIGGER RELEASED T WEIGHT AND HIS BODY SHOT UPWARD. SAVE FOR T CLICK THERE WAS NOT A SOUND. T BODY HUNG SUSPENDED AT A HT OF 12FT. T NECK VERTEBRAE HAD SNAPPED AND DEATH HD BEEN PRACTICALLY INSTANTANEOUS.

(IN WHAT WAY IS THIS DIFFERENT TO A MAN WHO TAKES T FIRST STEP TOWARD MURDERING HIS FELLOW BEING ANYWHERE? DOES NOT BUCKSHOT START TO ROLL FOR HIM TOO? I PUT THIS IN SO YOU CAN TELL HANS WHAT YOU THINK. C.S.)

What Kramer thought as he finished the last page would not have pleased either of them, and came nowhere near touching on the philosophical point which Strydom had raised. Yet once his indignation had passed, and he'd rescued the crumpled sheets from the wastebin, he realized that the Doc had, however inadvertently, given him a nudge in a new direction. This brief description of an execution had evoked in him a sense of the cold, impersonal part played by the man with his foot on the plunger. He began to visualize a hangman, to dismiss the notion of revenge, and see that the role might be a form of fascination with power.

Willie Boshoff looked up from the crate in the old storeroom and watched Ferreira returning in an apparent fury from the hotel across the yard.

"What did I tell you?" the hotel manager stormed. "It was him! Him making bloody snide allegations. I'll sue the bastard if he ever tries that again!"

"Lieutenant Kramer?"

"Who else? Didn't I say he'd gone all po-faced when I told him about the wops this morning? Didn't I say that the next thing would be him accusing me of bloody lying?"

"Take it easy, hey?" soothed Willie, lifting out a stack of old 78's in their paper covers. "Sarge Jonkers let it slip that this investigation, whatever it's about, is pretty big."

"Then why the hell pick on me?" Ferreira demanded.

"True, he must be getting a little desperate," Willie joked—and then checked anxiously to see if he'd pushed his new-found friendship too far.

But Ferreira was already intent on hurling everything out of a dusty washstand slumped in the corner. Metal mousetraps, light fittings, shoe boxes filled with brownish snapshots, two lampshades, a cigarette-card album, and a pile of piano music—half-eaten by termites—hit the floor.

"I am going to find that register," Ferreira muttered, tugging savagely at a pile of moldy rugs, trying to get at the squashed cardboard cartons beneath them. "I'm going to find it and stuff it right in his gob."

"Did you tell him we'd been looking for it?"

"Why should I've?"

"Well, I mean..."

"Huh! Then he'd have thought that he really had me on the bloody run! No, let him sweat a bit."

"Then maybe I—"

"So you only came down here to rook a free lunch out of me?" cut in Ferreira, very sarcastically. "I'll not forget that in a hurry the next time you offer to lend me a helping hand."

Then he gestured with two fingers, to show he didn't mean what he'd just said, and calmed down. It was difficult, once you had got to know him better, to understand why he and Jonkers were such big pals: not only could he be quite witty, but he was a nice, generous bloke as well.

Willie gave him a menthol king-size and they lit up.

"What did the Lieutenant actually say, Piet?"

"I didn't give him much of a chance to say anything, my friend. All he got out was some crack about me doing favors for him 'and who else?' by remembering the woman. How do you like that?"

"Ah," said Willie. "I see. Still, he's got to check every point, I suppose. You mustn't take it personal."

They continued the search. When you had a suitable excuse for it, there were few things more interesting than rummaging about among other people's belongings, and the ones they'd forgotten all about made the best goodie mines of the lot. There was also a sense of history and heritage to be found amid the cobwebs and mildew that made you envious of anyone with a heap of rubbish in their yard. Willie's sole relic of his own past was an elastic belt with a twisted-snake clasp, now barely big enough to fit round his thigh, never mind his waist, with which he'd been presented one Christmas at Underbrook Boys' Home.

"I think I've got it!" Ferreira announced triumphantly, upsetting a box of dented Ping-Pong balls as he pulled at something on top of the tool cupboard. "It's in with all the old invoices in this sod-ding rud-dy case under this pi-ile of crap here." He heaved at the case's handle and it snapped off.

"Need some help, Piet?"

"Ta, but I'll manage, thanks."

Willie reached back into the bottom of the crate and took another look at the small magazines he had just uncovered there. They were called *Lilliput*, after some kids' story he had heard about in General Knowledge, and yet didn't seem very childish when you tried to read the English they were written in. He flicked through a less buckled copy, searching for cartoons without captions, and was startled by the sight of a naked woman who had allowed herself to be photographed. She was beautiful.

"Come on, Willie, I've got the book open," Ferreira called to him. "Let's see what their names were, and show that clever bugger how to investigate."

156

So beautiful it scared him so that he trembled. Then Constable Willie Boshoff did a terrible thing.

Distracted by the suddenness and ferocity of the storm lashing Witklip, Kramer abandoned his ruminations, rose from the desk, and went through into the charge office to borrow a match—a pretext, he knew, for asking again if there was any news of Zondi. Perhaps he should have sent someone out to look for him, yet it had seemed a course of action fraught with unpleasant possibilities, whether or not the little idiot had got himself into trouble.

"Sergeant Zondi is coming," Mamabola informed him, turning from a window steamed up by the fug of police, public, and a goat.

"About bloody time! Is the young boss with him?"

Mamabola flinched as lightning struck close by. "No, sir. Goodluck suggests he may be at the hotel and has been captured there by the floodwaters. Hau, this is happening so quickly!"

"Ja, at least God doesn't bugger around," said Kramer, all too aware of the time that had been wasted that day.

He opened the door and stepped out onto the verandah, goose-pimpling in the hail-chilled air, and catching his breath as another fork of lightning blazed and banged. The raindrops were falling so hard they misted the lawn with splashes and the dirt pathway danced pink. Anything more than twenty yards away was lost in a luminous, swaying grayness, while water sheeted from the glutted gutter overhead, obscuring his view of the gate.

Walking through all this, really taking his time and soaked to the skin, came Zondi.

"Run, you fool!" bellowed Kramer.

Then, having moved to where he could see better, the truth of the situation came home to him. Mickey was dragging that leg a pace at a time, shuddering uncontrollably as his weight came upon it, clenching his fists tighter, and coming on. He staggered.

Kramer flicked his cigarette aside. "Wait, Mickey!"

"No, boss; men would see."

As faint as these words were, a hiss in the hissing of the rain, they halted Kramer like a shout.

He backed away from the verandah's edge. Zondi veered to the left, cutting across the grass beneath the flagpole, missing the path to the steps by miles. Then his faltering course made sense: he was trying to avoid the window.

His collapse came just as he reached to pull himself up by one of the posts supporting the verandah roof. But he didn't fall: Kramer grabbed the outstretched hands and swung him up, let go and altered his hold, cradling the poor bloody idiot in his arms.

"Mick?"

Zondi murmured, "No, boss..."

Kramer took a step toward the door with him. Then he retreated to where Zondi had tried to climb up, and laid his burden down very gently beside a puddle on the verandah floor. After dabbing away the blood from a bite mark on the lower lip, he went inside.

"Hey, you two!" he said, beckoning to Mamabola and Luthuli. "Something is the matter with Sergeant Zondi—you'd best fetch him into my office. He's lying out there like a drunk."

They carried him in and Luthuli clucked gravely.

"Where we put a boy in here?" he asked.

"On those dagga sacks," Kramer directed, pointing to the bulky marijuana haul lying labeled in the corner. "Have you got any brandy?"

Mamabola nearly had his supercilious smile punched off him, but came up with the answer nonetheless. "Sergeant Jonkers usually procures it from that drawer, sir."

"Get me a mug."

While the tin cup was being fetched, Luthuli fussed about, arranging Zondi comfortably on the bags of dried leaf. The patient seemed not too bad; it was always difficult to gauge the color.

"Here," Kramer ordered presently, handing half a cup of Oude Meester to Luthuli. "Start getting that down him."

Zondi choked and sat up, pressing the cup away.

"Drink it, Sergeant!" said Kramer from behind the desk.

So Zondi drank it, coughed, beat his chest with one hand, and subsided. He thanked the men for their help, and added, as they withdrew, some Zulu witticism with un-Zulu squeaks in it.

158

"What makes that noise?" Kramer asked.

"Igundane."

"Never heard of it. But tell me, what in God's name happened to you today, old son?" Kramer asked as he went over and half knelt by the dagga sacks.

"Much happened, boss," Zondi replied drowsily, his eyes closing. "Today I established that Izimu the witch doctor had committed a capital offense right here in..."

"Witklip? Who was involved?"

"A baby. He stole the child of Mama Buza."

"Sleep, you old drunkard," growled Kramer. "That is more than enough for now."

Then he rose and damn nearly danced for joy.

15

"KIDNAPPING?" WILLIE BOSHOFF said to Kramer. "Is that the capital crime you have in mind, sir?" And he handed his glass back across the bar at Spa-kling Waters for a refill.

Ferreira took the glass and snorted. "Ach, come on, Willie! Who the hell's going to pay two cents' ransom for a bloody piccanin?" He poured the tot. "Here, you put your own ice in. I'm doing you another double, Lieutenant, okay?"

"Child-stealing," said Kramer, before giving a nod.

The squirt of the soda-water siphon made an amusing sound effect to go with the sudden infusion of blood that turned Willie's face crimson.

"Still got a lot to learn," Ferreira stage-whispered wittily, passing Kramer his drink. "But he tries hard, Lieutenant, so you mustn't be too tough on him, hey?"

"I—I forgot for a moment, sir," Willie stammered. "There's so many of them and—"

"Ja, enough to force old Jonkers into taking both his socks off," Kramer said, then realized that not everyone might have heard of the Witklip computer. "You were just unlucky you didn't join the force when I did, youngster. Then there were only the three: murder, rape, and treason—all straightforward."

"When was that?" Ferreira asked.

"Mid-50's or so."

"Really?" said Willie, much impressed.

There the briefing lost impetus for the first time since Kramer had come bursting in, drenched by the last of the storm and tracking mud, about twenty minutes earlier. After an acrimonious start, caused by some indignity Ferreira felt he'd suffered, and remedied by a hearty slap on the back for initiative, it had seemed nothing would halt the reasoned flow. But now that the moment had arrived to actually make something of Zondi's breakthrough, Kramer faltered. It wasn't that he lacked material; his mind was sharp with new ideas, glittering theories, and a pricking of temporary oversights. It was simply that any attempt to think them into shape became like trying to arrange pins with a magnet—one move and the whole bloody lot leaped up in a willy-nilly clump, proving basic compatibility without achieving a sodding thing. Eventually, on the basis of things being easier said than done, Kramer decided to gibber on and see what came of it.

Willie was tapping ingenuously on the moldy, termite-ravaged hotel register that had so far been ignored as a remarkable piece of evidence, unearthed by sheer guts and determination.

"Ja, let's have a look," obliged Kramer, clearing a space on the counter before him. "Not that I doubt your word, of course, gentlemen. That one name was enough."

    & Master G. J. Vasari, Flat 27, 3 Bys St., Durban
    ignor A. C. F. Santelia, Via Civitavecchia 102, Milano

He read each line twice, solely for the pleasure of seeing it down in black and white, and then allowed the book to flop shut.

"Sorry the white ants ate the date and the room numbers off," Ferreira apologized. "But coming first on the line, right by the edge, it was bound to happen, hey? Still, we've got an approximate date, I suppose."

"Doesn't matter that much, man."

"What!" exclaimed Willie. "You're not interested in these Italians anymore?"

Kramer smiled. "Not to the same extent, now we've found another road to Rome that isn't so full of blind alleys and bloody pitfalls."

"Christ, it makes your bloody head spin, doesn't it?" remarked Ferreira, coming round to join them on the high stools. "Who could ever imagine such a thing? No wonder you first thought it was political!"

"Hey?" said Willie, frowning. Of his many lapses that evening, this was the most forgivable.

"Time we chuck out what's irrelevant and see where we go from here," Kramer suggested, as much to himself as to anyone else. "But before I do that, is there anything that strikes you immediately, gentlemen?"

"Ja; you could have saved yourself a lot of trouble by asking me about Izimu in the first place," Ferreira answered with affected pique. "I did very good business out of that search, I can tell you! You should have been here, Willie, man; we all—"

"Was it reported in any newspapers?" Kramer asked, not wanting to have this thrust down his neck again, but needing the information to wind up the first part of his argument.

"Newspapers? Hell, no! They didn't even put Tiens in, when he was crushed by his tractor."

"Uhuh? So it was entirely a local affair?"

"Correct."

"Which means that only somebody living locally would know of Izimu's unpunished guilt?"

"Correct again."

Kramer put down his glass and took out a crumpled sheet of foolscap which was covered in linked nooses. "Originally there seemed to be no pattern in this case," he said, smoothing the paper, "but Izimu has provided the key factor by making Witklip the center of activity. Let's take each of the three other cases I've outlined to you—forgetting the tramp, for whom we still have no information—and keeping in mind all the time that we're not dealing with an ordinary murderer. This man sees himself as a hangman, carrying out impersonal executions which the law has been unable to conduct itself."

"That's the bit I—"

"Shhh, Willie! Give the Lieutenant a chance, hey?"

"You'll notice, gentlemen, that the victims all fell within the area of this someone's experience. Izimu is the most obvious example, and close behind him comes Rossouw, the railway foreman. You did say that people came back talking about him, Piet?"

This carefully timed flattery won an eager nod.

"From what you've told me, young Vasari made himself very memorable as well the night of the barbecue—that 'little angel' stuff, remember?"

"Ja, only I don't get the paper except on Sundays if I'm in Brandspruit, so it never rang a bell."

"A churchgoer—which ties in on Rossouw again—might have recognized the name, though. Agreed?"

"It's very possible, Lieutenant. There's another thing to bear in mind, too: I was only around seven myself at the time."

"Point taken. Can you say what the talk would have been like in the bar if someone had noticed this trial and told the others?"

"Phaw! I reckon some could have been quite upset; they'd certainly have wondered about it, not knowing him like I did."

"What the other one did would seem unfair anyway," Willie got in, actually concentrating for once on what was being said. "The CID should never have allowed it, in my opinion. I can see those three now, but Tommy? He was here a hell of a time without anything happening and—"

"When did he come up with his story about the mission school?" asked Kramer, moving swiftly off thin ice.

"Mission school?" Ferreira repeated. "Oh, when he shot up those kids, you mean?"

"I didn't hear about that," said Willie.

"No, you wouldn't have," Kramer said with some cynicism. "That was one of Tommy's big mistakes, so I don't think Sarge Jonkers would want to impress you with it. He committed a mass murder for no reason at all."

"You mean even though they were just—"

"Even though, Piet; the man we're dealing with has a very literal mind, and murder is the taking of another human life."

A small shudder shook Ferreira. "Then the chances are he must have been standing here, right in my bar!"

"Can you remember when?"

"When Tommy told us that one? It must have been—ja, I can tell you exactly: three barbecues ago, the same night it started to rain and the men left the womenfolk on the verandah and came in here. Tommy'd just got in from a walk."

A sprint down from the Jonkers house, more likely, when rain had stopped play with a threat of the husband's early return. A more interesting insight was to be had in the fact that this date coincided with Erasmus's sudden nervousness.

"It's logical," Kramer reflected aloud, "that the hangman should see himself as a bit of a Supreme Court judge as well, and could have asked him some questions in private. I'll get Mamabola to see if that servant girl was ever questioned by someone about Izimu's identity, et cetera. Could give us an early lead."

"What if it doesn't, sir?"

"We've still got a lot else, Willie. Can I borrow your pen?"

Turning over the foolscap, he prepared to list the main factors as they emerged. "It's too easy to just say this hangman bloke is cracked—we don't know what started him on this, and there may be quite a few other cases, going much further back, we don't know about. The man who put us on to this investigation was working under primitive circumstances. But certain things do seem self-explanatory or whatever, and they can help us track him down. Most importantly, he does not see himself as a murderer. By using all the ritual and the paraphernalia, he becomes as innocent as the state's own executioner. In the same way, he exercises ultimate power without any responsibility for his actions, apart from seeing he does a good job."

Willie scratched under an armpit. "You mean he likes hanging people, sir? Is that it?"

Kramer realized he'd slipped into pomposity and nodded. "Ja, although he might not be aware of it himself. Or then again, perhaps he was the victim of a terrible injustice and feels this compulsion—perhaps he thinks God is guiding him. We could make religiousness our first characteristic."

1. "Good" Christian, he wrote.

"Secondly, we can assume that he has all the right trappings to go with his trade, gents. Not only would it be necessary for him mentally, but Doc Strydom says this standard of hanging isn't what you could get with a washing line and a bar stool."

2. Scaffold and gear.

"Of course, this stuff could be dismantled in between times, but certain conditions have to be met as regards the space available—could be in a barn or silo, for instance, if he hasn't made it part of his house."

"You can really see this guy, can't you?" observed Ferreira, trying to hide a sneaking smile.

"It takes one to catch one," Kramer said, giving the stock reply that the Widow Fourie had once suggested. "He won't be a blatantly criminal type either, you'll see." Then he cut short the laugh by saying gruffly, "This stuff is crucial, as any other evidence may be hard to come by, and that's why it stays among just the three of us for now. We'll make skills our Point Three. The necessary information is not available to the general public, which is a really strong lead. Either he was once in the prisons department, or he has some means of access. Any ideas?"

"Hmmm."

"Ja, Willie?"

"Well, I know a bit from when I was at police college and the blokes from Central used to come and play rugby. But I've never talked about it."

"Piet?"

"Nothing offhand. Sorry."

4. Assistant (one or more), wrote Kramer, twisting the paper round for them to read it.

"How can you know that?" Ferreira said, surprised.

"He dumped Tommy's car when he dumped him, so someone must have helped with the other vehicle, the one he carries them around in. That's on the evidence we have already. However, a hangman must have an assistant to be efficient, according to the Doc, and—"

"There are *two* of them?"

"How many killers were involved in the Vontsteen case? Or for something nearer to this, what about those mad bastards who buried all those kids in England? The Moors or whatever their name was? Conspiracy is nothing new, man, and the crazier the—"

"Why leave the bodies everywhere?" Willie demanded, driven by a conflict of reason to speak his mind, if a little slurrily.

"Gibbet," said Kramer, only then slotting this into his hypothesis. "It's what they used to do to hanged criminals to show the world what had happened to them. Highway robbers and pirates and suchlike. But the question you should be asking is: do you know two or more persons in this area that you automatically think of together? Strong ties, trust, old pals—have you got it?"

"Oom Jaap and Gladstone?" Ferreira murmured.

The pair of them guffawed, then explained that Gladstone was a wog foreman whom Oom Jaap Brenner allowed to sit beside him in the front of his lorry, instead of on the back.

"They're always chatting together," added Willie, "like Tarzan and the apes. We bluff you not."

"But to be serious, Lieutenant," Ferreira went on, "it isn't easy to find a quick answer to that, not in a country setup where so many people are—well—you know?"

"Unfriendly?" grunted Willie.

Ferreira gave Kramer an old-fashioned our-young-friend-is-tipsy look.

"Willie, I've got a job for you," he said, poking him in the chest. "On my desk at the station is a Telex, okay? Read it and make me a diagram of the *minimum* size this scaffold would have to be. Off you go, and I'll come up when I've finished picking Piet's brains."

The kid went crimson, put his glass down, and hurried out. Kramer stared after him—scarcely hearing Ferreira's suggestion of moving to his private closed verandah while Piet had a word with the chef about the diabetics—and stayed where he was for a time. There had been something very odd about the kid all the way through that. And then, at a touch, there'd been guilt written all over his face, with its heavy, sensual features.

"Dear God," mourned Kramer, helping himself to another quick Scotch. "Not one of those when I'm undermanned enough already."

Willie found a puddle guarding each door to the cab of the Land-Rover, so he crawled in through the back way. Flopping into the driving seat, he took several long, deep breaths, yet his heart went on thumping like a borehole drill. If every thief, he thought, had reactions like these, then police work would become a bit of old tacky.

"You're mad," he said distinctly. "Bloody mad."

Then he winced, uttering an involuntary whimper, as his mind recalled vividly that horrendous moment when the Lieutenant had poked him right in the chest.

This set Willie's fingers fumbling at his tunic buttons, which had parted as though they weren't there back in the storeroom, but now seemed too big for their buttonholes. Finally, however, he dragged out the *Lilliput* he'd hidden so effortlessly from sight.

His ears glowed hot. Christ, his brain had heartburn; it'd just done a searing repeat of the Lieutenant's mention of stealing—child-stealing, admittedly, but it had still made him blush like a bugger and fall about. The brandy hadn't helped him to concentrate either; quite the opposite. It had been pitiful.

He gazed at the thing in his hands. That's all it was: a thing. Yet it had already turned Constable Willem Pretorius Boshoff SAP 13408 into a thief for ever and ever, amen. From now on, every thief he caught could say, "Hyprocrite!"—and he'd have to let them go. Even the coons. He'd have to quit the force.

"Put it back, man—simple!" said Willie, and immediately felt easier. "What do you want this old rubbish for?"

He sighed at himself in exasperation and opened his tunic; he could smuggle the magazine back into the storeroom as easily as anything; no problems. He could say his cigs had fallen into the crate and he'd gone to look for them. Fifty to one he wouldn't even need to do that.

Wondering at his inexplicable folly, Willie flipped open the pages for one last cold and indifferent glance at the photograph of the lady with no clothes on. She filled him. Again a dizzy compulsion obliterated any thought or scruple; he hid the magazine with great cunning, winked in its direction, and saw his hand twist the ignition key.

Being so scared and excited was really quite nice, in fact—especially when no actual harm could possibly come of it.

There ought to have been a sign saying KLOZED-IN VERANDER or something. Kramer had found what seemed to be private territory—a screened-off section on one side of the hotel, which was equipped with four decent wrought-iron chairs and a table—but nothing vaguely resembling the apparatus of enclosure. The exposed red cement floor was covered with blisters of rainwater, and there wasn't even a piece of string between the pillars to prevent you falling over the edge into the flower bed.

"All seen to," said Ferreira, coming out through the French windows, followed by a wizened Zulu. "The boy's got dry cushions and he'll give the table a wipe. How do you like my spectacular view?"

Kramer turned about cautiously. He liked the view; the last glare of the upstaged sun was highlighting the great white stone, while throwing the rest of the landscape into deep, interesting shadow. The storm-clean air, heavy with the odor of wet earth and broken vegetation, was tuned to a shortwave sucksboo of twitterings, zingings, and pingings, chirrups, clickings, and croaks, dominated by the morse-chattering mynahs. So he liked what he smelled and heard, too. It was invigorating.

"The bar's beginning to fill up now—it's after six. Would you like to take a look at some of them?"

"What's that, Piet?"

"They've heard about you being here."

"And?"

"I said you were baby-sitting for Willie. Old Gysbert nearly bust a gut—he's one you can knock off your list right away."

"Why? Has he got one arm?"

"Ach, what I meant was you've never known a wild man like Gys! Here, you sit where the floor isn't so wet. A huge bloody thing, he is—big black beard; you'll know him. Farms about eight kilos out and drives a truck like a madman. Every time he goes into Brandspruit the traffic cop gives him another ticket."

Kramer's gut twinged. "Has he—is he married?"

"Widower," replied Ferreira, motioning the barman to put the tray of drinks down on the table. "Took up with Annie Louw after Tiens was killed, then she got TB and he was left with just the one daughter. Nice kiddie, blond the same as her mum. Goes to the government boarding school in 'Spruit during the week, comes home weekends and holidays. Hell, he's strict with her, though, and she's only—what? Maybe fourteen, fifteen? Like another?"

"Uhuh."

"Just lately he's stopped her coming to the barbecue because the Jackson boy took her into the old barn one night. It was nothing, only kids' stuff, bit of a fumble, but Gysbert nearly took off! Karl de Bruin—a nice old bugger—he had to talk reason to him before we had bloodshed. The Jackson boy was yelling— Gysbert had his hair, you see?—and saying he'd tell his father, and Karl was saying that kids would be kids and the boy had just been boasting. What a schlamozzle! Gysbert will knock any man down who crosses him, as Frikkie knows only too well, and that would include hard cases even like Tommy, who was there as well. About two years ago, he very nearly went on a charge over what he did to a guest who got fresh. But I mustn't give you the impression his heart is in the wrong place."

Ferreira, well-oiled himself, continued to talk about the man while making a production of pouring two more Scotches without a tot glass. Gysbert Swanepoel hadn't always been such a wild man, it appeared, but had undergone a personality change after the death of his wife. For some months he had remained his old, quiet self, then one night he'd arrived half-tanked already and had never looked back. But Kramer wasn't taking much of this in. It all added up: Wednesday had been the end of the school term in Natal, the description of the man and his driving matched, and the incident had taken place within nine kilometers of Witklip. Only by an outrageous coincidence could it have been anyone but the Swanepoels. And to think that, in his half-awake state, he'd superimposed his dream hussy over a fleeting glimpse of a giggling schoolgirl. Far worse, to think that he'd been on the brink of challenging Ferreira's claim there were no beddable females around—God, that would have sounded like an allegation of a statutory offense! He felt as though he'd just passed an ice cube.

"And so, you see," Ferreira was saying earnestly, "I think that should qualify him automatic."

"Who?"

"The Reverend Kotse."

Then Ferreira grinned to show he knew that Kramer hadn't been attending. He was not altogether correct, however.

"De Bruin acted as peacemaker?"

"Karl always does. He hates to see any trouble."

"What age is he?"

"Around fifty, the same as Gysbert, although you'd never guess it. A bloody good farmer—in fact, maybe our best. Him and his son have made pots of it, but they're not the kind of people to let it show. Hell, I see what you're driving at..."

Kramer looked at the white stone through the facets of his whisky glass, making it bulk and shrink as he turned the thing slowly in his hand. His stomach was expanding and contracting in much the same way: a sure sign of breakthrough fever in the intuitive male. He switched his gaze suddenly to Ferreira.

"I can't imagine it, Lieutenant. A more law-abiding—"

"Interesting, Piet, very interesting. Tell me, did he take on Gysbert Swanepoel all by himself, or was his son also present?"

Ferreira shrugged. "They've always been on good terms, despite the differences now between them, so it wasn't really—"

"He's a churchgoer?" Kramer asked.

"Er—ja. Nearly all the Afrikaner ones are. You know how—"

"Prisons? Connections with warders?"

"Not that I know of," replied Ferreira, frowning a little.

Kramer began to tread, toe to heel, along the edge of the verandah between the two pillars. One false move would have him in mud up to the ankles—one false move and he'd be in something similar, although a lot nastier, up to his nose, for Karl de Bruin was obviously a highly respected member of the community.

"I'm going to start with the search," Kramer said, returning to the table to finish his drink. "That way I stay winning whether we find anything or not. The subtle stuff can come later."

"Start searching right now?" Ferreira gasped.

"I'd prefer it to be in daylight while he's away from home," admitted Kramer. "Does De Bruin play bowls or do anything like that at the weekends?"

"Um—no. Tell you what, though: the barbecue committee will all be here tomorrow afternoon, fixing up the kids' holiday special. He's the chairman."

Such a long delay had little appeal for Kramer, then he remembered Zondi's condition and decided he might need the time for other things. "Fine," he said. "I'll be in touch again in the morning. Meantime, don't say a word about any of this, but keep your ears open."

"Don't worry, Lieutenant! I don't want to go on anybody's black list!"

"Ach, when did you ever kill someone and get away Scot-free?" Kramer reassured him jokingly and, with a mock salute, took his leave by jumping down into the garden.

A look on Ferreira's face, glimpsed just as he turned from the verandah, made him regret very much having said that.

That was the start of a dark mood which became darker and darker until, deciding he was achieving nothing by sitting up alone in the station commander's office, Kramer took the pathway to Jonkers's bungalow, passing close to the hut where Zondi was quartered. Although there was no light showing, he paused and listened for a while, hearing not a sound.

Kramer moved on, lethargic with a sense of absurdity. Exactly what he found absurd, he wasn't sure; perhaps it was the idea of having an early night. Or it could have been the fault of the Widow Fourie, who'd just accused him on the telephone of having had another woman; a more absurd conversation, based on a wild assumption made over a range of three hundred kilometers, was difficult to imagine.

The bungalow stank of floor polish, stale beer, and mail-order perfume. He pushed the door shut behind him, left the lights off, and followed the passage down to the end; on the right, the maid had said, was the guest room and his bed. A weak moon, shining in through the burglar-proofed window, dimly outlined a lot else: an ironing board, a sewing machine, a dressmaker's dummy on a stand, rows of melon preserve, cardboard boxes. He picked his way across, stripped to his underpants, and lay back on the coverlet. It was, in fact, a long time since he'd slept in a strange bed, let alone one with a stranger in it. Silly bitch.

He closed his eyes and his thoughts drifted, swirled, and became caught up in an eddy of too much drink and no food. He saw tiers of prisoners in brightly colored uniforms behind silver bars upsetting their water dishes.

He opened his eyes and took a fix on the far wall. The giddiness left him; he began to feel floppy, warm, and drunk. It was a good feeling, and eased away his anxiety over what might happen to poor bloody Zondi. It couldn't be ending...

That was a pretty little dress on the dummy. Short sleeves but a high-buttoned front; a teaser if ever there was one. He rolled onto his feet and bent to look at it. There was a scrap of paper, scribbled over with measurements that didn't make sense, pinned to the collar; *Suzanne* was the name across the top of it. Little Suzanne Swanepoel, who hadn't a mother to make her a pretty party dress, so kind Mrs. Jonkers helped out. Between tumbles with Tollie and frolicking with Frikkie, the woman had a heart of gold. Trouble was, with a dress like that, you could never be sure of what lay underneath. Not unless you undid the round buttons, starting at the neck, one by one. All the way down to the waist and then drew back the two sides and had a look. Like that. Too dark, much too dark to see a thing. Feel, then. Run the fingertips up over the patent adjustable form and fill your palm with such a pleasing small shape. Linger. Think about the search tomorrow. Yawn, button up, and go to bed. Trying to be filled with self-disgust, but failing.

16

MR. RAT DIED THAT NIGHT. By Saturday morning, he no longer gnawed on the bone, nor did he squirm, twist, and scrabble. Instead, giving off heat and bloating rapidly, Mr. Rat decayed. Zondi could just feel the swelling.

But uppermost in his mind, as he drove through the early morning mist toward the farm where Dorothy Jele worked, was the story of Mama Buza's baby. It had seemed a perfectly good story when told by a virtuous man like Absalom Mkuzi, and yet, within minutes of Zondi's leaving the headman's kraal, his instincts had taken him on that long trek to talk to Mama Buza's former neighbors. They had said nothing to alter the crucial fact that all of Witklip believed in Izimu's guilt as a child-stealer; they had, however, enlarged on one or two details that troubled an outsider unused to God's taking part in police work. Details such as the baby's miraculous condition—which could, as one old hag had observed, have been attributed to Izimu's foul designs, along the lines of the fatter the better. Then again, Zondi had seen his own infants restored to bouncy well-being overnight at the end of a lean week on staple rations. Notwithstanding any of this, it still seemed to him rather peculiar, and he was eager to hear what Dorothy Jele might be able to tell him.

The Chevrolet rattled over the cattle grid and followed the drive around to the front steps of the huge white house, which had very small, narrow windows. Two lion dogs rushed out, barking savagely, to be followed by Mr. Jackson, the farmer.

He was a big man with a red wobble under his sharp chin like a turkey. His bluey-gray eyes were the color of a dead sheep's and his nose was pointed, making him resemble the sort of white man a child would crayon at school, yet his voice was low, deep, and almost friendly.

"Yes, boy?" he said, noting the official look of the car. "What is it you want here?"

Zondi replied in respectfully murmured Zulu: "I wish to speak a little with your servant Dorothy Jele, master."

"Dorothy is helping the madam with her hair," Mr. Jackson told him, switching to Zulu himself. "You'd better go round and wait in the yard for a while—but first I will have to know what this is all about."

It was a pity he was bilingual; often a fluent burst of gibberish and a few clicks of the tongue would deflect an awkward question such as this without further ado.

"There is a new ordinance, sir," Zondi lied earnestly, building on a truth, "similar to the one which makes all Xhosa people into citizens of the new nation of the Transkei, irrespective of their place of birth. It requires registration of those—"

"Whoa! You're not trying to take her away from us, are you?" interrupted Mr. Jackson, returning sternly to English. "We've had Dorothy for thirty years, you know—she's one of the family. Never been parted from us for more than a week."

"On the contrary," Zondi replied, using English himself now out of politeness. "The ordinance is concerned with the maid's domicile at the termination of her employment only."

"But we've promised her she can build a hut here and we'll see she never starves or anything. Can't she do that?"

"It is not for me to say, sir. But has the boss considered nominal employment?"

"So that's how it's done?" Mr. Jackson chuckled, then went back into Zulu. "A man never knows what they will think of next! All right, off you go. She will be about ten minutes."

Zondi waited until the dogs had followed the farmer into the house, then he hobbled down the drive leading to the garages and the servants' quarters. The five domestics in the walled yard, seated on wine boxes and upturned buckets, spooning up mealie meal porridge, greeted him with reserve. He declined their offer of a seat and a share of their breakfast, and leaned against the trunk of an avocado tree, thinking over what he had just learned.

So Dorothy Jele had chosen to work for the Jackson family for a full generation without, it appeared, having ever requested more than a week at a time in which to turn her back on them. This deepened his interest in the case of Mama Buza's baby—although that wasn't, of course, what he was there for. At a guess, the Lieutenant would want to know if any had cross-examined her about the identity of the man in the forest.

Kramer overslept, to be awakened by the maid bearing a breakfast tray of fried bread and tomato. Intensely annoyed with himself, he leaped up, ate the bread while he shaved, and then dressed hurriedly, muttering recriminations. He left the bungalow shortly after eight and jog-trotted along the path, noting to his satisfaction that the door of Zondi's hut was closed and that all was as quiet as it had been the night before. But as he drew nearer to the police station, he saw that his car had gone, and this made him run the rest of the way.

"Where the hell's Sergeant Zondi?" he demanded on reaching the charge office.

Goodluck Luthuli stamped to attention. "He go by Jackson farm, suh!"

"Is that so? What's that you've got there?"

Goodluck handed over an envelope marked PRIVATE & CONFIDENTIAL, which Kramer tore open where he stood.

Dear Lt. Kramer, the note inside said. *Hardly anybody pitched up last night because of the roads and the trouble when the vet crashed. See you later. In haste, Piet F. (I've gone to get a new tire from Brandspruit, don't know how long I'll be.)*

The note—and the fact it was a note—somehow bothered him. But not half so much as the discovery that Zondi had helped himself to the Chev and buggered off. No doubt the cheeky sod was checking to see if anyone had tried to make Dorothy Jele swear to having spotted Izimu among the trees—only those hadn't been his orders, and things in that department were coming to a head.

"Morning, sir!" said Willie, strolling in smelling of horse. "I've got that diagram ready like you asked for."

That was slightly cheering; Kramer ordered him through into the office to see how it looked. Willie produced a sheet of white card—the shape belied its origin as the stiffener from inside a new shirt—and handed him a scale drawing that was remarkably good. Even the grain of the wood in the platform was there, and the lower figure—outlined in dots—had toes that pointed realistically downward.

"Not bad. But how's the arithmetic of this? Last night you were sitting here moaning like a stuck pig."

Willie hesitated. "Before you chucked me out, didn't you say I could go and do it in feet and inches?"

"Uhuh. But explain this figure of twelve-eight—that's a bloody sight less than I expected."

"Still higher than an ordinary room, Lieutenant."

Kramer sat down behind the desk, lit a Lucky, for breakfast, and motioned Willie to get on with it.

"Well, sir, I started by making the scaffold platform my fixed point. Then I proceeded to find the victim who had the longest drop—or, in other words, the one who took up the most room below that point in the 'after' position, so marked."

"Izimu: he was the lightest, according to his P.M. report."

"Ja, only he had a scrawny neck with no muscle tone. Although the tramp was heavier, he had shoulders like a buffalo, so Dr. Strydom reckons he took a six-foot drop. To that I added three inches for neck stretch, supposing the body was left hanging for twenty minutes for the heart to stop, plus another inch for clearance—both minimum amounts. So you could say that the bottom line of the sum is six-four."

"From the floor up to the platform?"

"Correct, sir. Then for the 'before' position, or the space required above the trap door, I simply took the tallest person—the railway ganger—and added on his height of six-one."

"Plus what?" Kramer asked.

"Three inches for the shackle attaching the rope to the adjusting chain."

"But what if the hangman stands higher than six-four?"

"He'd have to bloody stoop, sir."

Kramer was surprised into a short laugh. "You're a typical example of what Doc's expertise can do to a man, but I must say I'm impressed. Where did you learn to draw like this?"

"Ach, at the orphanage."

"Uhuh?"

"That's all there ever was a lot of—paper and pencils; sometimes crayons as well. A man used to bring us the old rolls from the newspaper and Matron cut them up."

This was a guilelessness quite different from that shown by the knobbly-kneed abortion at Doringboom, and Kramer looked Willie over carefully, wondering if he had got him wrong. The scrutiny was misinterpreted.

"I—I didn't mean to be rude just now, sir it's just..."

"Go on, man," Kramer murmured.

"I appreciate we're only trying for a minimum here, and that the gallows must be higher. It's not that. And obviously Dr. Strydom knows a lot about the theory, only—"

"He also did the P.M. at about seventy executions."

"Oh, I see," mumbled Willie, becoming confused. "Then it doesn't matter."

But the obvious conflict in the kid intrigued Kramer. He called out for Luthuli to bring them some coffee, and invited Willie to take a chair. "You know something about the practical side? Something he's overlooked?"

Willie cracked his knuckles. "Did you also mix with the warders when you were at police college, sir?"

"Occasionally." Voortrekkerhoogte's proximity to Pretoria made this inevitable.

"Then you know how they boast about the hangings. How they think it he-man stuff to watch those kaffirs getting the chop. Granted, it isn't a sight I would want to witness. With a white or a colored it must be even worse."

"Although they usually do them one at a time."

"That's true. But what I'm saying is that this expert advice here—ach, it seems somehow too posh."

"In what way?" Kramer asked, glancing at the Telex slips.

"For instance, one Saturday night after a Rugby match, we were in the bar at the Van Riebeeck when the prison blokes started having sport with this little chap—I think his name was Kriel. He was down for his first execution on the Tuesday and the others were trying to put him off. It was no use him saying it was only a black bitch who'd smothered her 'bambino' to keep her job. Hell, they were the worst, these others told him; not only had you got to strap her up between the legs, but to a bloody stretcher as well. There was no other way of getting her there. Jesus, those were the buggers who really fought."

"You're losing me, Willie."

"That's how it started, you see, sir. Then they began to talk about the gory things, especially when the executioner gave too much drop. There was always blood all over, they said, which was why he'd seen sawdust near the coffin room. Yet according to these notes, such things shouldn't happen."

"I'm lost."

Willie cracked another knuckle. "One warder said—it sounded true and he was drunk, so it made him cry a bit—he said that he'd seen the rope slip up and pull half this boy's face off. The noose got stuck under his nose, which meant his neck broke okay, but all this part was scraped clean. Where was the rubber ring? Dr. Strydom says there's a patent rubber ring that's supposed to hold the noose tight until you can pull out the pin and push the lever."

"If they were doing a big batch, then—"

"Not according to these notes, Lieutenant. Even with six on the trap there should be no difference. Then there's all this velocity times mass squared over acceleration. And the elastic module of the rope they're using."

"Hey? It sounds more like a bloody space launching!"

"Ja, you could call it that," Willie said, grinning. "Actually, it is part of the sums you've got to do if you want the drop to be right. But do you remember John Harris, the bastard who put a bomb on Jo'burg station? Their coach said they'd given him 'an extra-long drop,' just to make sure. They're still talking about Harris, said he'd gone well and—"

"Gone well? Hell, I remember that expression now. Nice and quick, Luthuli."

Kramer reached for his coffee and took a sip.

"The point is, Lieutenant, that you don't give 'extra-long drops' if you're using the correct tables—or so Dr. Strydom says. A good hangman gets the drop correct to half an inch, no blood and no mess."

"You're saying what?"

"I'm saying," replied Willie, searching for the right words, "well, we're working from an ideal here."

"But they've *been* ideal hangings, my boy—that's the point. Furthermore, I never heard stories like yours in my time. They must have seen you coming."

Willie was someone who colored easily: he turned a stubborn red. "With respect, they weren't even looking at us while this was going on! They could also have made up much worse stories—not so?"

Kramer had to concede that. "Uhuh."

"And when I saw Kriel, about two weeks later, and asked him how it'd been, he said she hadn't gone well. Or at least she had started going well, which had made them forget about the allowance they had made for the stretcher or strait jacket—I can't exactly remember. The drop ended up too short, she wasn't heavy enough, and so she had only strangled. Above floor level, Kriel said, so you could watch the hood as it turned slowly round and round. That was all he told me—he didn't say anything about blood. It would have been easy for him to come up with a really gruesome story, but you could see he wasn't in the mood."

Willie became absorbed in this recollection and lifted up his coffee cup without looking at it. He drank in noisy gulps, his eyes on the dagga sacks.

"Come to think of it," said Kramer, who was finding his own drink too hot, "I heard somewhere recently that the hangman was using a pick handle to finish off his botched jobs."

"Ach, that's nonsense!" Willie protested.

"How do you know? What means have you of finding out?"

"Because, sir, that's really stupid to get things so wrong! These blokes said the hangman was really good with the condemneds. Some of the kaffirs like to kick their slippers off and run all the way, and he lets them. Harris was singing 'We Shall Overcome' and nobody minded. It isn't he makes mistakes on purpose, only all this textbook stuff—"

"Books aren't allowed about prison procedures. Doc is speaking from experience and his specialist's study of the subject. Other medicos send him clippings and that."

"Ja, I know, but—"

"Certainly not in such detail. At most, all you ever get is pure hearsay. Are we agreed on that?"

Willie nodded.

"Then where has *our* hangman obtained his technical know-how, if it wasn't via Pretoria Central by some means or other? You answer me that!"

Kramer didn't wait for Willie's reply before reaching for the telephone. It had just occurred to him to begin his day with a call to the commandant of Pretoria Central; the odds of anyone local being the state hangman were terrible, but there was always the chance.

Dorothy Jele came into the yard with the hipless walk of a white woman. She wore a starched uniform, an immaculate white cap, and spotlessly white tennis shoes. Her skin was glossy with good living; her hands were not chapped. The other servants smiled up at her as if this would make their day easier.

"The master said you wished to see me," she said in accented English. "What is your business?"

Zondi studied her broad face, noting the tightness of the small mouth. The puffy eyes gazed on him with the fixity of a slow mind imitating authority; the arms barricaded a flat chest.

"Forgive me if I bring you from your work, my sister," Zondi said humbly in Zulu. "Already I have heard how greatly valued you are by your employers."

"From my master?" she asked, her expression softening.

"He instructed me to treat you with great respect."

This brought her hands down to smooth the sides of her uniform. She glanced over her shoulder at the other servants, frowned at a young housemaid who was looking their way, and took out a Yale key.

"Come with me," she said. "I have a more suitable place than this for our business. Is it more registration?"

"A few particulars."

They started toward the far corner of the yard.

"You are lame. I suppose that's why you have been given this job."

Zondi smiled.

And she nodded wisely, in the way stupid people do when well pleased with themselves.

Dorothy Jele's room was, he felt quite certain, very different from the others in the same row. Basically, it had the same cement floor, barred window, and whitewashed brick walls, and the electric light was possibly common to them all. There was nothing purely functional or improvised about its furnishings, however—and he thought fleetingly of his own packing-case dresser and of the lines Miriam had scratched in the rammed earth underfoot to simulate wooden boards. The carpet, bed, wardrobe, dressing table, table, chairs, easy chair, curtains, pictures, mirror, cabinet radio, and china ornaments all spoke of thirty years' unbroken and devoted service, rewarded on an exceptionally lavish scale. Not only was nothing secondhand, but every item had been so cherished that it still looked brand-new—even the radio, which dated back to the fifties, and would have been among the first enticements chosen by her employers. This newness gave the room a shoplike unreality to add to its dreamy, contradictory feel; contradictory in the sense it didn't have the sharp, acid smell of whites that you usually associated with such arrangements. Although, on closer inspection, the passage of time was evident in one corner, in a picture frame filled with the sort of postcard-sized, full-length portraits that families had taken of themselves at a stall in the Trekkersburg beer hall. In each of these Dorothy Jele stood alone against the painted backdrop of skyscrapers and thundercloud, and in each she was several years older.

"My, this is a fine room," Zondi exclaimed, bending to admire a two-bar electric fire. "Never have I seen one so complete and wonderful." And that was true.

"I am pleased."

"How fortunate you are, my sister! For most of us, there is

little beauty in our lives."

He was watching her face now, a little sickened by her delight in his words—even by the way her fingertips stroked the polished tabletop, moving in little circles on its smooth mahogany skin.

"Have you noticed the bedside lamp?"

"Hau, I have indeed!" he responded, coming to the high point of his flattery: "And are all these riches truly yours?"

"I hope so," sighed Dorothy Jele.

The wistful reply was so unexpected that Zondi needed a moment to grasp its implications; even then, he spoke before realizing them fully.

"What? You do not know?"

She shrugged, her face clouding.

"If they have not said, why have you not asked them?"

"I—I do not like to."

"Why?"

"They may think me greedy."

"And so?"

"Or that I am going from them," she mumbled, looking down at her reflection. "It is better to wait and please them by working hard every day. When I am old, then they must tell me, because it is promised I will move into a hut that—"

"Woman, is your life a deposit?"

"That is insolent! You have no right to speak to me in such a way!"

"Then how," said Zondi appalled by what he had heard, "should I address the foolish wretch who took Mama—" But he stopped there, unable to see how anyone quite so stupid could have been quite so cunning when it had come to framing the witch doctor for the crime she had herself committed.

Much later that morning, just as Willie and Zondi arrived back in the station commander's office, Kramer's call to Central Prison, Pretoria, was returned. The prison had insisted on ringing back, being understandably concerned that he should be who he said he was, and it had probably been checking on the Witklip telephone number, among other things. This did not mean, however, that the captain delegated to pass on their reply to his queries was particularly forthcoming. He sounded like a man who wouldn't give you a cup of sand in the desert.

"Captain Theron here. Your answer is no."

"That's all? What about those other connections I asked you blokes to—"

"No," Theron repeated.

Kramer looked at Willie, who was standing with Zondi on the far side of the desk, and asked, "I have a few questions about hanging techniques I'd like to have verified, if possible. Could you tell me what procedure is followed?"

"Exactly as laid down."

"Uhuh?"

"The judge says, 'You will be hanged by the neck until you are dead,' and we do it."

Theron put his phone down.

"Bugger me," said Kramer, "that was a great help. What have you to report? Zondi?"

"Dorothy Jele says many white bosses spoke to her about the sighting of Izimu. It would be impossible to—"

"But I've got something, sir!" blurted out Willie. "I was talking to my landlord—old Mr. Haagner—just casually, like you said I must do it, and he mentioned that Mr. de Bruin had been among those who were away during the war. He knows it wasn't fighting, but it had something to do with the government."

"You didn't push it too hard?"

"Hell, I hope not, sir. Also, I've been down to Spa-kling and all the committee's there already. De Bruin, Van der Heever, Swanepoel, Crowe, Wantenaar, Fouche—the whole lot of them. They're making up games for the kids, and George said it would take all afternoon."

"Piet?"

"Er—he isn't back yet."

Kramer got up and adjusted the wall clock to synchronize with his own watch: it was now one o'clock exactly. He turned and was stricken to see Zondi's leg shuddering in spasm—this had been hidden by the desk before.

"We move in one hour, so get Mamabola and Luthuli on standby. Show them your drawing. Is there anyone who can mind the shop?"

"Nyembezi, who's on nights. Actually, he's more use than old Goodluck."

"Wake him and swap them round. Try the hotel and see if Piet's back."

"But I've only just—"

"Ring him, damn it! And you, Sergeant—outside."

Zondi's exit was painful to watch. Once in the area behind the charge office counter, Kramer steered him into the half-empty storeroom, closed the door behind him, and raised a fist.

"This is what you deserve, Mickey!"

"For, boss?"

"For behaving like a half-witted kaffir, you stupid bastard! What the hell are you doing to yourself? I'm phoning the DS at Brandspruit and Mamabola's taking you in—and I don't want any arguments. I don't want to *know*. Got it?"

They looked at each other.

Kramer said, "All right, but here you'll stay until this thing is over. I'll get them to fix it up for you before we go. More brandy?"

"Hau, please not for me!"

"It's no trouble."

"You would not think that, boss," Zondi murmured slyly, as he slid slowly down the wall, "if you had my headache."

With a lopsided smile, Kramer left the room and gave instructions to Luthuli for a mattress and some blankets to be found somewhere. And then, realizing there'd be no red tape involved, he also told him to send for a good witch doctor.

"Sir?" interrupted Willie, displaying agitation. "Piet isn't back and his barman wants to know about closing time."

"Why ask me, for Christ's sake?"

"Well—um—Sarge is on the committee, too, see? And when all the blokes have to be there for the afternoon, he sort of tends to look the other way, if you—"

"Fine," said Kramer. "I'm not looking."

Not there at any rate, and the happier the committee stayed for the afternoon, the better.

17

ZONDI KNEW HE WAS DREAMING. He'd meant to say many things
to Dorothy Jele, and now he was saying them. He chided her for
thinking that a careless mother was necessarily an uncaring one.
He reminded her of the sweet fever turning to delirium as the
search had drawn closer. He laughed at her virtues as a true
Christian woman, a woman who couldn't be made to tell a lie.
She shrieked back that it wasn't her, wasn't her. She shrieked
and shrieked and coughed and whispered and there was
someone standing over him.

He had still to be dreaming. The man wore a lounge suit and
there were inflated pigs' bladders in his hair. His squint
transfixed you, his breath was aromatic. Herbs. He was gone
again.

Dorothy, Dorothy, Dorothy Jele.

Someone else in the room.

"Have I woken you?" whispered Goodluck Luthuli.

"Are my eyes not closed?" Zondi snapped, noticing he'd
succumbed to the peevishness of an invalid. "I am sorry, my
brother. What time is it? Is the Lieutenant—"

"They have been away the whole afternoon, Sergeant. There

is no sign of their return yet. I heard you were restless, so I brought you this." Luthuli held out a small horn with a wooden stopper. "It is the medicine left by Jafini Bhengu. He was most painstaking in its preparation, and ground up the ingredients to a special fineness. He says it would be better if you went to the nuns' clinic, but this will bring you relief until then."

Groggily, Zondi took the horn, uncorked it, and saw that it contained a gray powder. "All afternoon, you say? Then the sun is going down?"

"Soon. Is there anything else you would have brought to you?"

Zondi's attention had been taken by the way Luthuli was tamping down the tobacco in his cheap black pipe. He glared at the pipe, annoyed by the insistence of its detail: it was the kind with a perforated metal cap which fitted over the bowl, and there was a little silver chain, attached at one end to the pipestem, to keep this cap from getting lost. When he began to hate the pipe, his own delirium seemed not far off.

"A farm is not hard to search. The workers will know all the far corners, and they will also know where they have been forbidden to go. If I—"

"Mamabola is helping your boss, and he is a bright one," Luthuli said, replacing the silver cap. "Perhaps they visit many farms."

"Mamabola! That puppy!"

With a grunt, Zondi tried to rise—only to discover he hadn't the strength to take a grip on the ammunition box beside him. His head reeled and he slumped back.

"You must sleep," Luthuli coaxed gently, pulling up the blankets again. "I will be in the charge office."

The door closed. Zondi felt for his gun; it had been taken from him. He went limp. He thought about Dorothy Jele, and remembered how thin the walls of her room had been. Soon he was dreaming again, hopping frantically, seeing his children running fleet down a straight path to the barricades.

"Lieutenant!" shouted Zondi, this time waking himself up.

He fumbled for the medicine horn, tipped the whole lot into his mouth, and turned to the wall. Then his mind became lucid and he began to smile. A moment or two later, he was laughing.

His sophisticated taste buds had just revealed to him the secret of Jafini Bhungu's success. That gray powder was nothing other than wood ash and aspirin.

"I don't get it," said Kramer, as he and Willie finally boarded the Land-Rover. "That place definitely had a feel to it that wasn't natural."

"Where's Nyembezi?" Willie asked Mamabola, who was sitting on the floor in the back.

"He is coming now, boss; he just sprung a leak."

"Did you get the same impression, Willie?"

They looked back at the wide, low bungalow, at the barn and tractor shed and scattering of outbuildings. The large disused water tank had caused a brief flutter of hope. So had the milking parlor, with its pit between the machines, but by then things had been verging on the ridiculous.

"Can't say I did, sir. That old cookboy was a bit funny, but otherwise it seemed normal to me. I don't think he believed we were looking for an escaped prisoner." And Willie laughed. "How did Mrs. de Bruin take to you going inside?"

"She didn't bat an eyelid, went on doing her knitting. Of course, what I said was that I wanted to use the bog. Look, she's still there now; bet she's watching us."

A lumpy figure in a black frock went on knitting and swinging gently on a cushioned bench suspended from the verandah rafters. Tortoise-shell spectacles gave a glint.

"Ja, took it all in her stride, asked no questions about the man we were looking for, whether he was a rapist or what. But it was little things, like the keys."

"Sorry, Lieutenant?"

"When I was going through the rooms, checking the floorboards like you suggested, I noticed that there was a key in every keyhole of every chest, cupboard—or else the thing was open. What I'm getting at is that nothing was locked; I could have gone digging in anything I liked."

The back door slammed and Nyembezi's weight settled heavily on the metal seat. Kramer started up the Land-Rover and drove out slowly to the gate, turned left, and began the descent to Witklip. They passed a sign reading M. R. JACKSON—

PRIVATE. The next sign they came to was outside Gysbert Swanepoel's place. Kramer swung in there, just missing a gatepost.

"Hey?" said Willie.

"Best we do one other," Kramer explained, knowing damn well what he was up to. "If we just do De Bruin's, that's a bit of a giveaway." It was like being in rut.

"But Jackson's is in between!"

"He's also at home this afternoon, in all probability, my friend. And not a very nice man, by the sound of it."

"Hell, I.... Must I come in with you?"

The drive was relatively short and ended at the foot of some concrete steps ornamented with small palms set in tubs made from car tires.

"Must I, sir?" Willie repeated, very jittery, as the Land-Rover's engine was switched off.

"We'll make this a quickie," said Kramer, now committed. "You take the outside, me the in. Tell Mamabola to see the head boy, the induna, and Nyembezi had better stay here with the van. Same prisoner story as before. Got that?"

"Fine; will do."

"Then spread out, Willie, spread out."

The door was opened by a shuffling crone with a face straight out of a prune packet.

"Boss Swanepoel not home," she said, deeply apologetic. "Little missus she lie down."

"That's okay, auntie. You see my boy down there?"

"Hau, hau! Po-eesie?"

"Uhuh, police, But you're not in any trouble. Just you go to him and he'll explain."

She hurried off. It was as well Zondi wasn't around.

Kramer stepped into the house and took a glance into the living room. It had large sash windows and an enormous fireplace. The furniture was old, and so was the carpet; the effect was very homely. A muzzleloader hung over the mantel, pointing at the head of a dead buffalo on the same wall, and, above a homemade bookcase, was a faded world map. There wasn't a photograph of her anywhere.

The house was very quiet. Every door onto the long passage

stood ajar except one. He listened, tried the handle carefully, and found it was locked. But the key was on the outside, so he turned it, waited five seconds, then went in.

A low, green light, filtering through the drawn blinds, transformed a scene of mild chaos into the natural untidiness of a forest clearing. Scattered panties made vivid crinkles of fungi on the tree stump of a stool and around it; tights hung like torn spider web from chairback and mirror; other clothing and pop cuttings littered the floor underfoot, crackling and yielding. There was a faint, fecund forest fragrance, the sickly sweetness that tempts flies into fleshy petals, and the trapped, heavy air was sweat-prickle humid. Over on the far side, on a bank of mussed bedding, a slender figure was lying face down. Kramer circled the end of the bed. Her face was hidden by a fall of blond hair the right length for pigtails. Her arms were straight down at her sides and her hands underneath her. Her skin was tanned to the color of a young doe and there was a sprinkle of freckles on the near shoulder. She was wearing a sleeveless white blouse, a denim skirt which reached to midthigh, and was barefoot. Her legs were long and strong and very smooth. He wanted to touch them.

Willie kept as far as he could from the house. He expected the girl to come running out at any moment, followed by the Lieutenant, to accuse him of all the things he'd so often imagined doing to her. It didn't matter how irrational he knew this notion to be—that's what he felt. It had him scared and excited and sick to the stomach. He slunk into the vehicle shed and tried to get himself together.

There had been a time, way back in the home when the only rides he ever took were on buses, when he'd been mad keen on motor transport of any sort and had known all the names. But this chance of inspecting a diesel Mercedes saloon at close quarters was one he had no interest in taking. He pushed a finger along its dusty flank and wiped the muck off on an old refrigerator truck.

Then he noticed the blood. A spear-shaped splash on the mounting step at the back. He circled the truck and discovered that the cooling unit had been removed before the last paint job.

Puzzled, he swung back the elaborate latch—which someone had been modifying with a brazing torch—and opened the doors.

Vvvvvvvvvvvv. Flies filled the stinking air, which was like a belch from a hyena. *Vvvvvv—vvvvvvmmm.* They settled again to continue their feasting. There was blood everywhere on the ribbed metal floor, and a row of hooks had been screwed into a reinforced strip that ran the length of the thick, insulated ceiling.

"Impofu," said a grating voice behind him.

With a start, Willie swung round and found Mamabola and the farm's headboy standing there.

"The induna explains," said Mamabola, "that this is the conveyance used for the transportation of eland." He asked the man some questions in Zulu, and then added: "Boss Swanepoel has now fifty head of buck on the poor pastures; no other farmer in this district has so many. Boss de Bruin only twenty-nine and Boss Jackson thirty."

"Ja, I bloody know," Willie lied, feeling a terrible fool, "but that doesn't mean I can't be interested! How often does the boss shoot them? Doesn't it matter if they get a bit bad?"

After some mumbling, muffled by the woolen cap the induna held respectfully in front of his mouth, Mamabola came up with a hesitant answer: "He says the white masters in the big cities eat only buck that is rotten."

"Oh, ja? Tell him to pull the other one!" retorted Willie, looking at his watch. "Do all of them have trucks like this, hey?"

It was no good: Kramer couldn't leave without seeing what her face was like. He cleared his throat.

She stopped breathing. Her neat rump lifted slightly and a hand appeared stealthily at her side.

"Pa . . . ?"

She propped herself up on an elbow, flicking her hair aside with her right hand, while using the other one to keep her blouse closed. A kitten's tongue licked the perspiration from her downy upper lip; the large green eyes dilated, not telling her anything. He tingled with an uncanny sense of recognition; it almost frightened him.

"My warrant card," said Kramer, flipping open his wallet. "I'm a policeman, so don't catch a panic. We're looking for—"

"You gave me a scare! I thought it was him back."

"Sorry, hey? It didn't seem right not to tell you this boy was around. We're also telling the servants."

She smiled and he smiled and that took care of that. Except there was something secret about her smile that had nothing to do with him. He examined her face, still feeling the effects of his initial reaction to it, yet without being able to account in any satisfactory way for why he found it familiar. Perhaps his dream hussy really had looked like that—he couldn't really remember now; perhaps he'd registered a sharper picture of the passing schoolgirl than he realized. It was true, too, that her face was of a stereotype prettiness, found in every stock character from Bambi to Snow White to beauty queens, and built on the bossed forehead, big eyes, cute mouth, round cheeks, and neat nose of a baby. Very much the sort of face which would cause no resentment among her classmates if she was chosen to play the princess in a school play. And yet it might have been only the eyebrows, with their distinctive curve upward. He needed to look at her a while longer.

"Why was the door locked?" Kramer asked, half guessing her answer.

"He thinks I've been naughty."

"I thought it might be that. And were you?"

She looked down to do up two of her buttons, tightening the fabric so that the swell of her breasts showed; they were as big as shop buns, each with a currant-sized bump in the center. The action seemed unthinking. She giggled.

"It's the second weekend running I can't go out. I'm meant to learn this stuff." She nudged a book on her pillow.

"What about the barbecue tonight?"

"I'm not allowed," she said with indifference, making a face. "Still, I think they're boring. You should see the barbecues we have at school sometimes!"

Kramer sat on the edge of the bed, down where her feet were. He was conscious of his own warmth, of her warmth, of the room's warmth. They mingled together somehow, touching.

"Better games?"

"Hey? Oh, ja, much better. Was that you who came after lunchtime?"

"No; just arrived."

"I thought it was Pa, which just proves it. I wanted to ask him if I could have the radio—but he never takes any notice on purpose."

She drew back her right foot, scratched at a mosquito bite, and then replaced it so that her toes were gently touching him. She didn't seem to notice. But he did.

"Your pa has quite a temper, has he?"

"Not really," she said, appraising him as though wondering what his personality was like. "Pa's very strict, that's all. He does nice things, too, like he reads me books, turning it straight into Afrikaans from English sometimes. He's clever, my pa. Also, he's promised me a horse if I'm good now."

Kramer smiled. "What are your chances of getting it?"

Her toes wriggled.

The stimulus wrought a minor change in his circulation. The child had a self-proclaiming sexuality that would probably frighten her half to death if she were aware of it; it came over in the lazy movements of her limbs, in her need for casual contact, in the scent of her. His own awareness of this gave their touching an edge of irresistible tension; he knew he should go now, but couldn't see the harm in it. Her face was still a mystery to be solved, too, he told himself.

"You haven't answered my question."

"That depends."

"On what?"

"On who." She laughed.

Her toes were kneading his thighs like cat paws, taking their rhythm from the rise and fall of her breasts. She was watching him slyly. He couldn't believe it.

"I know a secret about you," she said with a smile.

"Which is?" Kramer waited, his blood racing.

"From your eyebrows I can tell your hair's the same color all over. I'm the same if you look."

She had drawn her feet up again, shiny knees parted.

"I must go now," he said, keeping his eyes on her face. "That must be some boarding school you go to."

"Go on, stay—please. You can see how bored I am."

Her foot came back to lie across his thigh, the toes reaching.
Then she gave a little kick.

"Push off, big man!" She giggled. "You're looking at me like
my pa does! I want my horse more than a ride with you, you
know. Although I wouldn't have minded till you did that."

"Jesus!"

"Can't take a joke? Now tell me what Pa does, that I'm the
lost generation."

"You're a whore," he whispered. "Where did you learn this?"

"That would be telling, hey? Now push off like I said, or I'll
call the girl. I don't like you anymore."

"Thank God for that," said Kramer with icy control.

Shaken, he rose and gave her a curt nod, forgetting there
were things about himself over which his control was limited.
She looked at his loins, saw what her power had conjured, and
burst into schoolgirlish laughter. He didn't move until her face
had a sulk on it. Then he walked round the bed and to the door,
where he could not help pausing for a last look back. She had
rolled over again and was lying very straight, with her hands
hidden beneath her.

"Hey, Lieutenant!" Willie called out, beckoning him to the lean-
to garage beside the barn. "It just could be something."

Blinking against the aching brightness of the afternoon, and
with his head full of pus, Kramer strode across to see what the
excitement was about. He saw a beaten-up refrigerator truck
which had been converted to carry game in; one very like it
called occasionally at the hotel across the way from the office. In
fact, for all it mattered, this could be the same one.

The truck was filthy.

"What could be something?" he managed to say.

"He could be using his one like this—in fact, the induna says
there are at least four in the neighborhood. The garage in
Brandspruit made them up and—"

"Like *this?*" Kramer exploded, slamming one of the heavy
doors shut. "Jesus bloody Christ almighty! What was the point
in getting you to read all Doc's bumf? A clean death, hey?

Whitewashed walls and new rope and scrubbed boards—look at that sodding floor! That's not just metal on top, but eight inches of bloody insulation underneath. Height? Nine foot? Eight? From the wheels to the top? Eleven?"

"Ach, no!" said Willie, gaining color. "I'm not such a fool. Be fair, sir!"

The kid was right to stand up for himself. Kramer took a deep, silent breath and then turned calmly to the awed black onlookers. "Mamabola and Nyembezi into the van. Tell the induna we'll be moving on to search for the prisoner down the valley." Then he said, "Carry on, Willie; I'm listening. My problem was that it struck me like a very messy murder, which isn't what we're dealing in at present."

Willie's grin was instantly forgiving. "You should have been here when I opened it, Lieutenant, hey? No; my idea was that here could be an ideal vehicle for transporting the bodies in to where he dumps them. In the notes it says that the blood wouldn't have all drained to the feet if the corpses hadn't—er—"

"Quote 'been maintained in a vertical or semivertical position'?"

"Ja, that's right. There's another thing, too: nobody notices these trucks moving at night or early in the morning, because of the time the meat markets open."

"And the loading hours around the hotels and restaurants. De Bruin's got one of these, you say?"

"A blue one on a Bedford chassis. I didn't look inside it when we were—"

"Willie," said Kramer, "I like it."

"So shall we go back up there?"

"I think the English would say that's putting the cart before the horse, my friend. And I can guarantee it won't be in the same condition as this one. God, Swanepoel is a pig."

"It's really the induna's fault. He should have had it cleaned on Tuesday. I told Mamabola to kick his arse for him. But why aren't we going just to take a look? We didn't find sod all else there."

Kramer suddenly knew what he'd felt about the De Bruin homestead. "You've put your finger right on it! They had nothing to hide—right? Why not?"

"Because it isn't them?"

"Because it isn't *there*, man! It's somewhere else. And I think I know how we can find it."

"Sir?"

"Time to put some pressure on, Willie. Let the bastard know what we've come to Witklip for. Either he'll crack and we'll see it, or he'll keep cool and try to sneak away to destroy it—providing he isn't madder than we realize. As soon as he makes his move, we nail him."

"What sort of pressure?" Willie asked, as they started back to the Land-Rover. "A Wanted notice?" But he was only joking, as his wink indicated.

"Something subtle. Something to really put on the mental thumbscrews, even if he's blocked out to the usual pressures. Something he can't resist reacting to."

"Quite something," remarked Willie, very dryly.

"Don't worry; I'll think of it."

Kramer got behind the wheel of the Land-Rover and noted that the sun, which had shone so brightly in his eyes, had touched the edge of the ridge. It would be dark soon. He started up and drove hard to the gate. Incredibly, as he turned away from one of the most regrettable things he'd ever done, he flinched with regret at not having accepted that open invitation. And part of his body said yes, it agreed with him.

The stones rattled loudly against the Land-Rover's steel plating. Willie was asking him a question, so he leaned over to hear it.

"Was—was his daughter around?"

"Too right, man! Do you know her?"

"Er—not—not really. I've seen her a few times."

"Then you should get in there," Kramer shouted back, but not loud enough for their passengers to hear him. "Christ, I've never seen anything so eager for it! Wants to give it to you on a plate. I nearly got raped, man, and I'm an old granddad compared to you!"

Willie was gripping the crash bar, really coming to life at last. "But she's only fifteen!"

"Doesn't matter to her, I can tell you. So why should it matter to you? I think that Jackson kid was bloody lucky to get out of that barn still able to walk. He should complain!"

"You've heard about that? I only—"

"Ja; Piet told me last night. But seriously, Willie, my friend, if ever you feel the urge, and the old man's not around, you have a go and you'll see what I mean. In the few minutes I was in there, she made sure I saw everything."

"No! Honest?"

"Honest. A real little nympho. No wonder he's keeping her away from the barbecue these days."

This outburst seemed to flush a sickness from Kramer's soul, but the space it left was immediately taken by a choking self-disgust. He eased up on the throttle, got a Lucky into his mouth, and offered one to Willie.

"Actually, it's nothing to make jokes about."

"Uhuh?" Willie said—and not for the first time; he'd made several unconscious imitations already.

"It's a kind of illness, and has maybe got something to do with having no ma. Or the effect on her when she died. It's also a fact that kids these days are definitely different, and those boarding schools were pretty wild even in my own day. Did you ever go to one?"

"No, I was always stuck in the boys' home."

Kramer flinched again, very tender all round. "The really terrible thing is that she's got mixed up with someone there who should be locked up."

"Bloody hell," said Willie, puffing out his smoke in a flurried blast. "That explains it! Everyone was wondering why that what's-his-name bloke got the sack. Usually they say, but one minute he was a house father in the hostel, next minute he was gone, vanished completely from Brandspruit."

"Who knows?"

"But she was really like that? Willing?"

"In heat," said Kramer, smiling for an opposite effect. "Shall I tell you what it reminds me of now? Of a time when I had to go through the loony bin in Trekkersburg and some inmates there held up their dresses as I passed. That's not sex, man. Agreed?"

"Ja, agreed. I like mine hot but not—er—what shall we say?"

Kramer let it die there. Emotionally spent, his mind achieved a new clarity, and he applied himself to the problem of finding the right thumbscrew. Willie drew on his cigarette thoughtfully. Dust billowed behind them.

"Can I say—" Willie began.

"Go right ahead, providing it's the case we're both back on."

"Not finding anything might also have something to do with me saying the notes were too posh in comparison, and we could be looking for too much."

"For the last time, man!"

This pigheaded quibbling by a credulous bloody teen-ager, who wouldn't notice a subtle nuance if you stuck it up his nose, was more than any grown man could be expected to tolerate. Kramer was about to let rip, when he realized how very true this was.

"Blasphemy—do you know that's what you're talking?"

"I don't care, sir. I've got to say what I believe."

"In that case," replied Kramer, looking up at the great white stone passing high above them on the left, "if you are prepared to be as principled in public, then I think we're ready to roll, Willie, my lad."

18

NEVER HAVING BEEN ONE to mix easily, Willie Boshoff felt daunted by the prospect of intruding into so much close-knit fellowship, but he was determined to carry out the Lieutenant's weird plan. And, as he skirted the games rigged up on the lawn for the barbecue party, his resolve was strengthened by the thought of at last getting out of Witklip. It seemed only just that the Lieutenant would help him with his transfer; he had, after all, been very impressed by the scale drawing, and had now taken to talking to him man-to-man—not only that, but he'd entrusted him with a delicate, possibly even dangerous mission. If the mission was a success, then SAP 13408 was as good as on his way.

Willie paused in the gloaming to straighten his tunic and press his hair down neatly. He wondered if the Lieutenant was in position yet, and where he had chosen to hide himself.

Then Willie walked on, approaching the steps which led up to the verandah and the public bar. How different life seemed now, all thanks to the big fellow who'd not appealed to him in the slightest at the beginning, but who had become one of the best blokes he had been privileged to know. Nothing worried the bastard; he did what he liked, when he liked, and sod them all. If he knew about him pinching the magazine, he'd just laugh; he'd not expect something dreadful to happen, and he would be right. Nothing had. A lovely bit of goose, that; pity she lived in England—he could do her right now. This was it.

Willie pushed open the bar door, took in a blur of faces and voices, and made for the counter.

"Hey, look who's here!" Karl de Bruin said with a laugh, slapping him on the back. "Wonders will never cease! What'll you have, son? A lager?"

"Ta, Mr. de Bruin—that's kind, man."

Samson, the Zulu barman who always wore his clip-on-bow tie upside down, brought a lager up from the shelf underneath. As he jerked the cap off, he said softly, "Boss is not back yet, young chief."

"Really?" Willie's mouth went a little dry.

"Long time he has been gone," Samson added, keeping the froth from coming over the top. "The party begins very soon."

De Bruin clinked his glass against Willie's and they drank. It tasted very good, especially when you hadn't stopped since early morning for anything. Perhaps the Land-Rover, which was a real heap, had broken down.

"Of course, you would have been even more welcome pitching up *before* the work was done," De Bruin joshed him. "Us blokes have only just finished the obstacle course for the over-tens. Gysbert made some lovely fish out of bean tins for the magnet pool—did you see them?"

"Er—no. I'll catch up on that later."

"You're coming tonight?" asked Swanepoel.

"Ja. Ja, I think I am."

"I see; when the cat's away...?"

Swanepoel's witticism won an undeservedly loud laugh.

"You mean when the..." Willie lost track of that. He had just realized that Jonkers and Ferreira were now both absent at the same time.

"Go on," Swanepoel encouraged him. "I don't mind what you call that fat little bastard."

"Easy, man, easy," said De Bruin.

George van der Heever and one or two others joined the half-circle; they nodded to Willie in a friendly way, making him feel very welcome. The whole idea of the mission seemed—no, he was under orders: it wasn't his job to think.

"To what do we owe this honor?" asked Hendrik Louw, a man you didn't see often himself.

"Celebration," said Willie, ad-libbing. "A kaffir I caught during my training has just lost his appeal."

"Never met one with any," Swanepoel quipped, getting his laugh again.

"Which means?" De Bruin asked, frowning at the other man.

"Ach, he gets the chop."

"How does that make you feel?" a strange face inquired.

"I don't mind so long as I don't have to watch it. They pull their bloody heads off sometimes, hey?"

"Oh, ja? What happens to them exactly?" the stranger said, moving in a little closer, touching the wart on his cheek.

In a minute or two, Willie had such an attentive audience that he only wished he'd done something like this before. And he didn't have to pay for his second—or third—lager either.

Kramer sat on a pile of beer crates in the bar's scullery and willed his toes to uncurl. That's what Willie's clumsy feed line had done to them, and now his teeth were clenched at the sound of the increasingly tipsy full performance. Except for an occasional prompting, not another voice had penetrated the plywood partition in the time it had taken to smoke two and a half Luckies.

He passed the remaining half to the washing-up boy, who was enjoying this unforeseen break in his activities, and took another swill of the Lion ale he'd opened. Zondi had been muttering about Jackson when they had called briefly at the station house; there had not been the opportunity to hear him out—which might have been a mistake. Something about Jackson having the brains and the motive.

"They keep the coons in one big cell so they can sing together," Willie was saying, "seventy or so at a time."

"It'll be less soon," a light voice observed.

"How's that?" Willie challenged.

"I saw in the *Sunday Tribune* that the Transkei has got its own two hangmen now—both wogs, need you ask."

"Ja, and did you read what the official said?" a wheezy bass joined in. "They got applications for the job from all over the bloody country, but the four whites who applied weren't given serious consideration. Christ, that makes you realize how independent we're making them, hey?"

"Perfect job for a coon," someone else said, laughing. "Good pay for unskilled labor you don't even have to do every day! I'm glad none of my boys got to hear about it!"

"It's not unskilled," a voice said.

"Huh! That wasn't what I read in my paper. When the official was asked whether they were getting any training for the work, he said, 'No comment.'"

"He wouldn't be authorized to comment on prison affairs of that nature," said the voice. "Of course these men will be trained."

The wheezy bass sniggered. "What with? Hundred-pound mealie bags?"

"They might use them to stretch the rope the night before. You've got to put some weight on it, or mistakes in the amount of slack will occur."

"Mealie bags?"

"Filled with sand."

"Ah! Now he tells us!"

There was a big laugh all round. Kramer placed his ear to the partition.

"Like I was telling you," Willie said, reclaiming the limelight, "if it's a white guy, then sometimes he gets a special program on the loudspeaker for a couple of hours the night before. There's a convict who acts like a D.J., plays him hits, his own requests, passes on messages from the others—mostly just saying 'Good luck.'"

"He can smoke, I suppose?" asked the light voice.

"Ja, he's permitted tobacco the minute his appeal fails."

"Like a sort of ration?"

"Not just any old amount, man! He's there to be punished, remember. But I reckon they would let him save it up for the last night," Willie explained.

"Where," asked the neutral voice, "did you pick all this up, youngster? I notice that sometimes you are a little unsure of your facts."

There was a brittle pause.

"Meaning?"

"I've heard differently, that's all. How about another one in that glass of yours?"

Here the voice became lost in a boozy hubbub that came up as suddenly as a twist on a volume knob; nobody, it seemed, had enjoyed that surprisingly tense little moment. Kramer felt a tap on his shoulder; it was the washing-up boy, returning a favor by pointing out a small peephole in the plywood.

Kramer peered through it. Gysbert Swanepoel was unmistakable as he towered over Willie on the left. Behind the black beard—there was enough of it to stuff a pair of size 6 boxing gloves—was a strong face with high cheekbones. His complexion was coarse and unevenly tanned, like the skin of a rice pudding dusted with cinnamon, and the deep-set eyes had a bright sparkle. The nose was narrow, the eyebrows distinctive, and the ears very thin. He was smiling indulgently.

On the right side of Willie was a man of much the same age, short and tubby, wearing a porkpie hat and braces. He had a head like a pink lollipop topped with gray fluff from a schoolboy's blazer pocket. His features had been licked smooth so that they tended to run into each other, leaving only the overhang of a long upper lip to stress the hard set of a mouth like a bite mark. He wore round spectacles with tortoise-shell frames over eyes that were a curious tawny. His expression was strained.

In between them, Willie stood twiddling his empty glass by the stem, trying to appear completely relaxed. But by the hitch of his shoulders, it was plain that he expected at any moment to have a noose dropped over him.

"Silly bugger," said Kramer, not wanting the initiative to be taken from them. "Go and fetch Samson, my friend—tell him the sink's blocked."

A white shirt blocked his view for a few seconds. When it moved aside, Willie and the short man had gone. In came Samson on tiptoe.

"Forget it!" Kramer said, raising a finger to his lips, then dived through the door into the inner passage.

"Hello," chirped the old lady with bandaged legs. "It *is* so nice to see you here again. Will you be staying long?"

He gave her a quick peck on the cheek and got by when she drew back in delighted surprise. They fly screen filling the doorway at the end of the passage gave him an ideal position from which to see without being seen. It wasn't needed: Willie and De Bruin were standing in among the kids' games with their backs turned to him, talking earnestly together.

"And these are the fish I was telling you about," De Bruin said as Kramer came within earshot. "He's very clever with his hands when he wants to be. Does that look like a bean can to you?"

Willie looked up at the tin fish spinning and glittering at the end of a short line. The magnet lost its grip and the fish fell. In picking it up, both men became aware of Kramer's long shadow on the grass.

"There you are, Boshoff; I've been looking."

"Er—hello, sir."

"Can I have a word with you for a moment?"

Kramer took Willie aside, and said quietly, "Well, Judas, which one was it?" He noted the jerked nod. "You've done a first-class job. Stick around here, watch for Number Two, and I'll handle this bastard." Walking up to De Bruin, he stuck out his hand. "Lieutenant Kramer, here for the weekend."

De Bruin's grip was unsure. "Pleased to meet you. Karl de Bruin is the name."

"I've just been speaking to Boshoff here."

"Ja?"

"He'd like to stay on for the party—in fact, he's got a message from Mr. Ferreira for the chef. But I've to get back to the station, so I wondered if it'd be too much of a favor to ask for a quick lift?"

For an instant, the man dithered. "Why, certainly, I'd be pleased to help out. My work here is finished for—"

"Ta, very much," said Kramer, giving Willie a dismissive wave. "Don't be too late, Cinderella, or you know what'll happen to your pumpkins."

Then he forced the situation by beginning to stride for the car park. De Bruin caught up, but said nothing until they'd reached the trees.

"You're standing in for Sergeant Jonkers, I hear?"

"After a fashion."

"Must be a rest cure after Durban."

"Uhuh. You farm around here?"

"About twelve kilos out."

"The place with the buck on it?"

"Could've been mine; ja, I keep a few head. Won't be a moment."

De Bruin did something Kramer had never seen done in the country before: he unlocked the driver's door to his Ford three-quarter ton. Then he reached across and released the catch on the other side.

There was a sheen of sweat over his forehead which caught the cab light. The doors slammed. In silhouette, the profile was that of a prim, introverted, sensitive man.

"Judas?" said Willie. "Cinder who?" said Willie. "Jesus," said Willie, "whatever will the bugger think of next?" And having reassured himself that none of these epithets had been derogatory in their intention, but merely good-humored banter, he settled for a score of five tin fish landed from the zinc tub of blue-dyed water. He tugged the fifth from the dangling magnet, wound the line a few times around the toy rod, and replaced them, ready for the children.

"Having good sport, Willie?"

He started. "Ach, Piet! Where did you spring from?"

"Had a tough day," replied Ferreira, standing there with his hands in his pockets, not coming any nearer. "They didn't have the tread I wanted in Brandspruit, so I had to go down the road until I found a place. And you?"

Willie closed the gap. "We nailed him," he said, pride thrusting aside the numbness he'd felt up till then. "De Bruin's already on his way to the station. But you mustn't tell anyone, hey?"

"God!" Ferreira was deeply shocked. "Karl? Kramer's made a hell of a mistake!"

"We tested him: he knows all about hanging."

"But last night—"

"Ja?"

Ferreira turned slowly to face the hotel. He began walking, and Willie tagged along at his side.

"Why such a reaction, Piet? You knew from last night, didn't you?"

"Hmmm? Huh, I don't know! I'll have to think about it for a minute. Did you search the farm?"

"Nothing, but we know he's got it hidden someplace else."

"How?" The question was asked sharply.

"Well, because," Willie said, then realized how imprudent he was being, "because of—I'm not sure actually."

They mounted the steps. Of course, thought Willie, it had been seeing Piet back again that'd put him right off his guard. Perhaps, on reflection, he had no need to feel he'd dropped a clanger. Now that they were together, it was impossible to see his new friend as part of the conspiracy. Fanciful nonsense.

"Is De Bruin's son here tonight?" he asked at the doorway.

"He's away. Left Wednesday for army camp."

"Oh? Tell you what, Piet—can I buy you one?"

"Ach, there's—"

"You gave me lunch yesterday, hey? Fair's fair."

With something of a smile, Ferreira followed him to the far end of the bar, away from the knot of jolly farmers and the few guests who had now joined them. Willie looked covertly at Swanepoel, wondering what it must be like to have a daughter like that. Wondering what it might be like to have her himself, and imagining the moment when she pulled him down into her. A fantasy like this, deliberately evoked within a few feet of the father, revived a mixture of feeling in him that he'd grown to like. He ordered two Scotches.

"What's up?" Ferreira inquired, trying to read his face. "You look like a cat that smells kippers."

"I smell my transfer, hey? The Lieutenant can fix it for me."

"Down to Trekkersburg? The CID? That's pretty good!"

A move quite so radical as this hadn't occurred to Willie, but suddenly he saw how just that would be. "Uhuh. It's just a shame we didn't get together before, Piet. I want you to know that."

"All the best," said Ferreira, clinking glasses. "I'm sorry, too, but—like they say—opportunity only knocks once."

"Very true," said Willie.

Then he raised his glass and drank. As he did so, his eye caught sight of an invoice tucked into the pocket of Ferreira's white nylon shirt. ᴙƎꙄ ᴙO⊥OW ⊥IᴙU˖ꓷꙄꓷИAᴙꓭ, he read through the thin fabric.

Karl de Bruin sat as invited on the chair in front of the desk in the station commander's office. He watched Kramer close the door, lock it, and return to sit opposite him, arms folded. He gave the appearance of being bewildered.

"Tonight in the bar at Spa-kling Waters hotel, you saw fit to contradict certain remarks made by my colleague. I think you will know which remarks I refer to, Mr. de Bruin."

"Ja; so what? Surely you haven't brought me in here to say that's an offense!" De Bruin laughed uneasily, taking his hat off to twist it by the brim. "The lad had got his head full of cock-and-bull stories."

"How would you know? What are your sources of information?"

"Usual place: newspapers, magazines, things I've read."

"Published in this country?"

"I don't buy papers from—"

"That is a lie!"

De Bruin made to get up.

"Sit down, farmer. Stay down until I've asked my questions. Why did you see fit to make these contradictions?"

"I don't like to hear talk like that, Lieutenant Kramer."

Kramer decided to sneer. "Oh, really? Too gruesome for you, is it?"

The pupils of the man's eyes were like flies caught in chips of amber. His lips—smiling so winningly a moment before—were tightly pressed together. A pulse ticked in his left temple.

"It *was* too gruesome for me. His comments could also have upset people who might think his account was accurate. Upset them very much."

"Ach, I see: sort of part of your duty as a leader in the community?"

"If you like," said De Bruin, tensed against the next move.

"How do you know Constable Boshoff was wrong? What are your sources of information?"

The hat revolved faster in the stubby fingers. "I just know it isn't like that. The state wouldn't allow it. To talk like that is close to treason."

"Treason? You interest me, Mr. de Bruin. What made you say that, may I ask?"

"What? It's nothing—a figure of speech. We all use it."

"Uhuh?"

"That's all. Are you finished?"

"So the state wouldn't allow it," Kramer repeated with deliberate sarcasm; acknowledging the fact that nothing need ever be wasted by adding: "All the state asks is that a condemned prisoner is hanged by the neck until dead."

"In one sense, but the people who do it *are* trained."

"When, where, and how, Mr. de Bruin? From your vast knowledge, you must be able to tell me that!"

With calculated suddenness, Kramer rose and went round to stand over the unhappy man in the chair. De Bruin tried to smile again, blinking against the light overhead, and licking his lips before answering.

"Well, it would have been some time ago, I suppose. Perhaps things have changed, perhaps there have been retirements. I may even be wrong, in which case I'd be happy to apologize to young Willie in private."

"Apologize?"

"Look, I've stood all—"

"Apologize? Kiss and make up, you mean? Then walk out of here? You're under bloody arrest, Mr. de Bruin, as you damn well know!"

De Bruin got slowly to his feet, dropping the hat on the chair behind him. "No, I don't damn well know. You asked for a lift and then started making this fuss. I think it's time you gave me an explanation, young man, or—"

"An explanation? That's your job, Karl."

"I'll not say another word until I'm informed as to what the devil you're playing at, and that's final."

The tawny eyes stayed steady, the big fists bunched; there was no fear in him, and, very obviously, he was tough. Filled with a righteous indignation that only the innocent or the insane would feel their right.

Someone knocked on the door.

"Go away," said Kramer, without looking round.

"It's me, Lieutenant! I've got a report that's urgent!"

De Bruin glanced at the door, giving Kramer an instant in which to lift his truck keys from the desk.

"Wait, I'll be back," he said, and left him standing there. Once in the charge office, Kramer gave his orders. "Nyembezi, by this door. Mamabola and Luthuli, get outside and search that truck. I want everything from it—tools, tow rope, sacks, maps, the lot. And now your problem, my friend?"

Willie pointed at the office door and made I-can't-talk-here signs. He looked fairly canned and rocky on his feet—ready for bed, in fact. But there was something in his expression that made Kramer hasten after him into the garden.

"Piet told a lie and I caught him," he said breathlessly. "Said he'd been down the road while all the time he was in Brandspruit, scared of seeing you until it was over. He wasn't sure if he hadn't buggered it all up. Stayed away as long as he could. You know what?"

"He tipped off De Bruin?"

"Hell, how did you—"

"Guessed, just this instant. The house this afternoon, the way the bugger's been taking it. Last night was it?"

"After you'd gone, sir," said Willie, getting his thumb caught in the Land-Rover's key ring. "Bloody hell—stupid, isn't it? Ja, he said he hadn't meant to, but you'd given him a—"

"What did he say to De Bruin?"

"He swears he only asked a few questions of a general nature, but hanging did come into one of them. This seemed to catch De Bruin's ear and—well—it's a bit of a muddle what came after that. The point is that De Bruin must have had warning. I thought I'd better tell you right away in case you were having trouble."

"What's Ferreira doing now?"

"He's running the party. He wants to say he's very sorry and will make sure nothing else goes wrong. He couldn't help himself. I'm just on my way back there, so if there's a message, I can take it for you. Yee-aaagh, that's better."

Kramer patted him on the shoulder. "A bloody fine job, Willie! I'm going to make special mention of this in my report. But there's a question I should ask."

"Fire away, Lieutenant!"

"With all the drawing you did last night, how much sleep did you get? We've an early start at daybreak looking for the evidence in this case; it really would be a help if one of us could be right on the ball in the morning. I can't tell you what to do with your off-duty hours, but..."

Acute disappointment showed first in Willie's face, then he made some adjustment and shrugged. "Say no more, sir! Boshoff is on his way. Will you be wanting these in the meantime?"

"Ta," said Kramer, taking the Land-Rover keys. "There could be a Bantu incident, I suppose. See you at sunup, Willie. Don't worry; this is being noted as well."

Willie grinned, waved, and set off across the road toward the Haagner household. He walked with his hands in his pockets and whistled off-key. Very briefly, Kramer was ashamed of treating him like a wad of gum that had lost its flavor, and then admitted how much less bother it would be with him safely tucked away. The mean-minded part of himself that did these things was always right.

"Hau, sir, look at this we have found," Mamabola said, hurrying over from De Bruin's truck. "Wrapped in newspaper under the front seat. Still very clean."

It was a loosely wrapped parcel of what felt like books. Kramer took the parcel, gave them orders to continue the search, and walked back into the light cast from the verandah. He paused and checked the date on the paper: it had been sold that morning. Gingerly, he uncovered the contents; as he'd thought, three books. The top one was black and as thick as a hymnal. There was no title on its outside, so he flipped two pages:

A New Handbook on Hanging.

Under which he read:

THE SUNDAY HANGMAN

Being a short Introduction to the fine Art of Execution, containing much useful Information on Neck-breaking, Throttling, Strangling, Asphyxiation, Decapitation, and Electrocution; Data and Wrinkles on Hangmanship; with the late Mr. Hangman Berry's Method and his pioneering List of Drops; to which is added an Account of the Great Nuremberg Hangings, a Ready Reckoner for Hangmen; and many other items of interest by CHARLES DUFF *of Gray's Inn, Barrister-at-Law.*

Next page: Published in 1954 by Andrew Melrose, Ltd., of London, New York, Toronto, Melbourne, Sydney, Cape Town.
Next page:

DEDICATED RESPECTFULLY
to
THE HANGMEN OF ENGLAND
and to similar
CONSTITUTIONAL BULWARKS
everywhere

Preface.
Then a wave of realization reared up out of the sea of alien print, curled over, and crashed down on him. "Jesus, the buggers who taught *us,*" he said.

19

ZONDI AND KRAMER WERE reading in the storeroom. The 25-watt bulb in the ceiling gave a poor light, but neither of them remarked on the fact. They had said nothing at all for a very long time.

"Listen to this, boss," murmured Zondi, making himself more comfortable on the mattress. "It is a section specially marked, and it goes: 'The jury system had been abolished two years before, a victim of its own inadequacy. The jury box had become a relic, now occupied by fashionable women spectators who had cajoled me into giving them a good place. Juries have proved to be a time-wasting luxury and their decisions were often shamefully biased.' Why should this interest him also?"

Kramer, who'd had eyes for nothing but the astonishing *Handbook*, looked up from a detailed description of the scaffold. "Which one says that?"

"*The Vontsteen Case*, by the lawyer who was the judge's—"

"Christ, give me that."

He ruffled through its pages, found underlined a press report on the new block at Central, and then, near the beginning, the very piece which the Widow Fourie had read out to him over the

215

telephone. The sentence about the bandage and gushing blood had been deleted, and *See AP 184* was written in the margin.

"Ah! AP 184?" inquired Zondi, rather smugly. "That is a cross-reference to this one, *Executioner: Pierrepoint*, which is by Boss Albert Pierrepoint, for many years England's master hangman. He is answering questions under oath at a royal inquiry, and his words are: 'I've never seen any blood.' He was truly a great man this, and very kind."

"Anything else marked in it?"

"Many, many things. His father called the work a 'highly skilled mystery.' It is impossible to hang more than two at once properly. There was 'no movement on the body,' he says, in the many hundreds of people—"

"It looks new," interrupted Kramer, reaching out. "When was it published?"

The date given was 1974—a little late in the scheme of things.

"And yours, boss?"

"You mean is it any use? Certainly! Gets a bit jokey at times, like you'd expect from those eccentric bastards, but the facts are all there. Here, look at this thing at the back."

There was a table of thirteen columns of figures; all you had to do was pick the one giving the weight of the prisoner, and read off the appropriate drop—which you then modified according to build, helped by such information as that a scrofulous neck (one having TB of the lymphatic glands) was apt to tear easily.

"Hau, that is mad to print so much!" Zondi exclaimed, taking the book from him. "What kind of people are these?"

"Read it and see if you can find out," said Kramer, getting up off the ammunition box.

"Lieutenant?"

"I want to make a quick call and then get back to De Bruin. Easier he tells us the rest than we try to work it out. Makes the mind bloody boggle, doesn't it?"

Feeling very detached, Kramer went out into the charge office and found there a man bleeding from a superficial spear wound. The three Bantu constables were grouped around him.

"This man reports a fight at a beer party, sir," Mamabola said, coming to attention.

"Big one?"

"Thirty to forty persons involved."

"How far away? Any firearms?"

"Five kilometers—no firearms."

"You want any issued?"

Mamabola glanced at Luthuli, who was testing the weight of his knobkerrie in the palm of his left hand. "No, thank you, sir. Goodluck says that could make the people all turn on us. It would be better with just the club."

"Off you go, then," Kramer said, tossing over the Land-Rover keys. "Take the walkie-talkie in case there are more than that by now, and you can't put a lid on it. Sergeant Zondi will be listening this end."

Luthuli, the veteran of such affairs, gave a casual order and they trooped out, taking the injured man with them. After making a scribbled entry in the Occurrence Book, Kramer put through his call to Trekkersburg.

"It's Tromp, Doc," he said. "What's news?"

"Ach, you wouldn't believe it, man!" Strydom said. "This television business is no joke. You remember how they used to say it would turn everyone antisocial? Not a bloody hope! I don't think I've ever seen so many cups of coffee made in a whole year before, and it hasn't been even a week yet. And yours? Anything come up yet?"

"Ever heard," said Kramer, turning the book over to read the title, "of Albert Pierrepoint?"

"Now, there was an expert!" enthused Strydom. "A man after my own heart! You should read what he says about the Americans and their standard five-foot drop and four-coil cowboy knot. *Twenty-six* minutes one poor bugger had to strangle. His own lowest time was nine seconds from entering the cell to the snap of the rope. The only annoying thing is that he never goes far enough into the detail."

"You've read his book, then?"

"Ja, I got it from the library some time ago. As a matter of fact, I noticed it was out only yesterday, when I was getting a note on the machine hanging to you on the Telex. That piece from the paper, remember? What were your own reactions to that?"

Kramer's detachment detached itself. "That wasn't a cutting sent to you?" he growled. "You might have—"

"In 1926?" Strydom laughed. "What kind of teen-ager do you

think I was? It comes from a collection called *By the Neck*."

"You didn't consider, though, that the existence of these books might be relevant?" Kramer said, dismissing his oversight.

"Hey?" There was a pause. "Ach, never. The examples they give are inadequate. Er—have you found someone who has read them?"

"Uhuh. And another book, too, by a barrister called Duff."

"Duff's *Handbook?* Man, isn't that a hoot?"

"It's meant to be funny?"

"Of course! My favorite part is where he suggests that there should be an exam for—"

"Funny? A lot of bloody nonsense?"

"What would be the point of that?" Strydom said in some bemusement. "If the facts he gives weren't accurate, then his whole—"

"Almighty God, Doc!"

"—sarcasm would be for nothing."

Kramer found himself actually speechless. He tried to articulate a home truth, but the sound wouldn't come.

"Ohhhh, *I* see what's got your Tampax in a knot," Strydom said with a chuckle. "You've found somebody with Duff and you think it might be him? Before you make a fool of yourself, Trompie, let me tell you something you must have overlooked."

"Ja?"

"That's a bloody *abolitionists'* book, man!"

Kramer gave Zondi the walkie-talkie set and a curt instruction, and went back into the station commander's office. He slammed the Pierrepoint autobiography down on the desk in front of De Bruin. The farmer turned white.

"Jesus, you silly bugger," Kramer said cheerfully, sitting down in the chair behind the desk and putting his feet up. "Look what I've found in your truck! You shouldn't have worried these books were banned, because they're not."

De Bruin swallowed, and tried to hide his confusion behind a weak smile.

"They're not?"

"To make sure, I've only this minute checked with the man in

Trekkersburg. A total misunderstanding all round, although I will make a full apology for my part in it."

"Well, naturally I wouldn't..."

"Good! And I mustn't forget to return your keys."

Kramer slid them to the midpoint of the desk. His strategy was crude, but, very roughly, it came down to this: the complete innocent would be only too glad to grab them and get the hell out; the sinner, for want of a better word, would suspect a trick. De Bruin squashed his hat onto the back of his head, and tucked his thumbs behind his braces—as if half of him wanted to go and the other half to stay. Very curious.

The keys remained untouched.

"Is that all, Lieutenant?"

"Definitely."

"I'm still lost to know quite why my remarks caused this reaction."

"Prisons Act, Number Eight of 1959."

"But that—" De Bruin began, as though he knew equally well that the act merely made it an offense to publish false information about prisons.

"Ja?"

"Doesn't mean a lot to a layman."

"Ah!" said Kramer. "Then take my advice and don't concern yourself with such dreary matters. Haven't you got a party waiting? Hell, I've kept you long enough!"

"Trying to get rid of me?" De Bruin joked without much conviction.

Kramer thought he caught a whiff of what was going on then: the man seemed to be acting compulsively, to be forcing himself, not only to prolong the converstion, but to take it into deeper waters as well. More than one self-confession had come his way with this sort of preamble.

"Not before you've had your compensation!" he said, bringing his feet down. "Now, I know Frikkie keeps a bottle of the same in here somewhere."

"Well, I won't say no," chuckled De Bruin, sitting again.

Fortunately Luthuli had seen to it that the two tumblers were clean, and the brandies were poured in a trice. That was another thing: for a churchgoer, De Bruin was being fairly intemperate, and his strained look had never left him.

"Cheers," Kramer said.

"All the best."

The brandy became a momentary preoccupation.

"So you must be an abolitionist, Mr. De Bruin? It explains why you're so chock-full of information."

"In a way, I suppose I am. I've got an interest, certainly."

"Uhuh."

"I—er—knew someone involved once."

"You don't say?"

"A youngster."

"In this district?"

"On the coast. Durban, as a matter of fact. Or, more exactly, I knew his mother—lodged with her during the war, while I was working at the post office. Tragic. It was terrible what it did to her."

"Uhuh?"

De Bruin stalled, sipping at his drink. His eyes had changed: the hardness had gone—now they were wary and expectant. Kramer, who had been under the impression he'd been holding the rod, realized abruptly that he was, in fact, the tin fish. The man was trying for a rise out of him.

"Of course, Mr. de Bruin, in my job you can't afford to consider that side of it too much. It's true as well that the people we get to know best are the victims, and we see how little mercy went into their big step into the hereafter."

"I can appreciate that, Lieutenant," replied De Bruin, relaxing before his eyes.

The transformation was striking; in a couple of blinks, the farmer was all Ferreira had described him as being: an easygoing-looking man, with a kindly mouth and the air of a peacemaker. De Bruin downed the rest of his drink, stood up, and held out his hand. "Must be getting back, as you said. At least you know where to come now if you're wanting to speak to the local expert on hanging, hey?"

"Is that what Piet Ferreira told you?" Kramer asked softly.

The hand trembled.

"Is that why you hid those books in your car?"

"You've—you've only just said there was no law against having them!" De Bruin blustered.

"True. But there are other laws concerning what you *do* with them, sir."

"Do with them? I'd lent them to somebody."

"In Witklip?"

"Brandspruit. I picked them up last night—"

"And wrapped them in this morning's newspaper?"

Kramer wasn't sure at all what was going on, but knew that he'd turned the game in his favor, and that—very soon—he'd have all the answers.

"It's no good." De Bruin sighed wearily, letting the hand drop and his shoulders slump. "I'm not cut out for this sort of thing."

"You lie very badly."

"I didn't exactly come prepared, Lieutenant."

"I can see that. I can also see that you're a man who isn't accustomed to trying to pervert the course of justice."

"I'm not trying to do that! God forbid!"

"This time, a full explanation?"

De Bruin nodded, returning once again to his chair.

A cockroach scuttled behind the dagga sacks. The night closed in tight, squeezing all that mattered into that small circle of yellow light. The horse clip-clopped in its stable.

"Where do I begin?" De Bruin began, "I'm in such a muddle—I didn't sleep for worrying over which course would be right to take."

Kramer gave him another double tot. It went ignored.

"Yesterday evening I called to see Piet Ferreira to finalize tonight's arrangements—I'm chairman of the party committee. He took me into his office and behaved so strangely, asking the most peculiar questions, that I tackled him—pretty hard, I'm afraid. One way or another, I found out that you were in Witklip looking for a man who knew about hanging, and that you'd decided it must be me."

"Just keep talking," Kramer encouraged him, leaning back with his fingers laced behind his head.

"Probably things would have worked out very differently if

he hadn't also told me who you worked for. I really don't know. But as soon as Piet said Security, I realized someone might be caused a lot of unnecessary distress."

As soon as De Bruin said that, Kramer's stomach fell through a trap on a very long drop.

"Because," the farmer went on, "whatever his other failings, nobody on earth could accuse Gysbert Swanepoel of any form of disloyalty to his country. I was going to say just 'a friend,' but I have to trust you, and give you the reasons behind the foolish things I've done today. At first, when I got home and talked things over with the wife, we decided to let you get on with it. Gysbert has never spoken about his obsession to anyone else, and there seemed little chance of him becoming involved. Then Piet rang me and said there would be a search of my farm—he still sounded very scared of me, which neither of us could understand—and that started me worrying. There was always the chance, you see, that you'd try other farms if you found nothing on mine. Lettie—my wife—suggested Piet's story sounded too incredible to be true, so we compromised. Did you go to my place today, by the way?"

"We did."

"Had she left everything so you'd not break—"

"She had," Kramer admitted. "Your compromise was?"

"To wait until Gysbert had left for the hotel this afternoon, and to remove his three precious books."

"It would only have been a matter of time before—"

"I see that now, Lieutenant. I can see that nothing could really have stopped you reaching him, but I felt—I felt it was a chance worth taking. Then, of course, I had to spoil everything by choking Willie off in the bar."

"Uhuh; why did you do that?"

"I *had* to. I had to say something before Gysbert went off the rails—you've no idea how much that kind of talk upsets him. It was the worst dilemma I've ever been in, God knows! And—huh—I thought I'd pulled it off, too."

De Bruin sipped a little of his brandy. The cockroach still scuttled; the horse had possibly dozed off. Except for that one scratching noise, like the first grooves on an old record, the night was deathly quiet.

"Now I have to explain why I did this, and I only hope you'll see some excuse for me. Gysbert and I have always been friends, dating right back to junior school. I was one of the quieter boys, and he was even quieter. This gave us something in common, understand? So when the war broke out, and we were wanted to help out with essential services in Durban, it was natural we should go together. We found a room to share in the house of a young Italian lady, whose husband had been interned. There were quite a few other lads there—from other parts, of course— and the atmosphere was very friendly. But Gysbert couldn't adjust to city life. The girls made him even more shy than the ones back here, and he dodged getting in a crowd whenever he could. As far as I was concerned, having so many new people to meet was a pure pleasure, and I changed quite a lot. This meant poor old Gysbert got left on his own with his books a lot of the time—he'd always been a big reader, and the public library was the one place he would go to. The lady seemed to understand him and his reasons for being the way he was, and often invited him into her parlor. Actually, we were entitled to the use of it, but you know what I mean. We all loved that lady—she was like a big sister to us all, but I think Gysbert loved her like a mother, his own having never much liked him. One night, I remember, he came up to bed and he'd been crying; you could see how red his eyes were, and I'm sure she had comforted him, because he talked to me for a long while about how wonderful she was. I was in bed with the flu. Ja, that was it. Then the end of the war came and, one by one, we started packing up. I only had to give a week's notice, but Gysbert's was a month. Something like that. Well, he came home, and got on with his job on the farm. His parents died—very close to each other—and he was left with no one. I admit I was the one who put the idea of marrying Annie Louw into his mind. With some men, especially Gysbert's sort, a widow can be ideal. But, man, he was so formal! Did his courting the old style, going round to her place and sitting at the table until the little candle he'd brought had burned down. Annie used to whisper to me on Sunday and say she wished she could put some saltpeter in it! They hit it off better than anyone had expected, and little Suzanne was born. Then came the first of the tragedies, when Annie died—must've got TB from one of the natives. We'll never know. Gysbert went into a terrible depression."

The cockroach stopped moving.

"Then, out of the blue, when Lettie and I were despairing, this lady arrived at the hotel to spend a long weekend, bringing her son along. She also had with her her husband and her brother. She and Gysbert had a long talk together in the first afternoon, and that did him all the good in the world. You know, I've often wondered if he'd written to her, asking for her help. Anyway, had she only told us they were coming, I wouldn't have had to give old man Ferreira such a blasting. He didn't—ach, it doesn't matter. Years went by without us hearing from the family again, then all of a sudden, one Sunday when Gysbert and me were picking up the paper after church, there they were again—and in terrible trouble. Ja, the youngster I was telling you about."

"What had he done?"

"The allegation was murder. He had just been brought up in the regional court to be sent for trial. Gysbert wanted to go rushing down there, then he decided this would be taking too much on himself. Finally, what he did was to offer to pay for the best defense in Natal, and I loaned him the money—all paid back now. But things went wrong and the boy was sent up to Pretoria. An appeal was useless, and there was nothing left but prayer. I used to go over to Swartboom three or four times a week with my Bible. That's when his obsession began: he told me he had to know what kind of death the boy would suffer, whether it would be merciful and quick. He dwelled on this so much he started taking trips to bars which prison warders frequented—or rather, he'd do this when delivering his venison to order. We get a call, you see, if they're going to have a special menu or whatever, and we shoot—"

"Please, carry on with this business of the bars," Kramer asked him, wondering if the wall was thin enough for Mickey to hear all this.

"That was a terrible mistake. He must have heard stories like young Willie was telling, because one night I went over and found him beaten up badly. He'd attacked some man. If you don't mind, I'm not going into the details."

"I get the point, Mr. de Bruin."

"I don't know whose idea it was to try and find out from books—perhaps it was his. His very first one was a Benjamin Bennett—you know the Cape crime reporter?—and he gave a very good account which set Gysbert's mind at ease. The day they hanged the boy, he spent the whole time by himself in the veld. We had him home that night, and he told us he had seen it happen, just like in a vision. It had been quick and clean; the boy had walked to the gallows singing 'Ave Maria.' He was at peace with himself for months after that. Then he came across, in some secondhand bookshop in Durban, the smallest of those books you found in my truck. Night after night I sat and argued with him, while he chewed over the shocking things that were in it. He withdrew into himself and there wasn't anything I could do. That Bennett book was an old one, you see, and by then Gysbert knew all the figures. He said he had begun to believe what a prison warder had told him, and blamed this on the 600 percent increase in hangings between 1947 and 1970. Suddenly, he went very silent on the subject, which worried me. I tried to get some account to contradict what he'd heard, but—huh!—we come back to the Prisons Act. It was almost becoming an obsession with me, because all the time poor little Suzanne was suffering; weeks would pass and he'd hardly notice her. She so craved affection. Then Lettie had a letter back from a bookshop we'd written to months before, offering us the book you have on this desk here. We bought it on spec and it was one of the best things we ever did. Let me show you."

De Bruin took up the book and turned to the preface, holding his finger against a paragraph he wanted Kramer to read:

"I operated, on behalf of the State, what I am convinced was the most humane and the most dignified method of meting out death to a delinquent—however justified or unjustified the allotment of death may be—and on behalf of humanity I trained other nations to adopt the British system of execution."

"Got that."

"And now, on page seventy-nine it should be—yes, just listen: 'Travel today seems to imply only long journeys—to *South Africa* or the Mediterranean or the Riv-something—*and I have made all these trips in my time.*'"

"Which doesn't necessarily mean—" Kramer began automatically, then stopped.

"Perhaps not, but the arguments are strongly in favor of it being the case, and Gysbert is able to take great comfort from the words of this man. They give him the authority to reject anything he finds unacceptable."

Kramer was staring at the master hangman's blurb on the back of the book, which De Bruin was still holding:

> *Capital punishment, in my view, achieved nothing but revenge.*

Suddenly, he'd had enough of books and of stories that didn't quite match in all their details. There was some irony in knowing that Swanepoel was guilty, without having any real evidence to prove it, but the final solution seemed only a hair's-breadth away now. He stood up.

"Do you believe me? Do you see what I'm trying to get across?" asked De Bruin.

"I believe what you've allowed yourself to believe, Mr. de Bruin. You have certainly told me most of the truth."

"What is that supposed to mean, damn you!" De Bruin exploded. "I've put all my cards on the table; now what about yours? Have I your assurance that, having heard the full story, you will not pursue any pointless inquiries in that direction?"

The temptation was too much for Kramer—and the truth would emerge soon enough; he palmed his small batch of photographs, just as that oaf had done back in the bar on Tuesday morning, and then dealt them out, one at a time, face upward on the desktop.

"Those are my cards," he said, and went to call Willie to action stations.

But Mr. and Mrs. Haagner, just returned from the barbecue, having been the last to leave, said they'd only that minute looked in on his room and he hadn't been there. Although, as a giggly Mrs. Haagner conceded, he might have been outside making a weewee. Kramer went to Willie's room and found a small magazine propped up at the foot of the bed to show off an old-fashioned nude to advantage. He took the magazine and brushed passed the Haagners, not saying good night. He checked to see if the Chev was there, and it was. He broke into a run and went round to the yard, yanking open the stable door and finding the stall vacated. He heard a telephone ringing. He saw, through the barred window of the station commander's office, De Bruin answer it. He sprinted to the window and heard the man groan.

"Quick! Who is it?"

An eternity later, Karl de Bruin clattered the receiver into its cradle, and stumbled over to hold onto the bars in a state of near-collapse.

"Suzanne. Pa came home, found her door unlocked. She said must've been servant girl. Hit her, wouldn't believe her. She said policeman had been there. Hit her. Swore it. Hit her, went looking. Found Willie. Hit Willie. Hit her. Only got to phone now, bleeding. Willie gone. Game truck. Said he was going to—going to ... Willie."

"Ambulance!" Kramer shouted over his shoulder.

As he raced to the front, the Chev's lights came on and it roared toward him, slewing round, the passenger door swinging open.

"Let's go, boss," said Zondi.

20

LIKE A SKULL ON a dunghill, the great white stone shone in the moonlight, becoming smaller every minute behind them. The Chev howled and slithered and clawed its way up to the pass. No dust showed in its headlights.

"Ten-minute start," said Kramer.

"Five, more like."

"Never make it."

"Before?"

"The fork down the other side."

Bracing himself against the movement of the car, Kramer lit two cigarettes and stuck one of them in Zondi's mouth. Then he flicked on the map-reading light and held the magazine beneath it.

"Dear God," he murmured. "This is so old she could be his bloody mother."

"Sorry, boss?"

"Sick."

"Not your fault, Lieutenant," grunted Zondi, missing the point and a sheer drop simultaneously. "You must take it easy, or you will do a foolish thing. What is the procedure when we overtake this vehicle?"

"Huh!"

"It is a good road for a puncture."

"Trust a kaffir!"

"Every time," added Zondi.

And they laughed.

It was the release Kramer had needed. "The procedure," he said, "is simple. If he won't pull up, then I'll do as you suggest and take his tires out." He placed his Smith & Wesson .38 on the map shelf in readiness.

"From the back or side?"

"Either. Willie will be all right—the doors and walls on that thing are so thick they'll stop any spare slugs."

He didn't go into what might happen if the truck, losing a tire at high speed, left the road; that smattered of trying to think too far ahead.

"Let us hope that his gallows place is far from here," said Zondi, making careful use of the ashtray. "The longer he drives, the better our chance will be."

"While you're at it, let's hope I'm somewhere near right with my bloody theory."

"That he must do the deed properly?"

"Uhuh. It depends on how far off the rails he's gone, I realize that, but I'm certain all the fiddling about is essential to him. He's got to weigh—"

"But what charge, boss?"

"I'll let you guess," said Kramer, and outlined what had happened after the visit to Swartboom.

They were nearing the crest of the pass by the time he had finished. There was still no dust suspended in the beam of the headlights, and unless they reached the fork on the far side in time to see some telltale sign of his passage, their chances of ever catching up would be halved.

"Well, Mickey?"

"Can the fire be blamed?" Zondi replied enigmatically.

Then he gunned the Chev into the final S-bend before the top and the plunge into the long descent.

Willie Boshoff lay on his back, cold sober and terrified. The floor beneath him bounced, tilted sideways, and rolled him over again, smashing his face against something hard in the dark.

Bound hand and foot, he could no nothing to save himself, and back he rolled again, tasting the blood and mucus from his broken nose. He retched.

The truck changed up. It began to move faster, more smoothly.

He should never have done it. The transfer would have been his without any extras. He should have told the Lieutenant instead of pretending to go off to bed.

His mind was repeating things. Playing over the way Swanepoel had questioned him when the Lieutenant and De Bruin had left. Making him see and hear again those little giveaways which had given him his idea. The Lieutenant can nail the hangman, he had thought, but I'll be the one who gets the credit for his assistant. All I have to do is ask his daughter a few questions.

The truck—it sounded like a Bedford—slipped back into a lower gear, and Willie rolled again, the victim of his own inertia.

He had never got near her.

He'd never know what had made him mad enough to risk what he had done; never. Never know why it had been something he didn't want to share. But to keep to himself, as he acted compulsively, slyly, stealing away on the horse and climbing in through the open bedroom window. To lose all sense of time when he discovered, left lying around quite openly, a leather demonstration carrying case of the kind that traveling salesmen use. A case packed neatly with all the tools of a terrible trade—the very same case and contents as described by Dr. Strydom in his Telex: the rope, with metal eye and rubber washer; a wrist strap and leg strap, unused; the black cap; fine copper wire; packthread; tape measure; two-foot rule; pliers; spare shackle.

The truck was slowing down. And down. And coming to a stop.

Pray God, a roadblock. Willie, who had recovered consciousness only momentarily, felt a greater darkness overwhelm him before he could find out.

Zondi snapped off the Chev's headlights.

"Why the—"

"Down there, boss! At one o'clock!"

Kramer looked and saw, far below them on the valley floor, a pair of stationary headlights. An instant later, they were switched off. No other lights shone anywhere.

"But that's bloody miles before the fork, man!"

"It must be where he has his place."

"Rubbish! How could he build on reserve land?"

"Some building that is there already?"

"That isn't used?"

Zondi gave all his attention to the road. His speed had dropped considerably, for the moonlight tended to play optical tricks with the sharp bends.

"Use full lights and just belt it," ordered Kramer.

"So he can see we follow him?"

"Wouldn't know it was us. No, wait."

The Chev crunched to a halt on the verge, held in check by the handbrake until they could resolve their dilemma: on the one hand, to continue in hot pursuit might be to precipitate events, while on the other, a more cautious approach might get them there too late.

"I think he must have seen Willie off already," Kramer said softly. "He's stopped now to set up his side show. We've no idea of how long ago he left the barbecue party."

"Or he has already seen our lights," Zondi suggested.

"Not a chance. He was facing the wrong way to get anything this high in his rear-view mirrors. Bugger, *why* has he stopped?"

Now that they had been in the dark for a minute or so, their night vision was improving; the valley was beginning to roughen up as areas of different tone became more distinct. There was a crescent of fairly pronounced shadow about two hundred yards to the right of where the truck's lights had gone out.

"Hau, pillbox!" said Zondi, using English.

"And 'pillbox' to you, my son."

"No, boss! That is what throws the shadow. The pillbox the English soldiers poked their guns from—round, with small windows."

"Of course! Ja, I can see it now."

The ubiquitous bloody pillbox; so much a part of the landscape in parts of Natal, you never noticed them.

"Which is where he's got his scaffold, Mickey!"

"Maybe he just wants to hide on the side road."

"No, man; that's got to be where it is! Can you think of a better spot?"

Everything was making sense again. For a time, Kramer's theory of a cool, impersonal hangman had been irreconcilable with the bitter, impulsively violent character of Gysbert Swanepoel. One of the chief reasons for this being the actual evidence they'd had of a humane, carefully conducted ritualism, which didn't go at all with what Swanepoel was alleged to be capable of when crossed. And yet, in this very conflict of opposites, lay the knowledge that Willie was still very much alive.

"There's no hurry," said Kramer, lighting another couple of Luckies. "We're not dealing with one man here, but two. The way he knocked Willie down was his straightforward, surface reaction to a problem—he avenged himself in a way not uncommon among country folk. Now his obsession with capital punishment has taken over—there can be no doubt he caught Willie in the act—and he cannot imagine a policeman being made to pay the ultimate penalty for such a crime. So he has decided to execute him, deluding himself there is nothing personal involved in the matter. You follow?"

Zondi's grunt was noncommittal. He put his hand back on the handbrake handle.

"I know what you're thinking, man—that he's just a bloody killer—but if he saw himself that way, then why all this complicated fuss? Because he needs to delude himself he's no more a killer than the state executioner! And for the delusion to work, he has to kill without murdering. What's the only way you can do that?"

"Legitimately? But his—"

"By not using a murder weapon, for Christ's sake! He can't use a gun or a knife or his hands—it has *got* to be the gallows. It doesn't stop there either, because to sustain the delusion, the deed has to be taken very seriously, with the proper attention being paid to every detail, just like the real thing. And every time he succeeds in carrying out a perfect execution, he feels more certain in his mind about what happened to Vasari. That's really what lies behind all this."

"Why should he care so much?" Zondi said, releasing the handbrake.

"The old, old story: he didn't see what happened to the sodding victim. You have; you've seen the pictures. You know that old man was just as alive as the little bastard who shoved him over the railing—Vasari."

The Chev picked up speed as it free-wheeled on down the slopes of the ridge.

"A long drop," observed Zondi.

"Ja, and they say he screamed all the way down onto the rocks. Didn't die either, until the coolies had called the ambulance. I reckon we'll make it with five minutes to spare at this rate."

"Yebo?"

"Has to check the traps and fix the slack. Huh, might even have the whole night, if he's decided to stretch the rope properly, but I wouldn't like to bet on that."

"Maybe Boss Willie will give trouble as well, increasing our chance."

"Oh, wog of little faith," Kramer sighed, quite certain the right decision had been made—and for the right reasons.

Then he sat back to see what he could remember of the only pillbox he'd ever bothered to look at closely. The height would have been ideal—a good fifteen feet, even before you started to dig a pit into the earth floor—and there'd been stout wooden beams across the top. The windows and door had been bricked up, but not very effectively, and a good kick had given him access. These windows would also be bricked up, of course, to prevent any light from showing, and presumably the door would be some sort of restoration job. This left the roof as his most likely means of entry, providing it, too, was falling to bits like the other one. And that was some provision. With another sigh, Kramer realized he was saddled with a problem that had sorely taxed his forefathers, and that had seldom been solved without a considerable quantity of dynamite. That was, of course, why the bloody things were still about.

Willie came around again and knew that he had been moved. He was sitting, propped up in a corner, with something made of black material over his head. The change of position had relieved the congestion in his nostrils—he could feel the snot and blood sliding down his chin—and he could, very faintly, smell things. There was the shop freshness of the material, and, coming through it, an odor of disinfectant. He identified this as Jeyes Fluid, with which prisons and station-house lockups were traditionally saturated. The association paralyzed him.

Then a dark shape moved aside from his line of vision, allowing a bright, if slightly orange, light to penetrate the cloth and make it partially transparent. Like a child trying to cheat at a party game, Willie could see very little through it—except for the silhouette of something that hung between him and the light source. It was a noose.

A noose, Willie noted, with no slack taken up in the rope and neatly tied with packthread; a strangler's noose.

He screamed, hoarsely.

"Nobody outside could hear you, even if there was anyone there," said the voice of Gysbert Swanepoel, looming with the return of the dark shape. "I'm sorry you have to have the cap on so early, but I haven't had time to make my usual preparations. I didn't want you unduly upset."

Willie tried to kick at him.

"Don't make it harder for yourself, Boshoff. I've never had to tie anyone up before, and I'm hoping you'll try to be a man when the time comes. Your execution will be at midnight, by the way, right on the dot."

When Willie heard that, he stopped feeling terrified. He ceased to believe in what was happening. He sniffed and—as delicately as he could—spat.

"Shall we talk?" Swanepoel asked. "I'm afraid I have no assistance, so I have to play several roles at once. Let us suppose for the next few minutes that I am your kindly warder."

"That rope's wrong," said Willie, amazing himself.

"In what way?"

"No drop."

"Ah, but there is a drop, I assure you. I had you on the mealie scales before we came here. Eleven stone would give a standard American drop, as it happens—rather a fluke—but I've added three inches extra for reasons you may not want me to go into."

235

"Can't see it," said Willie.

"It's tucked away, Boshoff. Don't worry, please; all will go off very smoothly, and you will feel no pain."

"What about the stretch? Is the rope stretched?"

A large hand patted Willie on the knee. "Trust me, Boshoff, trust me. I use a steel cable for linkage—a little refinement of my own, as my procedures cannot be as leisurely. You seem to be showing a much more intelligent attitude tonight. What you said today really upset me. I can't tell you how much."

"Is that why you've got me here?"

The dark shape walked away, making the floor tremble at each pace, then returned.

"Ja, I suppose it must be, Boshoff—although I couldn't have done anything about it, if you hadn't given me an excuse."

The man was either completely mad or the Lieutenant so terribly wrong that he deserved to die in Willie's place. Mercifully, there was no reality in any of this—in fact, playing along with Swanepoel was like talking in a dream in which you felt perfectly safe.

"What excuse? What have I done?"

"You know quite well, Boshoff. You must have been that police friend of Tommy McKenzie's he threatened me with. Deny you decided to step into his shoes, having heard all his stories."

"And do what?"

"Fornicate with my daughter. Teach her evil, take advantage of a condition that had already caused me enough concern. To commit, in short, Constable Boshoff, a statutory rape."

"No, I bloody didn't!"

"Oh?" replied Swanepoel, without any real interest. "Then I shall have to use my alternative charge—in your presence at least. When I came on you in my bedroom, you attacked me: the charge under which you were convicted was one of house-breaking with aggravating circumstances."

"You're the judge, too?"

"For the meantime, until this matter comes before a proper court."

"I don't understand that," said Willie. "And you don't seem

to understand that we're on to you. We know all about everything! Oh, ja, and if you touch me, then the Lieutenant will know for certain who the hangman is!"

Swanepoel laughed; the sound was mocking. "I hope you're right," he said. "It's taken them long enough. Would you like me to be the chaplain now? Five minutes are all you have left."

The Chev stopped on the road where the track led off up to the truck and, a couple of hundred yards beyond it, the pillbox. If Swanepoel heard its engine, then he would simply suppose it had passed on by.

"Get on the walkie-talkie and tell Goodluck and his lot to drop everything and come down here fast!" Kramer told Zondi, opening his door. "All I'm concentrating on is getting Willie out to begin with, and then we might be able to do with some additional help."

"I could create a diversion, boss."

"Mickey, I'm sorry, but you're not up to it, man. You have already done a fantastic job. Okay?"

Zondi reached over the back of his seat for the radio.

"It would take you," Kramer said, impatient to go but unable to leave him like this, "five minutes to reach the bloody truck, Mick. Be reasonable!"

He felt a dry palm squeeze his fist briefly.

With his throat constricted so it hurt, Kramer turned and sprinted up the track, keeping on the grass. As he drew near the truck, his hand brought the revolver's nose up, just in case. But the cab was empty and the back locked, with the great latch snug behing its cleats. He reached a barbed-wire fence and looked for where Swanepoel had passed through with his burden. This wasted time, so he vaulted over before finding out.

"Priorities," he muttered with conscious grim humor. "Probably hasn't got the drop right yet—no bloody table to check it against. Hey ho for the Witklip computer."

The slope leading up to the pillbox, squat and evil against the moon, was treacherous with loose stone. He tripped and went down hard, making one hell of a clatter.

The absurd, wild, fervent hope that help was on its way had

taken possession of Willie. If only he could keep Swanepoel talking long enough, the nightmare would suddenly—and very sweetly—come to an end.

"You mustn't think I haven't my eye on the clock," Swanepoel said abruptly. "The law is very particular in these matters."

"You're the law? If you're the law, then what did you charge Ringo Roberts under? Tell me that!"

"Murder."

A starburst of pain in Willie's nose made him pause, then he gamely went on: "But that's where you're wrong, see? The law decided that the charge should be withdrawn."

"Ach, not *that* murder," Swanepoel said casually, moving away to make a final inspection of the noose.

Willie watched his shape move the rubber washer thing up and down. He also became aware that he had wet himself. This had been a serious offense in the home, and it made him feel very ashamed.

"Which murder?" he demanded angrily.

"My son's"

"Who?"

"Anthony Michael."

"Jesus!"

"I knew you wouldn't know that, and, for obvious reasons, I don't mind you hearing it from me now. I like to tell people when I have the chance, which isn't often. You know, I saw him once, as a matter of fact—I think she brought him for that purpose. Perhaps to see the land of his father, so he'd have it in his mind always, because she was like that. A strange, lonely, beautiful woman, who knew me like no other person has ever done. She also knew what was right. She knew that we were of two cultures, and our lives would run on along separate lines. All she ever asked in return was that baby, and I gave life. I gave life, I can take life; I am a man!"

Loudly, mockingly, Swanepoel laughed. His insanity was established, but through it ran a steel wire of logic that suddenly snapped taut, choking off the breath.

"Have you a father?" he asked, laying that great hand on Willie's left shoulder.

Willie shook his head.

"Good! I thought not—it is also something I always try to find out. The father suffers terribly, I can promise you. I suffered even when seeing my man-child, who had been nothing to me but sperm I had spilled, and knowing we would always live apart. Which was nonsense! Nonsense! I had made love—I loved that woman—I had made love, and they killed my love. She went away broken. I've never understood why others could not see he was mine. I wondered if the man guessed; I caught him watching me strangely. At times, I've been sure that Karl guessed, but he would never say so. Tenderness is not widely accepted; he would expect me to bear the stain of sin. It wasn't sin. I had to stay on until we were sure it had happened. 'I'm pregnant,' she whispered, 'you must go now. I have part of you for always.' She crossed herself. I wept. I used to be a proper crybaby!"

Desperately, Willie said, "But Vasari *wasn't* murdered!"

Swanepoel grabbed him by the shoulders, dragging him to his feet. "Wasn't he? What happened to him? Can you tell me that?"

"He—he was hanged."

"Ah! A subtle difference? I'm glad you have spotted it! You know why?"

Again Willie shook his head, dizzy with fear and nausea.

"Because it is one I use myself," said Swanepoel, laughing very loudly. "Let's see the bastards talk their way out of *that!*"

There wasn't a sound in the shadow of the pillbox. Kramer circled it, moving in a crouch, absolutely silently. The windows had been bricked up and so, it appeared, had the door.

Then he came upon the thorn tree. It grew right beside the thick wall, branching off asymmetrically, before heaving its canopy over the top. With luck, it would make a prickly but adequate scaling ladder. He holstered his revolver, reached up, and dragged himself into the lowest fork. Testing each branch

239

carefully, he progressed from there, rising barely six inches at a time, his hands sticky with the tears made by the thorns. He kept pausing to wipe them dry, for fear of doing the butterfingers when the moment came to draw. A dry branch cracked under his testing tug.

He froze.

There wasn't another sound.

Swanepoel stopped laughing. He pinned Willie hard against the wall. He turned him round and took hold of his wrists.

"So you see, I *want* them to catch me," he whispered in Willie's ear. "I've always wanted that, ever since Roberts. He was the only one I hid, because I wasn't ready then. I didn't have an impressive enough number. But they were such fools! Such fools! I left the cap as a clue last time; did they find it?"

Blubbering, Willie managed to say, "They'll—they'll hang you, too!"

"Of course, Boshoff. How else will I ever know the truth? Ever know what happened to my man-child? They won't tell me themselves and the books all contradict. The Englishman I respect; he may even, as Karl says, have taught our hangman his skills. But when? How long ago? He has retired—has our man retired also? What of these stories of the white pickax handle? Of the short drops? The drops too long? When that trap opens, just before I die, I will know. Nobody will stop me."

He brought Willie away from the wall.

"But—oh, Jesus save me!—it—it won't work with me, Mr. Swanepoel! I did nothing capital! You won't be able to claim that in court. Make fools of them! *Please stop this! Please let me go!* I'll give you anything! I've never even been with a woman!"

"It's best not to, Willie. Hold still while I undo your feet; only beasts should be dragged to their death. You must stop struggling now and show dignity. Walk tall like my boy did; make me proud of you."

Panting, pouring with a stink of sweat as sweet as rotting flesh, Zondi staggered as far as the truck and could go no farther. The walkie-talkie, which had proved useless because of the high ridge between him and Luthuli's party, was still clutched in his hand. He tossed it down.

There was no sign of the Lieutenant up at the pillbox.

Zondi looked into the cab of the truck. The open door and the keys in the ignition switch indicated that Swanepoel had abandoned it in a hurry. Perhaps all that theorizing had been too fanciful, too reverent about executions in the way that white people often were, trying to turn killing into pulling teeth. Perhaps it was all over, and there was blood in Boss Boshoff's mouth.

There was a scrambling noise.

The noose was around Willie's neck. It was being tightened and the rubber ring drawn down into place. The floor beneath his stockinged feet felt absolutely solid; he couldn't detect the crack. Just bumpy lines.

"You're right," Swanepoel agreed. "It has driven me a little mad. The doubt, I suppose. Still, each time I see it work perfectly, I know it must have been quick for him, providing it was done properly."

"You don't need me, too," Willie whispered, not being able to speak any louder, having curled away in a far corner of his mind. "You don't need another. You've proved it five times."

"Any scientific experiment requires many repetitions for the result to be of any significance, Willie. I could have performed five flukes. Shall I tell you why you're different from the others? And more like my son?"

Willie nodded. Another second—anything!

"They gave me no trouble because their guilt would make them yield to what must inevitably happen. But, like Anthony Michael, you do not feel guilt. That is why I want to see if you can still take this like a man. I am going to say goodbye now, then I am going to walk—"

"A prayer! I can't die without a prayer!"

Swanepoel sighed. "Our Father," he said.

Kramer looked over the top of the pillbox and saw the top branches of a thorn tree growing inside it. Below that, silvered by the moon, weed. Broken beams, brought down by termites, lying where they had fallen.

"Ach, no!" he gasped.

Then began climbing down, ripping his clothes and his skin in his haste, feeling nothing. Ten feet from the ground, he jumped and rolled, cracking his head on an anthill. Dazed, he staggered up, stumbled, ran.

Round in a circle, not knowing which direction to take. He stopped. Looked all around and saw nothing but the truck.

Despair dashed aside reason. "It's in the truck!" Kramer shouted. "In the sodding truck! Must be!"

He started to run again.

The truck was too low.

He jogged.

Too low and bulletproof.

Gravity was bulletproof, too; once the falling body began to fall, there would be no stopping it.

He paused and took aim. Aimlessly.

This pause seemed providential, because he suddenly noticed, for the very first time, a small thicket of plane trees on the far side of the truck. Tall, densely packed plane trees which could be hiding anything in their midst.

"Amen," said Gysbert Swanepoel, touching Willie again on the shoulder. "I have five steps to take, my son, that is all."

The air in that stifling cloth bag was foul.

And for a man breathing his last, this became the greatest injustice of all.

Tears ran down Willie's bruised cheeks.

One. Two.

"Go well, Willie."

He shook. The whole world shook.

The floor jerked violently beneath him.

21

ZONDI KNEW ONLY ONE way of defying gravity to do its worst, and that was by changing its direction. Not in relation to the center of the earth, of course, but within the design of death which man had placed upon it.

Whether his move would come in time—or a split second too late—he had no idea. Nevertheless, it seemed worth trying.

So he half stood on the throttle of the truck, his right leg locked at the knee, and aimed the left front at a bank. The truck leaped toward it.

By swerving to the right as he left the track, he'd throw the truck fractionally off balance. Its list would increase, however, once the left front tire struck the bank and, if the angle was correct, the truck would become momentarily airborne. After that, it would crash down on its side.

Or, as the Lieutenant would say, such was the theory.

When Kramer saw the truck suddenly start up and roar off, he cursed himself for an idiot: Swanepoel had never left the vehicle, but had hidden in the back with Willie.

Kramer knelt on one knee, braced his gun hand in the crook of his left elbow, and fired five shots.

Then whooped when the truck swerved, struck a low bank, heeled over, and banged down on its side, bursting the big back doors open.

There was a bright orange light shining inside it.

Kramer approached the truck with great curiosity. He found Gysbert Swanepoel lying on the ground pinned down by a large mealie bag of sand, stunned and smiling stupidly.

"Is it heavy?" he asked.

"Eleven stone exactly," Swanepoel answered.

"Uhuh."

Down the other end of the truck, Kramer found Willie with the noose around his neck. As the distance from the center of the ceiling to the wall was a mere three feet or so, he was sitting there quite comfortably, with plenty of slack to spare. The noose slipped off easily; the bag—being stuck to his face—was a trifle more difficult.

"I'm St. Peter," said Kramer. "Harp or electric guitar?"

Willie stared blankly.

"You're all right, kid. You'll live."

"I want a transfer," said Willie.

This struck Kramer as being exceedingly funny. But he knew that if he laughed, he might go to pieces. "I'll get a knife for the straps," he said. "Fingerprints wouldn't thank me for handling them. Just try to relax now."

Willie, trusting as a puppy, nodded.

Kramer traced the rope back. It went over a pulley, which had replaced one of the meat hooks in the ceiling, and was joined at the shackle to a steel cable. This cable then went over another pulley, situated at the back of the truck, and was fixed to the mealie bag.

"Machine hanging," he said to Swanepoel, who hadn't tried to get up. "What put me off was that the only example I'd ever heard about had taken place in a room thirty-five feet high. But you don't need much height when you use two pulleys."

"Not if your truck is long enough to have the slack tightening horizontally," Swanepoel agreed. "You just need enough for the prisoner and the drop to be side by side, on the same level. It's all a bit crude, but it works—which is the main thing. Usually I add a few curtains and that to give it more atmosphere."

"How was the bag released?"

"Nothing fancy. This bit of nylon rope kept it suspended until I sliced through it with a knife. Then it would drop, take up the slack—and crack! I'm very keen to tell you everything."

"I've noticed. Why?"

"I want it all to come out in court."

"Uhuh?"

"And then I want to see how they do it for myself."

"On yourself?"

"That's the idea!"

"Sorry," murmured Kramer. "All you'll ever see is the inside of a loony bin. You aren't fit to plead, Gysbert Swanepoel."

Even as he said this, Kramer noticed the curious upward turn to the man's eyebrows, and realized that it matched what he dimly remembered of the face of Anthony Michael Vasari. An unlikely association, perhaps, yet one which now fitted neatly into the context of a Catholic woman married four years without children, having a war baby and then adopting two others. This might explain what had drawn Tollie to the man in the first place—it certainly explained what a backveld farmer was doing with a world map in his living room. Kramer was aware he really ought to have thought of all this before, but there had always been so much else to think about, and that story of the prisoner of war had been just weird enough to sound true. God, what a terrible torment the man must be suffering, yet supplying him with his answers was—

"Bastards!" bellowed Swanepoel. "I *must* know!"

The mealie bag was tossed aside like a feather pillow. The huge farmer scissored Kramer's legs from under him, then took hold of him by the throat. Kramer fought back, kneeing him in the groin, and they rolled over and over, crashing against the rocks. Finally Swanepoel broke free and rose, pulling out a knife, cursing and sobbing, demented.

Kramer seized the excuse. He fired, killing the man instantly. Mercifully, he thought.

The shot didn't echo.

It brought total silence, like the crack of a clapperboard.

Then out of that silence came a deep, low laugh; a laugh quite out of proportion to the size of man who made it. A laugh

Kramer knew well, having heard it where children played, where women wept, where men died; always the same degree of detached amusement.

"Zondi, you old bastard! So it was you?"

He hadn't wanted to ask this before, just in case there had been no reply.

Leaving Willie in his hell for a little longer, Kramer put away his gun and strode to the front of the truck. The cab was empty. He twisted round. Zondi was lying against the bank, his right leg out straight and the other bent under him; he was trying to get a Lucky out of its packet. The clown laughed again, very softly, and shook his head.

"Give here," said Kramer, kneeling and taking the packet from him. "You're in shock, man—are you hurt?"

"A beautiful pain, boss."

"Hey?"

"My leg is broken."

"Christ! Right one again?"

"Left."

Kramer lit the cigarettes, drew on them thoughtfully, then handed one to Zondi.

"Mickey!" he said, grinning. "Mickey, you cunning little kaffir! And just how many weeks off do you reckon this'll entitle you to? Enough?"

"Enough for both, Lieutenant—for how can one rest without its brother?" Zondi chuckled. "How do you feel yourself?"

"Now I come to think of it, not so good," said Kramer.

Peter Lovesey

The False Inspector Dew   71338 $2.95
"Irresistible...delightfully off-beat...wickedly clever."
—*Washington Post Book World*

Keystone   72604 $2.95
"A classic whodunit."   —*Philadelphia Inquirer*

James McClure

"A distinguished crime novelist who has created in his Afrika-ner Tromp Kramer and Bantu Sergeant Zondi two detectives who are as far from stereotypes as any in the genre."
—P.D. James, *New York Times Book Review*

The Blood of an Englishman	71019	$2.95
The Caterpillar Cop	71058	$2.95
The Gooseberry Fool	71059	$2.95
Snake	72304	$2.95
The Sunday Hangman	72992	$2.95
The Steam Pig	71021	$2.95

William McIlvanney

Laidlaw   73338 $2.95
"I have seldom been so taken by a character as I was by the angry and compassionate Glasgow detective, Laidlaw. McIlvanney is to be congratulated."   —Ross McDonald

The Papers of Tony Veitch   73486 $2.95

Poul Ørum

Scapegoat   71335 $2.95
"Not only a very good mystery, but also a highly literate novel."   —Maj Sjöwall

Julian Rathbone

The Euro-Killers   71061 $2.95
"Well-written....the ending is sharp and bitter."
—*New York Times*

A Spy of the Old School   72276 $2.95
"This deserves consideration right up there with Le Carré and company."   —*Publishers Weekly*

Vassilis Vassilikos

Z   72990 $3.95
"A fascinating novel."   —*Atlantic*

Per Wahlöö

Murder on the Thirty-First Floor   70840 $2.95

Look for the Pantheon International Crime series at your local book-store or use this coupon to order.

Quantity	Catalog #	Price

$1.00 basic charge for postage and handling $1.00
25¢ charge per additional book
Please include applicable sales tax

Total

Prices shown are publisher's suggested retail price. Any reseller is free to charge whatever price he wishes for books listed. Prices are subject to change without notice.

Send orders to: Pantheon Books, PIC 28-2, 201 East 50th St., New York, NY 10022.

Please send me the books I have listed above. I am enclosing $_____ which includes a postage and handling charge of $1.00 for the first book and 25¢ for each additional book, plus applicable sales tax. Please send check or money order in U.S. dollars only. No cash or C.O.D.'s accepted. Orders delivered in U.S. only. Please allow 4 weeks for delivery. This offer expires 9/30/85.

Name _____

Address _____

City _____ State _____ Zip _____